ACROSS THE SAPPHIRE SEA

LEE COLGIN

Content Warning

Reader beware, this novel contains mature scenes intended for an adult audience. Main characters have troubled pasts that have led to a verbally abusive relationship that could be triggering for some people. If you have further questions, please don't hesitate to contact the author.

ACKNOWLEDGMENTS

My deepest thanks to my dear friend and trusted critique partner, author Kat Silver. Do check out her romping MM Urban Fantasy, Dark Flame, it's fantastic.

Thanks also to all my wonderful early readers. Without their encouragement, guidance, and advice, this book wouldn't exist. Stephanie Briarton, Sierra Charleston, Barbara Leftih, Nicole Renee, Jen Bass, Hellie Heat, & Laura Lane.

Thanks to Dextre for always cheering me on and for doing my chores so I could get this finished. You're the best.

PROLOGUE

Mahu, 564 Before Common Era, Egypt

*S*ilken black hair so dark it gleamed blue in the desert sunlight drifted in the current of the Nile's flowing water. Mahu beamed down at Dakarai, smile wide as Ra's golden rays. The scent of nearby juniper and hyacinth floated on the warm afternoon breeze.

"How is it you've never learned to swim?" asked Mahu, admiring the shining onyx hair as it danced in the ripples. He stood waist deep in the river, holding beneath Daka's shoulders and thighs as Daka learned to float on his back.

Daka's eyes, midnight blue and black as his hair, glistened with joy. "It never occurred to me to try. Perhaps that's why I need you, to do my thinking for me."

Mahu gave a rumble of laughter. "You often leave me incapable of higher thought when you're done with me and disappear to wherever it is you disappear to."

Daka reached beneath the water's surface and took Mahu's phallus in his hand. "Would you have it any other way?"

Mouth open on a sigh, Mahu caught Daka's vulnerable expression before the incubus could hide it behind a smirk.

1

"Never."

"I thought not."

Walking deeper into the water, Mahu continued the lesson. "When you're ready to float, you must take in a great breath of air and hold it. I'm going to take my hands away. Ready?"

Daka's grip on Mahu's cock tightened. "I have this to hold on to. Wood floats well enough."

Mahu arched his brows. "I'm going to drop you."

Daka's grin was wicked. "At least I'll have something to swallow before I drown."

A burst of laughter escaped his lips. "Stop it."

Daka's expression turned perfectly serious. "Never."

1

Elias, Present, 1432 Common Era

The crash of water breaking against the rocky banks of Wolin faded as they sailed farther out to sea. Gulls squawked in the gray sky above. Elias stood on the stern of the cog ship watching a dense fog encase the land they left behind. Sapphire waves rippled between ship and shore. He missed solid ground already. His stomach didn't appreciate the churning tide.

Though resigned to the journey, dread sat heavy in Elias's gut. He'd no desire to return to his homeland—a frigid place where bad memories drowned out the decent ones. But Valeri had insisted he come along, wouldn't dream of leaving him behind in the safety and comfort of Bran Vigny Castle where he might actually make a friend other than Valeri himself. Couldn't have that.

He took a deep breath of salty air and let it out slowly, relaxing his stomach muscles in an attempt to ease the nausea. Who ever heard of a vampire getting seasick?

Raised voices broke his peace, arguing loud enough to be heard over the wind battering the sail.

"Mahu wouldn't want us to be reckless on his behalf," said Laurence, irritation in his tone.

Elias didn't know what to make of him yet—Valeri's estranged fledgling. The tall, dark-haired vampire with the barreled chest intimidated him, so he'd kept his distance.

"And you're the expert on Mahu's wishes, are you?" Valeri's voice, crisp and angry as usual. His chestnut curls bounced as he gestured. He had to look up to meet Laurence's annoyed stare.

"It doesn't take an expert to know our magic isn't necessary." Laurence indicated the sail. "The winds are in our favor."

Valeri rolled his eyes. "The only reason you and your milksop are here is to be of some help with your magic."

Laurence stepped in front of his own fledgling, Remy, blocking him from Valeri's view.

"If you won't cast a spell, you may as well take a rowboat back to shore."

"You're not listening—"

"I wish I didn't have to," Valeri griped.

"—the wind blows in our favor," Laurence finished, ignoring the interruption. "Magic isn't needed."

Remy sidestepped the pair and approached Elias while their sires continued arguing.

"So that's for you to decide then?" Valeri continued. "The rest of us don't get a say?"

A flutter of unease coiled in Elias's stomach. This would be a dreadful time to gag. He caught Remy's gaze as the young vampire joined him at the boat's rail. He was shorter than Elias, and slighter too, but there was a fierceness in his eyes that radiated power.

"No," Laurence growled. "And why would we risk the crew becoming suspicious for nothing?"

Remy opened his mouth to speak—

"Fuck the crew!" shouted Valeri, entirely too loud.

Elias cringed.

Remy shut his mouth, whatever he was going to say lost to Valeri's outburst.

Elias gave an apologetic shrug.

"Charming," said Remy instead.

"Indeed," said Elias. Remy didn't know the half of it. Valeri could be quite loving when he wanted, but his possessive streak always spoiled it eventually. Remy was lucky to have a sire like Laurence, who appeared kind, gentle, and protective. Watching Remy and Laurence together made Elias jealous. Could he ever find companionship like that with the hot-headed Valeri? He'd begun to doubt it.

"Are you all right?" Remy's concern sounded genuine.

Elias nodded. "Just getting used to the ship."

"However did you meet such a charmer?" asked Remy, his golden-brown eyes glowing in the dim light of late evening.

Elias sighed. That was an interesting story, wasn't it? Difficult to answer in pleasant conversation with a vampire he'd only recently met. "I was a farmer working the field when he noticed me."

"A farmer?" Remy gave a polite smile.

Nodding, Elias explained. "Slash and burn farming, yes."

Remy's expression turned curious.

Elias continued, "Cut away the brush, burn the debris, then next season the soil is primed for growth. The barley needed to be harvested before the frost, but Valeri found me first." Elias paused. He didn't want to tell the next part. Instead, he changed the subject. "How did you meet Laurence? He seems nice."

Remy's polite smile broadened to a real grin, puffing his pink cheeks and revealing a gleaming row of white teeth. "He's very nice. Laurence saved my life."

Elias already knew some of their story. The tale was fast becoming legend. But he was curious to hear it from Remy's own mouth.

"He saw me cast the arc. Afterward, I collapsed. There was a werewolf who would have slaughtered me, but Laurence dove in to thwart him."

Elias imagined the scene. "How daring."

"And that was just the first time he saved my life. Apparently I have a habit of finding myself in harm's way," Remy said with a hint of a chuckle.

Elias envied him. "How very lucky for you that you have a protector."

"Very." Remy leaned back against the rail, yellow hair blowing in the wind.

Elias admired the tawny waves. He'd have liked to have long locks. But his own dark hair had been sheared rather short, and Valeri turned him into a vampire before it could grow, so short it would stay.

Remy scanned the people on deck. Elias followed his gaze. Valeri and Laurence continued their heated discussion, albeit quietly, thank the gods. The last thing they needed was for the crew to overhear.

On the other side of the deck, Aella, the red-haired head witch of Bran Vigny, spoke with the ship's captain. Ash, an older vampire who'd never uttered a word to Elias, also watched the argument, the expression on his face bordering on amusement. Ash was the delegate sent from their rulers, The Dozen, and the only official ambassador on the mission. Hopefully Valeri would let him get a word in when the time came.

Five vampires, one witch, two weeks confined to this ship, and none of them thrilled over the prospect.

"Is Mahu worth all this trouble?" asked Elias, but the moment the words escaped his lips he regretted them. It was a selfish sentiment, to want to stay somewhere safe when another so desperately needed their help.

Remy considered him.

If Elias could still blush, he would have. "I'm sorry, I—"

"No need to apologize. I understand. This journey is a lot to ask of us, a dangerous voyage, an outcome unknown. But yes, I believe Mahu is worth the risk."

"Of course," Elias rushed to agree. He didn't want to offend Remy.

But Remy didn't look offended. "Did you have a chance to meet him? Mahu? Before…"

It was well known Mahu's descent into madness had progressed faster over the cold season. No one knew why the disease's symptoms had spiked, only that his remaining time dwindled along with his sanity. He lingered abed, calling out nonsense from fevered dreams.

"No, I haven't met him," said Elias. "I saw him once, from a distance, but he looked like he wished to be alone so I didn't greet him."

"If it wasn't for Mahu, my transformation would have failed." Remy's tone grew serious. "Laurence would have watched me die in his arms. We owe him a debt. But you don't. Why are you taking this risk?"

As if I ever have a choice in anything I do. Elias put a hand on his queasy stomach, trying in vain to cure seasickness with touch. "The mission is important to Valeri."

Remy's gaze was tinged with scrutiny. "Why?"

"He wants to get back into The Dozen's good graces, earn a place at court. He thinks acquiring a cure for the aging sickness Mahu suffers will accomplish those things."

"Yes, but why risk your safety also?"

Elias gave a sad burst of laughter. "Would you tell Laurence no if he asked you to do something you didn't want to do?"

Remy pressed his lips into a tight line. "If Laurence asked me to do something I didn't want to do, I suspect he'd have a very good reason. I wouldn't say no without talking to him first. I trust him."

Must be nice, thought Elias.

7

Whatever their sires had been fighting about, they'd finished. Valeri stormed over, took Elias by the arm, and said, "Come."

Elias cast an apologetic glance to Remy and left without a word, knowing if he didn't follow along, Valeri was likely to drag him. A look over his shoulder showed Remy returning to Laurence's side. Laurence's arm went around his waist in a move so practiced he'd surely done it a thousand times.

A flare of longing panged Elias. Valeri had gentled his hold on his arm, but it paled in comparison to the sweet, loving touches Remy and Laurence shared.

They crossed the broad deck of the ship, Valeri in the lead, and took the stairs down to the cabins below. The stale air of the narrow hall smelled dank and salty. Small capsule rooms with wooden walls, floors, ceilings, and bunks lined the galley. Brown, damp, cold, and not much else. Their luggage had already been deposited in the corner.

Valeri closed the door behind them. Elias's stomach protested all the movement. It didn't seem fair; he hadn't eaten a morsel of food in the four years since he'd been turned into a vampire, yet seasickness could still claim him within minutes of boarding a ship. Feeling sorry for himself, he reached for his lover.

Valeri closed his arms around Elias's shoulders and rubbed his back. "Sick already?"

Elias clutched his waist and nodded against the cool skin of his neck. He breathed in the coppery scent of blood flowing close to the surface and suppressed the urge to bite.

"You can if you like," Valeri offered.

"Thank you, but I'll wait until later." Drinking now might make the nausea worse. Instead he kissed the juncture at Valeri's neck and shoulder.

"What were you and the little witch talking about?"

There it was, the paranoia Elias had grown to expect. "His name is Remy."

8

Valeri pushed him back far enough to stare into his face. "I know that. I asked what you were talking about."

Elias shrugged out of his hold and sat on the chest at the foot of the bed, clutching his belly. "Not much. He asked how we met. I told him about the farm."

Valeri narrowed his gaze, a cloud of suspicion in his eyes. "And the rest?"

Elias shook his head. "Not the rest."

"Good. It's none of their business."

"They're stronger than us, but you're older than Laurence. You made him. How is that possible?"

"It shouldn't be, but his fledgling is witchborn. Turning a witch is unnatural."

Elias thought they were all unnatural, but he wouldn't say so. "Their eyes glow like the ancient ones. Is it true Mahu gave them his blood?"

"Where did you hear that? Who've you been talking to?"

"No one in particular. Everyone's saying it. Remy mentioned that without Mahu's help, he would have died."

"If you want to know something, you ask me."

I just did, thought Elias sadly.

"I've work to do. Stay put. I'll return soon."

"Try to get along with the others, Valeri, please. We're stuck with them for weeks; we ought to make friends."

"You have me. You don't need friends." Valeri spun and left without saying goodbye, shutting the door harder than strictly necessary.

Elias heaved a long sigh and wondered, not for the first time, if their relationship could be saved.

Four Years Ago

9

The setting sun stole the day's warmth with its departure. Elias felt the chill creep into his bones as he continued to work under moonlight. His muscles ached, and his empty stomach groaned in protest, but the barley would not harvest itself.

Fingers clenched around the heavy scythe, Elias scanned the windswept fields. They'd planted the grain late in the season, and the first frost threatened an early arrival—an unlucky combination. Not that Elias cared. These weren't his fields. This wasn't his crop. Little more than a slave to the overlords, Elias did what he was told or else he'd be beaten and starved. More than once he'd learned that lesson.

A glance over his shoulder revealed two men cresting the hill on horseback. Overlord Makinen sat astride a roan mare with his chest puffed out and his chin held high. His primary joy in life was looking down on everyone else.

The other man, not so big or intimidating as Maks, was a stranger, though he'd come around often lately, always in the evening. Chestnut brown curls, arching cheekbones and deep-set brown eyes Elias often found focused solely on him. Maks preened under the stranger's attention, so he must be of some importance. The stranger wore fine leathers cut to fit his muscular frame and a flowing woolen cloak dyed a black so dark it would have disappeared into the night had Elias not already committed the man's appearance to memory.

The stranger caught him staring. Their eyes locked. A pleasant flutter erupted in Elias's chest. The stranger's lips curled to a sly smile, and Elias knew he should look away but found himself pinned by the weight of that loaded gaze.

"Ho there," Maks's booming rumble echoed over the fields, startling Elias to urgently hide the trespass. It was a punishable offense to stop working and stare idly off into the distance. Elias swung his scythe toward the barley, knocking down a neat row, but the effort came too late. Maks had seen him lollygagging and there would be consequences.

"What do you think you're doing, standing there while the others work?" A scowl etched across Maks's face. "Lazy wretch. I feed you, clothe you, house you, and this is how you repay me? Twiddling your thumbs in my field?"

Elias hunched. "Sorry, my lord." He furiously wielded the scythe, working double-time to make up for the error. Shame coiled in his gut to be so chastised in front of the handsome stranger, but worse than that, a deep fear Maks wouldn't stop with a lecture, not when he could lash a servant in front of a man he clearly wanted to impress.

Hoofbeats approached, each thud intensifying Elias's terror until his muscles trembled.

"Put it down," Maks ordered, gesturing to the scythe. "Five lashes, then back to work. Maybe next time you'll think twice about stopping before the crop is in."

Elias squeezed his eyes shut and let the tool fall from his hands. Five lashes. He tried to take comfort that it was not ten or twenty, but even five would leave him bloody and vulnerable to infection.

The other bondslaves continued to work the field as if none of this were happening. Elias didn't blame them. If they paused for a second, if they threw him even a glance of concern, they'd meet the same fate.

"Come. Present your arms," Maks demanded from atop the mare.

The stranger's horse, a dappled-gray gelding, stomped as Elias approached. He knew better than to hesitate. He ignored the horse and its mysterious rider to hold out his wrists.

Maks bound them together and yanked the knot tight so the skin pinched. Elias held in a whimper though he couldn't stop from flinching. Maks gave the rope a sharp tug. "Walk on."

Elias felt the stranger's eyes on his back as he followed behind the mare to the closest tree, but he dared not turn to look. He didn't want to anyway. Not when the stranger was about to watch him be beaten. Then his voice, a resonant tenor, pierced the tense atmosphere.

"Let me do it."

Elias's head whipped around before he could think better of it, the words landing like a blow. The stranger stared right at him and tipped his head, flashing a predatory grin that said, *why watch a man be beaten when you could do it yourself?*

Maks, who rode ahead, had not seen their exchange. "By all means."

The stranger winked.

Elias's jaw dropped along with his stomach. He cast his gaze downward, struggling to swallow both disappointment and the mounting terror of the lash's sting on his flesh. He didn't know what he'd expected from the stranger, but it wasn't this.

Maks dismounted and dragged Elias to the tree. He threw the loose end of the rope over a low sturdy branch and tugged until Elias's hands were pulled high overhead and he had to stand on his toes. His panting breaths grew erratic as his threadbare shirt was ripped from his back. A cool breeze teased the sensitive skin along his spine, already striped with the scars of previous punishments.

Five lashes. He could take five lashes. Vowing not to cry out, Elias grit his teeth.

Maks took the whip from his belt. The leather uncurled to its full, intimidating length, the end dragging in the ashen soil.

Elias watched while Maks's back was turned. The stranger landed neatly on two feet, clucked to his horse and patted his rump, sending the big animal sauntering away.

Maks handed the weapon over. "Don't go easy on him or he'll never learn."

The stranger arched his brows. "Is that so?" He took the whip and gave it an experimental crack. Though Elias had seen it coming, the resounding boom startled a twitch out of him. The stranger caught his gaze. "You're familiar with this punishment?"

Elias was too smart to answer, but he refused to avert his eyes. He doubted the stranger wanted to hear from him anyway. Probably preferred the sound of his own voice. Just like Maks.

"This one needs to be reminded often," Maks grunted.

"Does he?" The stranger prowled closer, a sway to his step that brought to mind something feline. He strutted a slow circle around Elias, whistling when he saw the mess previous whippings had made of his back. "Ah, this won't be his first time. Pity."

Elias felt the man draw close, a solid presence behind him radiating power. Breath ghosted against the shell of his ear. Fingertips tickled his naked spine. Elias stayed perfectly still, his heartbeat thundering in his chest.

Then, quietly, for Elias's ears alone, the stranger whispered, "I'd have liked to have been your first."

2

Elias, Present, 1432 Common Era

*B*ored, sick, and feeling abandoned, Elias had waited hours for Valeri to return to their cabin. The seasickness abated somewhat when he stayed below deck, so at least he had that small comfort. He felt marginally better when Valeri came to retrieve him to convene with the others.

They met, all six of them, in the kitchen galley while most of the crew slept.

"I'll guard you during the day," said Aella, the only one of their number who wasn't a vampire and could therefore be above deck during sunlight. "The captain has been well paid not to ask questions about the odd hours his passengers keep."

Laurence gave a nod. "Thank you. If you hear any rumblings among the crew, let me know. Seafarers are a suspicious lot. Rather they think us rich and eccentric than something supernatural."

"Won't they wonder about the donors?" asked Remy.

Because Elias and Remy were new to the blood, they'd had to bring four willing human donors from Bran Vigny along on the journey. Young vampires had to feed often, and there weren't a lot of options when stuck on a ship for two weeks.

"No," said Aella. "The donors wear fine clothes and jewels. They were well instructed on how to blend in. As far as the crew are concerned, we're all wealthy merchants crossing the Baltic to strike favorable trade arrangements."

Elias's gaze flicked from Aella to Ash. The elder vampire's cool blue eyes focused intently on the redheaded witch. She noticed Ash watching, and color crept into her cheeks. Aella spoke directly to him. "Can you think of anything else we need to discuss?"

If Ash intended to say something, they'd never know because Valeri spoke up instead. "We ought to use magic to sail faster. The sooner we get to Kemi, the better."

Elias grimaced. He got the sense this would soon become a stale argument, but it wasn't like Valeri to let something go when he thought he was right.

"The prevailing winds of the Baltic blow from the southwest," said Ash, perhaps to keep Laurence from rehashing this point himself and stave off another sparring match between the adversaries. "They'll push us straight to our destination under the watchful eye of the captain. Tiring our witches for the sake of a few less days at sea is counterproductive. We'll need Aella, Laurence, and Remy at full strength when we make landfall."

Valeri opened his mouth in rebuttal, but Remy chimed in first. "Valeri, could you please go over what you've learned of the cure to the aging sickness thus far? I'm afraid the details are still foggy."

Whatever Valeri had been planning to say was abandoned in favor of lording his firsthand information over the others. "The vampires of the court of ancients are rumored to be twice as old as Mahu's two thousand-some years, yet they remain healthy and sane. As far as it's known among our kind, they're the oldest vampires in existence. The secret lies with them at the Arctic Circle north of Rovaniemi."

"But is that all you know?" Remy probed.

Elias didn't blame him. He only knew a little of what Valeri held back and suspected there was more Valeri wasn't saying, some crucial detail he didn't want to reveal. The secrecy drove Elias mad.

Valeri gave a careless shrug. "Is that not enough for you? The location of the ancient creatures who hold the secret? What more should I have discovered while exiled and alone, tell me that?"

Elias suppressed the urge to point out that Valeri had not been alone. Elias had been there all along, even if his sire insisted on keeping secrets from him.

"My apologies," said Remy with diplomacy. "No one denies the importance of your contribution. We only seek to go in with as much foresight as we can muster between us. No one wants to fail Mahu."

Elias startled as Valeri took his wrist and rose suddenly. "If that's all, we'll retire for the day." He urged Elias from the room without giving the others the courtesy of waiting for a reply.

Back in their cabin, Elias tugged his wrist from Valeri's fingers and muttered, "You were rude to them. I asked you to get along, and you were rude."

Valeri whirled on him. "Now you're going to harass me too? I must tolerate their condescension, but I'd hoped for your support."

Elias held both hands up. "I didn't mean to upset you. It's only that the voyage would be more pleasant if we weren't all at odds."

Valeri shrugged out of his black leather doublet and toed off his boots. "You're dreaming if you think any part of this mission will be pleasant with Laurence and his boy-witch along."

"His name is Remy." *And he's older than me.* Neither of them were boys, but he'd learned to pick his battles with Valeri. He sat to remove his own boots and prepare for bed. "And he seems perfectly nice."

Valeri took one step forward, which was all that was necessary to loom over Elias in their tiny cabin. "Keep away from them. Nothing good will come from you believing their drivel."

"You doubt my ability to think for myself?" Elias inflected his tone as if the words formed a question, but really it was a statement because he knew them to be true. He wasn't in the mood for Valeri's bickering. Casually, he peeled off his shirt.

"Your trusting nature leaves you vulnerable. If you'd stop relentlessly questioning my authority for even one night, you'd realize I only want what's best for you."

Elias unfastened and removed his breeches, leaving him in only his smallclothes. "Have you ever considered asking me what I think is best for me?"

Valeri huffed and stripped to his smalls as well. "Enlighten me, Elias, with your twenty-three years of wisdom to my one hundred and sixty-three. Pray tell, what's best for you?" He stood, naked chest puffed, daring Elias to challenge him again.

Elias let out a breath and crawled into bed. There was no winning when Valeri was like this. He arranged the layers of heavy wool covers over his legs, then turned down the side for Valeri. "You are best for me, of course. Come to bed."

It was no great hardship to invite Valeri to lie with him. His stomach was still queasy and he wanted the comfort of his lover's arms, even if his words sometimes hurt Elias's feelings.

Valeri joined him on the thick pallet barely wide enough for two grown men, but they would make do. Lying on his back he opened an arm for Elias to curl up against his side. Elias lined them up from ankles to hips, throwing a leg over Valeri's thigh and resting his head on his chest. He relished the weight of Valeri's arm over his back, the hand holding his waist. It was the cozy way of sleeping they'd settled into from the beginning of their relationship. No matter how turbulent things got between them, the position brought Elias comfort.

Body to body like this, Elias could feel Valeri's every breath. The motion of it lulled him into a peaceful doze. He brought his hand up to Valeri's face to touch the soft hairs behind his ears. Curling the locks through his fingers, Elias sighed and closed his eyes. Perhaps tomorrow night would be better. His body would acclimate to the ocean's current, and the six of them would find a way to get along.

One could dream.

Valeri took his wrist.

Elias's eyes fluttered open. "What?"

Removing his hand from the curls, Valeri set it on his chest instead. "You should quit that habit. It's childish."

Elias tucked his hand beneath his chin and mumbled an apology. "I thought you liked it. I won't do it anymore. Sorry."

He squeezed his eyes shut and willed himself not to cry. Twirling hair wasn't important, but he loved Valeri, and though he knew Valeri loved him too, in his own way, his sire wasn't an easy man to get along with.

No tears, not tonight, thought Elias. *Save them for when you finally get the courage to leave him, because then there'll be no stopping them.*

Four Years Ago

"I'd have liked to have been your first," the stranger whispered. He still held the whip intended for Elias's back.

The words filtered through Elias's panicked mind like the scythe had gone through the barley, slicing it clear in two. One half, the sane bit, was horrified at the implication, but the other half? A spark of arousal sent blood rushing to his groin. He shivered. Behind him, the stranger chuckled. His breath ruffled Elias's hair.

Insanity.

Elias stared at the ground and willed himself under control. Five lashes, then back to the field. The bondslaves would work well into the night to protect the harvest from the threatening frost.

The stranger completed a slow circle, wrapping the leather whip loosely around Elias's torso as he went. He stood directly in front, toe to toe with Elias, demanding his full attention. Maks spoke in the background, but Elias didn't catch the words. He could do nothing but stare.

This close Elias could see every dark eyelash, the freckle on his upper lip, the flash of sharp incisors when he opened his mouth. The stranger was taller, even with Elias on his tiptoes, but only by a little. He was broad where Elias was slim. He tugged, and the whip pulled Elias even closer.

"I've been watching you." The voice rumbled from ruby lips like distant thunder, ominous and full of promise.

"I know." Elias dug deep and found courage. "I've seen you, for all the good that's done me." His eyes flitted to his bound wrists.

The stranger smirked. "Do you like what you see?"

"A lunatic with a whip?" The question flew out without thought. Elias didn't know what had gotten into him. He courted the devil with those words.

The stranger's smirk widened to a smile and a burst of laughter tumbled forth. Elias felt the gust of it on his face.

Maks approached. "Get on with it."

Annoyance marred the stranger's sharp features, but his attention never wavered. He ignored Maks and spoke only to Elias. "I can end this. Take you with me." Subtly, he increased the tension on the whip, forcing Elias forward. "Would you come?"

Elias blinked. "Where?"

"Does the location matter if the alternative is here?" His gaze flicked to Maks then back to Elias. "Under that idiot's lash?"

"*You* hold the lash."

"So I do." He tugged. Their chests bumped. "Would you come?"

"I'll come."

The stranger gave a hum of approval. His tongue wet his bottom lip. "Ask me to kill him."

Elias nearly lost his balance. He'd have stumbled save for his arms tied overhead, which were beginning to ache from the restraint.

Kill him? Elias hated Maks but didn't wish him dead...did he? He considered. Would the stranger really kill his master? Surely not.

Tempted, Elias let curiosity overrule fear. He would always have fear but curiosity came in short supply. He wouldn't waste it.

Elias glared defiantly at the stranger's glittering brown eyes and deduced the curiosity to be mutual. The stranger's gaze was pregnant with it. He didn't know how his prisoner would respond.

Elias whispered, "Do it. Kill him for me. Take me with you."

A pleased grin curled to reveal a row of white, sparkling teeth, two of which were sharp as razor blades.

Not teeth.

Fangs. A shiver rocked Elias where he hung.

"Fast or slow?" the stranger purred.

"Fast." Elias commanded like a dare.

The stranger pulled the whip from where it rested against Elias's bare skin. He whirled around, graceful as a cat, and drew the leather in a powerful arc over their heads. The tendons in his neck strained with the effort. His brown curls bounced as he struck.

The mighty blow landed across Maks's shoulders. A stunned expression flashed on his face before the pain set in, and on its heels, rage. "What—" he stuttered, but was cut off when another strike—this one to the back of his knees—sent him stumbling to the ground.

Dropping the whip, the stranger followed Maks down. "You're lucky the pretty slave said *fast*." He grabbed Maks's jaw with both hands and snapped his neck. The sharp pop made Elias cringe. As

Maks slumped in a heap, the stranger glanced up, a grin still pulling his lips from his terrifying teeth.

A demon. But a demon whose cruelty just spared him five lashes. *My demon.*

The stranger rose and stalked forward.

Elias fought a threatening wave of panic, forced himself steady, and cleared his throat. "What's your name?"

"Valeri." He drew a blade from his belt. "Yours?"

"Elias." Had he avoided the whip only to be stabbed to death?

But no, Valeri reached high, took Elias's wrists in one hand, and cut the rope with the other. When his arms tumbled free, he lost his balance and landed with a thump against Valeri's chest.

"I've got you," said the demon, holding him with gentle hands. Hands that just slaughtered Elias's cruel master. In cold blood. In front of witnesses.

Numbness in Elias's arms gave way to pins and needles, but he found his feet. He made to pull away.

Valeri tightened his hold. "Not yet, you'll catch a chill." He unclasped his dark wool cloak and brought it around from his shoulders to Elias's. He refastened the clasp and smoothed the thick fabric along Elias's collar bones. "Better."

"Thank you," *my lord* lingered on the tip of his tongue, but Elias didn't want a new master, so he dared use his proper name instead, "Valeri."

"You're welcome." Valeri raised a brow as if he recognized the bold choice Elias had made. "Elias." The syllables rolled from his lips slowly. They stared at one another, eyes locked, until Elias gave in and lowered his gaze.

The whip was tucked into Valeri's belt. So they'd be keeping it, then.

Elias threw a glance over his shoulder. As he suspected, the other bondslaves had stopped their fieldwork and stood gawking at the events transpiring before them. What would they think of a stranger murdering one of their overlords? Did they know Elias was complicit? They couldn't have heard the exchange, but the whole thing would look suspicious.

"What if we're caught?" asked Elias, his focus back on Valeri.

"We won't be." Confidence dripped from Valeri's tone like blood from the jowls of a predator.

"What happens now?"

"We leave."

Elias's heart thudded in his chest. He wanted to follow. "And go where?"

Valeri gave a casual shrug. "Wherever we want. But for now, to my sanctuary because you're hungry and should eat."

"It's that simple?"

"It is."

The demon wanted to feed him. Elias wouldn't say no; it was too late for that anyway. And they couldn't stay there. Maks lay crumbled in the dirt, deathly still, because Elias had said the words, *kill him for me,* and Valeri had obeyed.

"You're free," Valeri murmured, taking Elias firmly by the arm.

Elias wished he could believe him, but even though it wasn't true, he'd no urge to argue.

3

Elias, Present, 1432 Common Era

*V*aleri's stirring woke Elias from his slumber, but he pretended to stay asleep as his lover carefully inched out of the bed. Valeri's age allowed him to get up sooner and stay awake later than Elias, who had to hide from even the dimmest of the sun's rays.

Elias secretly loved this ritual and stayed perfectly still so as not to ruin it. He had a feeling that if Valeri knew he was awake, he wouldn't do these little things Elias cherished.

Once out of bed, Valeri gently tucked Elias back in, arranging the covers just so, making sure to shield him from the cabin's chill. Then he bent over and pressed a soft kiss to Elias's forehead before dressing and leaving the room.

After he'd gone, Elias stretched and rolled over onto Valeri's pillow. He took a deep whiff of Valeri's lingering scent. He adored that smell. Then he closed his eyes and promptly fell back to sleep.

When the rocking of the boat woke him later, Elias knew instinctively the sun had retreated far enough for him to rise. Already his stomach protested the movement, but once he'd fed he could go up to the main deck. Perhaps fresh air would help him feel better.

Elias dressed and departed his cabin to visit the four humans they'd brought along for himself and Remy. A young vampire's thirst for blood hit hardest first thing in the evening.

The men and women of Bran Vigny's donor pool were well treated. When not stuck on a ship in the middle of the Baltic, they were free to come and go as they pleased, free to live their own lives, and given all the support required to do so.

In exchange, they provided safe meals for the fledglings who needed frequent feedings. Elias had great appreciation for this system. Unlike Valeri, he didn't take joy in hunting for his food; he much preferred willing people who knew what to expect over strangers he had to lull into a hazed stupor.

Knocking upon their cabin door, Elias waited until he heard a woman's voice call, "Come in," before he entered.

This cabin was larger than the glorified closet he and Valeri shared, with two sets of bunks, a table big enough for a card game, four chairs and even a small round window that would let in natural light during the day.

Aside from the two men, Mir and Rasz, and the two women, Bruneta and Damra, Remy was also present. Just finishing up, apparently. He still had an arm around Rasz's slender shoulders, and the man looked pleasantly drunk.

Elias bowed his head in greeting. "Good evening."

Remy stood, a kind smile on his lips. "Hello, Elias."

"Remy." Elias returned the smile. He wished Valeri hadn't asked him to stay away from this vampire. He'd very much like another fledgling for a friend. "Could I ask you a favor?"

"Certainly."

Rasz had shaken off the dazed sensation most humans experienced when feeding a vampire. He buttoned up his collar and took the mug of warm broth Bruneta offered.

"Have a seat." Damra offered her own chair and went to sit on one of the low bunks instead.

"Thank you." Elias took the chair as Remy reclaimed his spot next to Rasz.

"What can I do for you?" asked Remy, his expression open. His eyes glowed gold after the recent infusion of blood. The phenomenon was unlike anything Elias had ever seen. Spectacular.

"I'd appreciate if we kept this between us," said Elias in a room full of five other people, knowing the request was hopeless.

Remy considered, probably thinking the same thing. "All right."

Out with it. Just get it over with. "Valeri's jealousy is easily provoked. He doesn't like me to drink from male donors." Elias cast an apologetic glance to Rasz and Mir. "It's nothing personal, just my life is easier when I don't poke the sleeping bear. Meaning, I'll only be drinking from Bruneta and Damra if that's all right. To ensure they aren't overused, would you mind mostly feeding from Rasz and Mir?" It was embarrassing to even have to ask, but if he could work this out, the hassle would be worth the effort.

"Of course," said Remy, his tone laced with concern, then softly, "Are you all right? Are you safe with him?"

Elias hurried to nod. "Oh, yes, perfectly safe. I didn't mean to imply he'd hurt me. He wouldn't. He's just...a lot sometimes."

"If you need anything—"

"No, thank you, I'm fine. I promise."

Remy's intense gaze searched his features. Elias tried to reflect only calm and gratitude, but underneath the facade, he'd become frazzled.

"You know what?" said Remy brightly, changing the tone of the room with his beaming smile. "My friend Clara sent me with loads of reading material. I have bundles of pamphlets and a few books. She thought two weeks on a ship would certainly be boring. Shall we search through them later? You could borrow one, and I'll bring several to leave in your care," he said, gesturing to the small group of humans.

"That would be lovely," Damra chimed in. "We'd be delighted with a new story to read."

"Good, then it's settled. I'll bring them by later on. And, Elias, when you're done feeding, come find me, and you may pick your own."

Elias fought to keep his tone level. "Thank you, Remy, that's a generous offer, but I'm sorry. I have to decline."

Remy arched his brows. "Why? Surely Valeri can't be jealous of a book?"

"No, no, it's not that." His shoulders sank. "I can't read. I never learned."

"Oh," said Remy, drawing out the sound so it lingered between them along with Elias's shame. Remy stood from his place on Rasz's bed and knelt in front of Elias with a hand on his knee. "That's nothing to be embarrassed about. Lots of people have never been taught to read. Instead of choosing a book, we'll begin your lessons. All right?"

Elias felt the shy smile as it formed on his face. He'd always wished to learn to read. "Really?"

"Of course. It would be my pleasure."

"Thank you."

Remy stood. "You're welcome. Now, I've kept you from your breakfast long enough. I'll leave you to it."

"Goodbye." Elias was still grinning as Remy left.

Damra pulled her chair up to his. "That Remy's a good lad, is he not?"

"He is," Elias agreed.

"And you are too, my boy." She brushed aside long brown waves of hair, exposing her neck. "Come on now, drink."

Elias eyed the pretty blue vein pulsing beneath her creamy skin. "Thank you, Damra."

Then he leaned in, and ever so gently, he bit her.

Four Years Ago

"Take my horse," said Valeri, clicking for his gelding to come. "I'll take the mare. Can you ride?"

Elias eyed the gray gelding with no small amount of longing. He loved horses and enjoyed caring for them, but he'd never been on one. Bondslaves didn't ride; they walked behind to shovel shit from the overlords' roadways. But riding didn't look difficult. He thought he could manage.

"Probably," he answered.

Valeri cast an amused glance over his shoulder. "That'll do." He left the mare where she was and approached, gesturing to the horse he'd ridden. "This is Pavel. He's an easy goer, and with some encouragement, should follow me anyway. You won't have to do much but stay on."

"Hello, Pavel." Elias held his hand out for the horse to sniff. His lips tickled Elias's fingers. Giving Pavel a gentle pat along the solid muscles of his neck, he thought the two of them would get along fine.

Valeri hovered close, gathering the reins and handing them to Elias. "Left foot in the stirrup, reins in your left hand."

Elias's gaze flitted back to the slumped body of Maks. His stomach clenched, and he forced himself to look away. Taking the soft leather reins from Valeri, Elias did as he was told. Was he really leaving the fields, leaving the other bondslaves, and escaping his servitude? The punishment for runaways was death, not even considering the body they were leaving behind. So he'd better get on with it and not get caught. He grasped the saddle with his right hand and felt Valeri's touch at his waist, ready to help if it turned out Elias was inept at horse riding after all.

Pavel stayed still as he mounted, and Elias found himself on the back of a horse for the first time. A grin tugged his lips, despite his fear and their circumstances. Valeri's hand squeezed his calf, catching his attention.

"Sit up straight. Relax your hips. Good. Be gentle with the reins, don't pull on him or use them for balance. Let your body move with his rhythm. Keep your heels down in the stirrups; don't let them slip out. Eyes ahead. I'll lead."

That was a lot to keep in mind at once. "All right."

"Oh, and Elias," Valeri caught his eye as he strode back to the fidgety mare, "don't fall off."

"Don't fall off. Got it." Pavel shifted his weight, and Elias stiffened. Remembering Valeri's advice, he took a breath and relaxed. *Move with the horse's rhythm.* He'd always wanted to try this. And the challenge of it kept shock's icy tendrils from digging in.

Valeri mounted in a graceful movement, turned the mare about, and glanced to Elias. "Ready?"

Elias squared his shoulders. "Ready."

With two crisp clicks of his tongue, Valeri signaled to Pavel, and the gelding's ears twitched forward. Valeri tapped his heels to the mare's flanks, and she was off.

The powerful animal between Elias's thighs sprang to motion, unwilling to let his master ride away without him. Elias bounced at first, clinging with his legs. Though his fingers clenched the reins, he was careful not to pull.

Move with the horse. Move with the horse.

As luck would have it, the rocking motion was somewhat predictable. Elias didn't have to bounce. He let his weight settle in the saddle and kept his eyes ahead like Valeri had instructed. Riding wasn't as easy as he'd thought, but nor was it impossible.

Valeri took them past the slash and burn fields Elias had spent years slaving over. Whether or not the barley got harvested before the first frost was no longer his concern. They moved away from the clustered village of hovels the bondslaves slept in and into the great forest beyond. Less moonlight shone through the dense canopy of pines, and Elias could see very little. How was Valeri managing so well in the dark?

Ahead of him, hoofbeats thudded evenly, and Elias simply trusted Pavel not to lose them. Their pace had slowed, making it easier to stay balanced in the saddle. The combination gave his mind more opportunity to wander.

Was he safe with Valeri? Probably not, but the demon was enticing, a mystery in a world that had become dull. Elias wanted to unravel him, to see what hid beneath the bold words and deadly actions. A shiver took hold of his spine. He clutched Valeri's cloak tighter around his shoulders. Under it, his chest was bare. The material didn't scratch his skin like the wool he'd grown accustomed too. The fabric was softer, of fine quality, and warmer too.

As night wore on, the nervous energy from expecting to be whipped, from watching a man killed before his eyes, from agreeing to follow a demon into the unknown, began to wear off, and in its place a heavy drowsiness loomed. From sunup to sundown Elias had toiled in the field. Exhaustion threatened to overwhelm his body even as his mind raced.

What sort of creature was Valeri? Where had he come from and why had he shown up to inspect the farms with the overlord? Was Maks his first kill? Elias doubted it. The act had been too easy for him. Natural. A predator.

Perhaps fear would keep exhaustion at bay after all.

Pavel swayed steadily beneath him, content to follow behind the mare who carried his master. Elias risked a pat to the horse's neck. His ears flicked, and he let out a friendly wuffle.

"Good boy," said Elias. "Thank you."

From ahead, Valeri's voice pierced the quiet night. "Enjoying the ride?"

"Yes," said Elias honestly. "Especially now that we've slowed."

"It's not much farther. You're doing well."

Heat crept into Elias's cheeks at the praise. He battled a

churning mix of emotions. Terror, gratitude, anxiety, and something he didn't care to admit—lust. He found Valeri's confidence alluring. A handsome demon, powerful when necessary then patient when doling out horse riding tips to a beginner.

His stomach growled, drawing him back to reality. Elias was starving, and despite Valeri's cloak, he was beginning to get cold. It must be after midnight. His rump had grown sore, then numb. His muscles ached.

"Almost there," said Valeri, as if sensing his discomfort.

At least he would not go to bed bloody from the lash.

The terrain became hilly as they drew closer to the fells of Yllas. Miles ago they'd turned off the obvious path. Elias's eyes had mostly adjusted to the lack of light, but he had no idea how the horses picked their way over roots and brambles and through the thick copse of trees in the darkness. Pavel proved sure-footed as they approached a steep embankment.

Elias expected Valeri to turn the horses to walk alongside the wall of earth, so he wasn't ready for their abrupt halt at its base. He lurched forward, bracing his hands on Pavel's neck to stop himself falling. The horse, bless him, made no protest.

Glancing around, Elias searched for some reason they'd stopped: a house, a barn, anything. But in the black of night, he was at a loss. He looked to his demon rescuer for answers.

Valeri had already dismounted the mare. With her reins in one hand, he reached to Elias with the other. "Come, I'll help you down."

Elias took the gloved hand in his own, braced his weight in the left stirrup and drew his leg over Pavel's rump. He landed with a jolt, his body stiff from the ride, knees weak.

Valeri caught him at the waist, standing close. "Welcome." His hand lingered at Elias's side.

"Where are we?"

"My home." Valeri cocked his head and grinned. "Well, one of them." He gave a gentle squeeze before releasing Elias's waist. "I'll show you in, then I must tend to the horses."

Elias's skin tingled where Valeri's hand had been. He saw nothing but shadowed tree trunks. The air smelled of damp soil and pinesap. Would they sleep under the stars? It was far too cold for that.

Valeri collected Pavel's reins and indicated Elias should lead, though to where he didn't know. They were headed to a wall of earth for all he could tell. The horses followed behind, and just when Elias was certain they could go no farther, a wooden door appeared in front of him, framed by a shallow overhang. The entrance blended in so well he'd never have noticed had he not been guided straight to it.

"If you would, please." Valeri gestured to the handle. "It isn't locked."

Elias pulled the door open. Inside loomed a black hole. He turned and nearly bumped into Valeri. "I can't see." A tinge of panic edged his voice.

"Ah, it's all right. Here, take the horse. I'll light the lamps for you."

Elias took the reins. His chest loosened with relief upon hearing the word 'lamps.' At least if Valeri's home was a cave, it would be a lit one.

Pavel's nicker brought a smile to Elias's lips. He gave the horse an affectionate scratch on the neck while they waited. "Thanks, boy. You were wonderful." The mare, less overtly friendly, swished her tail and shifted her weight. "I'm sure you're wonder-ful, too." Elias reached to scratch her, but Valeri's low laughter caught his attention first.

"She's probably irritated to still be working, whereas Pavel has grown accustomed to being awake nights," Valeri explained and reached for their reins. "I'll need some time to see to their needs. Go on inside and make yourself comfortable. Eat whatever you like. It's all for you."

"All for me? You won't be eating?"

A sly smile formed on Valeri's lips. "Perhaps later."

"Thank you."

With a click of his tongue, Valeri signaled to the horses, and they were off to god knew where, because Elias saw no fence, no barn, no stalls. He watched them depart until their shadows disappeared into the night along the embankment, and he was alone.

A growing sense of anticipation churned in his chest. What had he gotten into? He turned and saw the flickering of the lamps inside. Then Elias let his curiosity and hunger drive him into the mysterious den of the demon.

4

Elias, Present, 1432 Common Era

*R*ain drove the six of them below deck where they crowded in the kitchen galley over a game of cards Aella had taught them to play. Karnoffel was a four-player game, with teams of two, so Elias and Valeri sat out the first round and would play the winners.

In the meantime, Elias went over his letters in his head. Remy had been teaching him to read in secret, and Elias was still memorizing the basic sounds and how they fit together to form words. Having something to focus his mind on had eased the seasickness to a tolerable level.

"That's our trick," said Aella, pulling the cards into her and Ash's pile.

Ash's cool blue eyes studied the remaining cards in his hand. He threw down an eight of shields. At this rate, they'd win the trick and likely the whole hand.

"Hell's bones," Remy murmured. "I'm out of shields. Laurence, save me?"

Laurence glanced over his cards. "I'm afraid all I can offer is to go down with you."

Remy tossed down a ten of bells and winked. "I'll take you up on that."

"Later, you two." Aella took a gulp from her mug. "Not until after we've beaten you at cards."

Laurence also threw bells, while Elias thought to himself, *B - E - L - S, bells.*

Ash took the trick for their team, winning the hand. He collected the deck to shuffle.

It was surreal to be in a room with both Valeri and Laurence and witness civil behavior. After arguing at precisely all of their planning meetings, they'd run out of insults, though the tension between the two hung in the air like a bad smell. Valeri was no fan of Aella either. When he'd learned they must take a ship because she would not risk a portal, he'd judged her lazy.

Though from Elias's perspective, her reasons were sound: the distance was too vast, she'd never been to the destination and therefore did not know its essence, and there were no witches to help on the other side. The combination made the task insurmountable. But rather than be grateful she'd be able to portal them all home when their mission was complete, Valeri held a grudge. And it wasn't the only grudge he held.

Elias had asked Valeri what happened between him and Laurence to cause so much hostility, but he'd never gotten a full answer. Only complaints of Laurence being petty and disloyal. Valeri loathed disloyalty. Which was why Elias had kept the reading lessons secret. He'd been told not to speak with Remy, but he would not let Valeri's jealousy stand in the way of making a friend.

"I call acorns," said Ash with a glance to Aella. "Six tricks."

Her lips curled to a grin. "Seven."

Ash nodded. "Seven it is."

Remy gave an exaggerated sigh and pushed Aella's cup closer

to her free hand. "You should drink more. It's our only shot at beating you."

Aella drank the ale and set the mug down with more force than strictly necessary. "I can beat you just as well drunk as sober. Watch me."

Grinning, Laurence threw the two of acorns. "My money's on Aella no matter how much ale she drinks." His gaze flitted to Remy fondly. "You never told me you're terrible at cards."

"I'll make it up to you later." Remy tossed the three of acorns, assuring they'd lose this trick too. He shrugged. "Maybe sooner than later."

Acorns. A - K- O - R - N - S, acorns. Elias wondered if he'd spelled the word correctly. He'd have to ask Remy sometime when the vampire-witch wasn't jovially losing at cards.

Aella collected the trick with glee, sharing a conspiratorial smile with Ash. They seemed to read each other well. She called acorns again, and he led with six, betting Remy and Laurence couldn't beat it.

They couldn't. And Aella and Ash's winning streak continued.

Valeri leaned into Elias's side. "Looks like we'll be playing Aella and Ash."

Ash. How would you spell Ash? A—

"Are you any good at cards?" asked Valeri, interrupting Elias's thought.

"I don't know. I've never had a set to play with before, though this game seems simple enough."

Aella sent him a sly grin and raised her cup in his direction. "Happy to wipe the floor with you next."

Elias didn't care who won. He was just glad to see everyone getting along. They'd have to spend at least another week together on this ship, then who knew how long trekking through Lappland to Rovaniemi and the Arctic Circle. The trip would be better without the endless bickering Valeri provoked.

"Where did you learn to play?" Remy asked Aella.

"My parents taught my sisters and me when we were children. We used to bet ginger candies." She smiled at the memory. "I once won so many of them I got sick from eating that much sugar before my mother could tell me to share."

"I've never had ginger candy," said Ash. "What's it like?"

Elias had never had it either. He just remembered one type of candy, peppermint, and the thought brought longing. He'd only ever gotten a couple pieces as a child and only at the winter solstice. A shame peppermints would make him sick now that he had the means to buy them. Or, well…Valeri had the means to buy them.

"Oh, it's excellent. Sweet and spicy. As a child I had hard candies, but at Bran Vigny the cook makes them chewy. I don't know how. Must be magic to taste so good."

Elias leaned into Valeri. "Did you ever have candy? Before you were a vampire?" Elias knew Valeri had been wealthy as a youth. Nobility. Second son of a lord. Surely they had enough coin for treats.

Laurence's gaze flitted to Valeri, a curious expression on his face.

Valeri didn't notice it, thankfully. He put his arm around Elias's shoulders and sighed. "I remember…a candied sauce of milk and sugar. The mixture was brought to a boil, allowed to thicken, then spread thin upon a tray. As it cooled, the sauce would harden and you could snap off pieces to eat."

Elias imagined a youthful version of Valeri, waiting for the candy to harden. "Sounds delicious."

His dark eyes glistened at the memory. "It was."

"You're all making me hungry," said Aella, taking another drink instead.

Ash laughed. "You started this."

"I did, didn't I? Well, it's good we aren't betting. We'd have taken Remy and Laurence for all they're worth."

Laurence stood from the table, his eyes on Remy. "That's the truth. Good thing we're not betting men."

"Speak for yourself." Remy also stood. He took Laurence by the hand and tugged. "You mentioned going down on me, and I plan to collect the debt."

"Going down *with* you, like a sinking ship, not—"

Remy arched his brows. "Are you saying no?"

Laurence grinned and shuffled him from the room. "No, I am absolutely not saying no."

Next to Elias, Valeri stiffened. Elias laid a hand on his thigh. "They're gone. Shall we have a go at the winners? I'm feeling lucky."

"The game is not just luck, but skill," said Aella. "There's strategy behind each call. You must communicate well with your partner."

Elias and Valeri took their places at the table. Communication was not their greatest strength, but here was an opportunity with low stakes.

Ash dealt the cards.

"Your bid," said Aella to Elias.

Elias looked to Valeri and caught a hint of lust in his stare. Perhaps they would communicate fine after all. "Flowers. Eight tricks?"

"Flowers," Valeri confirmed with a nod. "Eight tricks."

With any luck, Elias could tug Valeri from the room and to their cabin just as Remy had Laurence moments ago. He held Valeri's gaze while he wet his lips.

Lips. L - I - P - S. Lips.

Four Years Ago

Elias ate his fill from the stacks of food set neatly on the center of the small square table. Dried figs, nuts, hard bread and leathered fish, enough to feed him for days. Valeri had come in mid-meal on silent feet and lit a fire in the wood stove. Already the cozy den began to warm.

He'd never seen a dwelling like this one, hidden in a hillside. Unsure what to expect, the luxury within came as a surprise. Though the space was small, the furnishings were decadent. A thick, emerald-green carpet cushioned his feet. Gleaming black stone rose from beneath the wood stove and behind it up the wall to the vent. Next to it, a lounge of gold and silver brocade dominated the room. Wood slated walls had been stained a dark cherry red, and Elias got the impression they strained to keep out the earth behind them.

Even in the low light, the richness of the colors dazzled his senses. This room didn't belong in a carved-out mound of dirt, it belonged in a nobleman's keep, or a castle in the clouds. The decor was the stuff of stories, not real lives.

So was the house's master with his chestnut curls and wicked teeth.

Valeri had disappeared to another room and returned with an armful of folded fabric. "For you." He set them within Elias's reach on the table. Clothes.

Elias ran fingertips over the blue shirt, the fawn-colored trousers. Soft. Not scratchy like his own. And smaller, to fit Elias, not Valeri. "You want me to wear these?"

"If you like." Valeri stood close to him, watching.

Elias had sat in the only chair, for the table just had one. He'd eaten more than his fill because he didn't trust the food would be there tomorrow, though Valeri had said, *it's all for you*, and even now had offered to clothe him.

Had he known Elias would be coming? Had he orchestrated tonight's events? Elias raised his gaze to meet Valeri's.

The demon loomed over him, the expression on his face fond,

though they were little more than strangers. The gentle expression did nothing to make him seem any less dangerous—or any less tempting.

Elias wanted to touch him. To feel the muscles of his arms, to brush his hand over the sharp cheekbones, to pull his lips back and get a closer look at the fangs they hid. Such a mystery was impossible to resist. But he sat perfectly still, charting the man before him with his vision alone and keeping his hands to himself until invited.

Silently, Valeri returned his gaze, perhaps conducting an inspection of his own.

"Did you plan this?" asked Elias.

"Some of it."

"Feel free to elaborate."

Valeri inclined his head. "I couldn't have known your master would order you lashed. That bit was merely a bonus."

"For you."

"For me, yes."

Elias stood to meet Valeri eye to eye. "You enjoyed killing him?"

"I did." The answer came with no hesitation. "And I'd wager you enjoyed watching."

"*Enjoyed* isn't the word I'd use."

"No?" Valeri stepped closer. They were no more than a foot apart. "How would you put it?"

"Shocked. Relieved…" Elias let out a sigh and chose to be honest. "Awed."

Smiling, Valeri reached forward, placing his hand inside the cloak to touch the bare skin of Elias's waist. With gentle pressure, he pulled. Elias took the cue and closed the gap between them, close enough to bump chests. He gave in to the urge to connect, taking Valeri's shoulders in his grip.

Valeri smelled of horse and leather, and Elias breathed deep, taking the scent into his nostrils and committing the moment to memory. Beginnings had a way of being tenuous. Elias wanted to pin this one down. Define it. Solve the mystery of the stranger for himself.

"What do you want from me?" Elias whispered.

Valeri's lips parted. "Everything."

Eyes wide, Elias dropped his gaze to Valeri's mouth.

"Ask me what I shall give you in return," Valeri ordered. The alluring resonance of his voice raised the hairs on Elias's neck.

"What will you give me in return?"

"Everything."

That one word held more temptation than all the others that had come before. He needed what Valeri offered.

Elias leaned in to kiss him. A soft press of lips, no more, but the touch sent fire to his groin.

Valeri moved to deepen the kiss, but Elias held back, his restraint a tattered cloth threatening to rip. Any attempt he made to resist would be futile. The demon had saved him from a lifetime of hard labor and suffering. Elias was half in love with him for that alone. He didn't want to resist, but there was something he had to know first.

Elias searched Valeri's face. "What are you?"

"What do you think?"

"A demon," Elias dared to say.

Valeri let out a low rumble of laughter; Elias could feel it in his own chest.

"Not a bad guess, but no, not a demon."

"Then what?"

"I am a vampire, sweet Elias. Do you know the word?"

Elias froze, air caught in his throat. "I do."

Valeri's eyes glistened with interest. "Do I frighten you?"

Elias kissed him again, feather soft, his answer mumbled against Valeri's lips, dangerously close to those terrifying teeth. "Yes."

"Yet you do not run."

"Would running save me?"

"No."

"Do you drink blood?"

Valeri's eyes were positively gleaming, acorn brown and intensely scrutinizing. "Yes."

The question ran through Elias's mind before he said it out loud. He already knew the answer, but the words came tripping out anyway. "Will you drink my blood?"

"Would you like me to?" Valeri made the act sound like an offer, a gift.

"I should say no."

Valeri lifted a finger and placed it on the tip of Elias's nose. "You should say what you'd like."

Elias shook off the condescending touch, taking the gesture for the dare that it was, and growled, "Then do it. Bite me. I want you to."

A smile broke out on Valeri's face, the dagger points of his two eye teeth on display. Elias drew in a breath. Before he could exhale, Valeri's fist closed around a swath of his short hair and tugged, bending his head sideways, exposing his neck.

Heartbeat thundering in his ears, Elias fought not to whimper. He'd asked for this, yet a wave of panic urged him to beg mercy. He braced for pain, stiffening against the length of Valeri's body.

"Relax, or it will hurt," breathed the demon against the sensitive column of his throat.

Of course it would hurt. He was about to be bitten!

A token effort at loosening his muscles was all Elias could muster when instinct demanded him to push Valeri away and flee for his life. But something else loomed alongside that instinct. The desire to stay, to offer himself, to make a place for himself at the demon's side, in his bed, and that urge wouldn't be denied.

"Do it," Elias cried out between gritted teeth. Waiting to be pierced was torture.

Valeri's low chuckle sounded from very close to his cheek. He ran his tongue from the tender skin behind Elias's ear to the junction of his neck and shoulder, leaving a wet trail in its wake.

Then he bit.

Elias had expected pain, and there was some, but it was muted under a pleasure so deep as to steal his air and curl his toes. He melted against Valeri's chest, pressing himself in tighter for more, arms wrapped around the vampire to hold him in place. Keep him there forever.

Fire sang in Elias's veins, liquid hot and molten, lighting up his every nerve and thrilling his senses. His nipples pebbled, and his cock swelled in his breeches. A moan escaped his lips. His eyes fluttered closed.

Lost in sensation, Elias didn't know how long his demon suckled, only that he never wanted the miracle to end. If this was how he died, locked in a vampire's embrace, he could make no protest. Death would be easy, to drift off in Valeri's powerful arms, teeth buried in the flesh of his throat, and their cocks pressed together, trapped between them and pulsing. Elias could let go. He could sink. His body grew light.

Valeri tore his mouth away, and Elias cried out at the loss, boneless, unable to support himself without help. But Valeri didn't let him fall. Strong arms held him up and steadied his balance. Elias leaned into the touch.

Valeri was kissing the place he'd bitten, laving it with his tongue, warm now from Elias's blood.

His skin tingled. His balls ached. He held onto Valeri with what little strength remained.

When their lips met again it wasn't the soft, gentle kisses they'd shared before the blood. It was fierce and claiming. Valeri's tongue in his mouth, fingers squeezing the flesh of his lower back. Elias sucked and tasted salt and copper, the metallic tang of his own blood. He moaned.

"So sweet," Valeri crooned between kisses. "So eager."

Dizzy from blood loss, Elias sagged on his feet. "You took too much."

Valeri's laugh didn't surprise him, but the savage incisors puncturing his bottom lip did. Elias let out a yip of pain even as the demon drew his injured lip into his mouth to nurse the wound.

"Sorry, but you're impossible to resist." Valeri licked the punctures closed, then kissed him again.

Arousal flared. Elias pressed their hips together. "I want you."

"You're exhausted. You're barely standing." Valeri bent down, thrust an arm behind his knees and another around his shoulders and scooped him up.

"Don't care," Elias mumbled.

"I do," Valeri said into his hair as Elias's head flopped against his neck. "Now, we sleep. Tomorrow, I'm yours."

My demon, thought Elias as he was carried off to bed.

Mine.

5

Elias, Present, 1432 Common Era

$\mathcal{T}$he cog ship rocked with the swell of each surging wave. In the distance, thunder rolled, drawing closer. The bitter tang of pine tar rode on the wind. Elias stood on the deck, hands on the rail, Valeri at his side. He wanted to watch the storm come in before escaping to the galley, and Valeri didn't like him wandering around alone.

Around them, crewman dropped the sail in preparation for the incoming weather. If they wondered why their passengers were awake and above deck in the dark hours of the early morning, Elias couldn't say.

"How is your stomach?" asked Valeri over the rattling of the wind against the rigging.

After a week aboard the ship, Elias had grown used to the constant queasy rumbling in his gut. But tonight the waves swelled to enormous heights, like nothing he'd seen the first time they'd made this voyage, and his stomach paid the price.

"Getting worse, I'm afraid." Elias gazed out at the churning sea, searching for the horizon, but it was obscured by dense fog, impossible to see where water ended and sky began.

Valeri slipped a hand to his lower back. "We should go below. We'll be in the way soon, and rain approaches."

"Just a little longer?" The tiny cabin and cramped galley had begun to feel like a prison. Elias longed for solid ground and open spaces.

Lightning flashed in the sky, sideways bolts jousting on the backs of churning clouds, putting on a show. A loud clap of thunder boomed too close for comfort, shaking the boards beneath their feet. Perhaps Valeri was right.

"All right," said Elias. "Let's go."

They turned from the rail just as a sailor hollered from atop the stairwell. "All hands on deck."

A nervous jitter skittered along Elias's spine. That sounded rather serious.

The captain bellowed orders. "Set the lines!"

"Set the lines!" repeated a crewman farther down so the others could hear.

Rain began to fall as Elias and Valeri crossed the deck to head below and out of their way. A sudden swell thrashed the ship, tilting the ground beneath Elias's feet at an angle he couldn't have anticipated. He stumbled, lurched sideways, and would have fallen, but Valeri caught him easily under his armpit.

Too easily. He'd plucked Elias, a grown man, mid-fall with one arm as if he weighed no more than a kitten, lifting him clear off his feet before gently setting him down. A sailor who'd witnessed the save stopped in his tracks. The man's eyes widened, and he took a step back. One man shouldn't have been able to lift another so effortlessly, and this sailor knew it.

Elias clung to Valeri as they hurried to the stairs. "He saw that."

Valeri arched his brows. "You'd rather I let you fall?"

"No, but he will suspect."

"Shall I throw him overboard?"

Elias blew out a frustrated puff of air. "Of course not." That Valeri could say such things in such a casual manner would never fail to stun him. It was something he hoped he'd never grow accustomed to, lest he become as callous as his sire.

The rain went from the first misting drizzle to spewing angry pellets in the span of a breath. Water sprayed Elias's face. Taking cover downstairs, they narrowly avoided a drenching. The ship's passageways bustled with crewmen rushing in the other direction to assist. They crowded to the side to avoid them.

A sailor shoved into Elias's shoulder in his hurry to get by, jostling him.

"Watch it," Valeri snapped.

The sailor didn't even turn to look back.

"Perhaps you should throw him overboard too," Elias mumbled.

"Don't tempt me."

Amid the chaos, the others had gathered in the galley. Elias and Valeri slipped in from the hall.

Valeri caught his gaze. "All right?"

Elias nodded. He was rattled but fine. Valeri guided him to an empty chair and pushed him into it, then he took a cloth from his pocket and would have wiped Elias's cheeks for him had Elias not grabbed the cloth himself.

"Thank you." He dried his face and stuffed the cloth in his pocket while Valeri hovered over him.

"Why were you on the deck during a storm?" asked Laurence, his tone clipped. He and Remy were already seated. Across from them on a bench, Aella inched closer to Ash.

Elias would have admitted his desire to watch the weather change, but Valeri answered quicker and with a sharp tongue.

"To get away from you."

Elias glared at him. "Don't fight."

Valeri returned his glare, lips pressed to a thin line.

Elias reached for him and tugged. "Please, just sit with me."

Valeri sat, and though the anger never left his face, he draped an arm around Elias's shoulders and squeezed. Elias leaned into the embrace.

The room felt stifling despite the cold. No one wanted to be there.

"Will the ship survive the storm?" asked Remy, voicing the concern in Elias's own mind.

Ash answered, his low voice soothing, "Of course. Cog ships were made to withstand this weather. We'll ride it out, then the captain will bring us to the nearest port to assess damages. No need to fear."

The boat churned violently, causing all six to sway sideways before righting themselves. The rise and fall of the ship brought Elias's nausea back with a vengeance. His gaze flitted to Valeri.

"You're all right," said Valeri quietly. "I'll keep you safe."

Elias took the words to heart. He needed the gentle assurances. Between the mounting panic and his upset stomach, his nerves were on edge.

"Where is the nearest port?" asked Remy. "Why don't we go there now?"

"It's safer to ride out the storm at sea," Ash explained. "The waves along the shoreline will be worse."

Worse than this? Elias's fingers gripped Valeri's thigh for support.

"This isn't so bad," said Laurence, who held Remy much the same way Valeri held Elias. "I've been in worse. Try not to worry; the winds will soon pass, and the water will calm."

Aella's normal complexion was pale, but she'd gone ghostly white. Elias couldn't actually vomit, but Aella probably could.

"Ash," said Elias, motioning to the storage closet, "get Aella a bucket. She might be sick."

Ash turned to Aella and studied her. "Are you ill?"

She gave a one-shouldered shrug. "I've been better."

Ash retrieved the bucket and passed it over. He sat down closer to her. "I'm sorry you're not feeling well."

Setting the wooden container in her lap, Aella nodded gratefully.

Thunder clapped loudly, rattling the walls. The air was alive with the storm's energy. Elias hoped the crew were all right.

Another jolt sent them all lurching.

Waves pummeled the hull. Elias clung to Valeri and resisted the urge to shut his eyes and pretend this wasn't happening. Valeri held him in one arm and gripped the counter with the other to keep them steady.

"Laurence," said Elias, though he knew addressing his sire's first fledgling might anger Valeri. He wanted the distraction a story might bring, and actually talking with Laurence might make the vampire less intimidating. "You said you've been in worse? What happened, and why were you at sea?"

Laurence's eyes met his, gray pupils shining like polished silver.

Elias rarely traded glances with him, knowing Valeri would hate it, aware of the animosity between them, but not its cause. If Elias could discover what had led to the rift, maybe he could avoid it happening to them. Valeri dodged questions, but perhaps Laurence would answer one day. For that to happen, Elias would have to speak to him.

"I've served as messenger for The Dozen for nearly forty-five years," said Laurence.

Valeri tensed against Elias's side. It went unspoken that Laurence's service to their rulers was in trade for protection from Valeri himself, though Valeri no longer held any sway over him due to the powerful infusion of Mahu's blood.

Laurence continued, "In that time I've been on many sea voyages."

"So this is normal?" asked Remy.

"Aye, unpleasant perhaps, but normal enough. The captain will keep the bow pointed into the wind until this blows over."

"Will you tell us about your journeys?" asked Elias. "To keep our minds off the storm?"

"I'm not much of a storyteller."

"Go ahead, Laurence, we're all curious," said Aella, clenching the bucket in her lap with white fingers.

"Please." Remy's doe eyes fixed lovingly on his sire.

Elias's spirits lifted a fraction because he knew the case had been won. Laurence would deny Remy nothing. Ash remained silent. Valeri was stiff next to Elias, but he would get over it.

"All right." Laurence sighed and glanced at the low ceiling, gaze unfocused as he recalled a tale. "Shall I tell you of my trip to Malmo, Sweden?"

"Please," said Remy.

Laurence began, "Did you know the name 'Malmo' translates to 'ground up maiden'?"

Remy's mouth dropped open briefly before he spoke. "I most certainly did not. Why in the world would they name a town after a ground up maiden?"

"Because her specter demanded the tribute. It was the least they could do, don't you think, after she'd died such a gruesome death?"

Aella's face was a picture of revulsion. "They ground a woman in a millstone?"

"Not they. *He.* A jealous lover, scorned by the maiden in favor of another man," said Laurence. "But the townspeople didn't stop him from his bloody revenge. They knew he was dangerous and turned the other way because his money facilitated trade to the area."

The tale that followed, as ghastly as promised, kept Elias from dwelling on the storm. Though now he would fear nightmares of bloody millstones and vengeful ghostly maidens.

By the time the storm abated, it was near to sunup and the

vampires were forced to stay below deck. Only Aella went above to speak with the crew and take in the fresh air. She returned with news that the ship had sustained minor damage, and as Ash had predicted, they were headed to port for repairs.

Though the delay would slow their journey, Elias couldn't help but to be eager for solid land beneath his feet.

***

Four Years Ago

Sleeping through the entire day had been a breeze. After working in the overlords' field for near to twelve hours straight, almost getting beaten, watching a man murdered, then riding halfway through the night with the vampire who'd done the killing and offering him his blood, it was fair to say Elias was exhausted.

He'd passed out easily enough, head pillowed on Valeri's chest and shoulder, and had woken only to use the chamber pot then returned to bed until sundown. If the little puddle of drool he'd left on Valeri's skin bothered the man, he didn't say anything as he rose and began to dress.

Elias watched him cover his naked chest with a gray shirt then a black leather doublet. He combed his fingers through unruly brown curls. Thick trousers went over his smallclothes, and all the while Elias stared.

Valeri had a lovely form. Muscular without being brawny, a bit of a soft stomach, lean legs and narrow hips. Deep set dark eyes over prominent cheeks. Brows arched in amusement at Elias's open admiration.

"Will you be getting out of bed tonight, or just watching while I do?"

Unease churned in Elias's belly. Though he felt drawn to Valeri, he also feared him. His entire life others had told him what to do. When to wake, what to eat, how to work—he'd had very few important decisions of his own. Very little control. Would Valeri allow him to lounge in bed? Did he even want to?

"What would you like?" asked Elias, opting for a safe choice. He was aware of his dependence on Valeri. Food, shelter, clothes, work. He'd abandoned all he'd known when he said, *Do it. Kill him for me.* Not that it mattered; he'd never known anything good.

Valeri sat on the bed next to him, picked up his hand and clasped it between his own. "I wanted you here, and here you are. The rest is up to you."

"Why did you want me here?" Elias couldn't read Valeri's closed expression. Couldn't peek beneath the veil.

Valeri opened his mouth but hesitated before admitting, "I was lonely." He shrugged. "And I liked the way you looked at me. I like how you're looking at me now. As if you're trying to decipher a code and haven't quite worked it out."

Elias squeezed his palm. "Tell me what I should know then."

Valeri blinked. "I don't have all the answers. Especially not before breakfast. Aren't you hungry?"

Letting the change of subject slide, Elias nodded. He was always hungry, and the thought of the figs and bread from last night made his mouth water. He allowed Valeri to pull him from the bed to his feet.

Standing before him, face to face, Elias remembered their kisses, the sting of teeth slicing his flesh, and the euphoria that followed. The desire to pick up where they'd left off simmered in the space between them.

"Not yet," said Valeri, reading both appetites from his expression. "You need to eat."

Elias's stomach rumbled on cue. Right. Food first, then maybe a stream to wash in. He felt dirty there in the middle of Valeri's finery with a day's sweat and a night's ride still lingering on his skin.

"Can I wash?"

"Of course. I should have offered earlier. I'll set water to boil." Valeri left for the main room.

Elias followed. An indoor scrub sounded even better than an icy stream. Afterward, he would wear the soft clothes Valeri had provided. He'd never had new clothes before. Always hand-me-downs, tattered upon receipt.

He ate his fill from the food left on the table and began wondering. "Valeri?" He tried the name for the second time, smooth on his tongue. He'd rejected *m'lord* or *master,* and Valeri had yet to correct him, which Elias thought of as a good sign.

Glancing over his shoulder from tending to the stove, Valeri either didn't notice the lack of title or didn't care. "Yes?"

"Do you eat food?"

Valeri's gaze dropped to Elias's neck. "You know what I eat."

"So no food?"

"No food." Valeri returned to his task, adding wood to the stove, then water to the pot above it.

It occurred to Elias the entire reason he was there might be solely for Valeri's nourishment. The idea carried a trace of disappointment. "How often will you drink from me?"

"Why? Are you worried or eager?"

"Both," Elias admitted, taking a huge fig into his mouth so he wouldn't have to explain further.

Finished with his task, Valeri approached. Elias didn't flinch when he reached out to trail a finger from ear to collarbone, leaving a path of oversensitive skin in its wake. Instead, he tilted his head to offer better access. Valeri's hand lingered at his throat.

"You're quite bold for someone so young. How old are you?"

Elias had to finish chewing and swallow before he could answer. "Nineteen."

"You've had lovers before me?"

The insinuation was not lost on Elias. He'd wanted it from the start, but the confirmation they would soon be lovers coaxed a flutter from his stomach. "Yes."

"Women?"

Elias gave a nod. "And men."

Valeri's lips curled at that. Elias snuck a peek at the twin daggers they revealed.

"I prefer men, myself," said Valeri. "But to each their own."

At a loss for words, Elias could only stare.

Valeri's heavy gaze matched in intensity.

Elias blinked, clearing his head. "You never answered my question."

"Didn't I?"

"How often will you dri—"

Valeri stopped him with fingers over his lips. "Shh, don't fret over that. I didn't bring you here to drain you dry." He took his hand away and gestured to the food. "Finish eating, have a wash, and get dressed. I must tend to the horses." And with that, he shrugged on his cloak and left Elias alone.

Valeri's words felt an awful lot like commands. Not that he was wrong, those tasks were exactly what Elias planned to do, but he'd hoped his days of being ordered about were a thing of the past. He wished, perhaps in vain, for Valeri to treat him as an equal.

Could he be Valeri's equal? His mind cast doubts. Could a person be equal to one whom they feared? Would he always fear Valeri as much as he desired him?

With a sigh he focused on the bubbling water rather than the churning feeling in his chest. A scrub would do him good. And with hot water. Such luxury...even if he did have to answer to a demon to get it.

6

Elias, Present, 1432 Common Era

The solid feel of land beneath his feet eased the stirring in Elias's gut. Grateful for a break from the seasickness, he bent side to side, stretching his back and legs before reaching up with his arms to stretch them too.

Valeri had escorted him off the ship at nightfall amid the hushed whispers of the sailors. The crew were becoming suspicious after all. Elias caught the words *demon, night stalker,* and *cursed,* but he was so eager to get to dry land, he paid them little attention.

Elias heaved in a deep breath of salty, coastal air as he took in their surroundings. The small port town of Rauma sprawled before them, bathed in the darkness of the waning moon. Piles of seaweed had washed ashore in the storm. The pungent stink of fish filled their nostrils. Valeri grimaced in distaste, which drew a chuckle from Elias.

"Don't care for the smell?" asked Elias.

Valeri led them farther into town. "No. Do you?"

"I'm in too good a mood to care."

Repairs would be finished sometime tomorrow afternoon, so they had the entire night to explore. Come early morning, they'd return to the ship.

Valeri strode confidently along the main cobbled road. Elias admired the way he carried himself, head held high, shoulders back, chest proud. Dressed all in black, he'd blend in with the night were it not for his gleaming chestnut curls.

Elias could never walk like that; he'd feel silly trying. Not that he slouched or appeared timid, he kept his back straight and his eyes forward, but he was ordinary. Just another man on the street. Valeri stood apart: mysterious, magnetic, and exceptional. Elias was caught in the tug of his orbit.

Low wooden buildings clustered at the center of Rauma. Oil lamps burned at thresholds and in windows. Valeri would be looking for a pub with an inn. Elias grabbed his wrist.

"Don't kill anyone." If there was a silver lining to being stuck on a boat at sea for weeks, it was the absence of this particular argument. Elias never wanted the humans they fed on to suffer, but Valeri...well, sometimes he did.

Predictably, Valeri rolled his eyes. "I'm not planning on it."

Those weren't the words that would soothe Elias's fears. "Promise me, please, or I'll go back to our donors. I don't want anyone to die on our account." When Valeri hesitated, Elias repeated the plea from his soul, squeezing Valeri's fingers. "Please, lover?"

Valeri scowled but agreed. "Fine."

"Thank you." Elias had little sway over Valeri, and what power he did have was tenuous. Each small victory must be relished. Each battle chosen carefully.

They'd found a pub, brightly lit and with boisterous sound spilling out onto the streets. Valeri held the door open for Elias. The room they entered was too small for the amount of people it held, but the jovial atmosphere made up for the cramped interior.

Fishermen crowded the tables and lingered at the bar. A fire blazed under a hearth along the far wall.

The barmaid eyed them from across the space, taking in their nice clothes, shining boots, and well kept hair. She made straight for them. "Good eve m'lords. Ale?"

Elias let Valeri answer for him while he studied her. A tall woman with straw yellow hair, intelligent brown eyes, and plump pink cheeks. The sort of woman Valeri might choose for a meal, depending on his mood, but it seemed he had another agenda.

"No, thank you, m'lady," said Valeri with a suave bow, turning his predatory charm on her without shame. The combination brightened the flush across her face. "Do you have a room with a bath? Or a sauna, perhaps?"

Her smile was genuine. "Aye, we have both for a man willing to part with his coin."

Valeri pulled money from the inside pocket of his doublet and handed it over. From the look on her face, the sum was more than enough.

"Have a seat while I make the arrangements. You're certain I can't bring you a couple of ales or plates? Cook's serving fried fish and potatoes."

"Most certain, thank you," said Valeri in parting. He scanned the room, chose a destination, and led Elias to a long bench at an already crowded table. The men stank of sweat and alcohol, but underneath...the coppery tang of blood. And Elias was hungry.

He both loved and hated this part: hunting for his dinner. Though reluctant to steal from an innocent person, the demon inside him—not to mention the one he sat next to—demanded to be fed. He couldn't help the thrill of anticipation stirring in his chest, but he could make sure Valeri didn't go too far.

Already Valeri had struck up conversation with the men. "You're right. We're not from around here. Sailed in from Stockholm, headed to Mussor for the fur trade, but the storm had other plans." A mix of a lie and the truth.

A hearty middle-aged man with a red face raised his mug. "Aye, brought in the herring drifter before she hit." He grinned. "Been half-drunk ever since."

"And him?" Valeri gestured to the younger man beside him. If the first man was half-drunk, this one was all the way there.

Red Face gave the drunk a playful punch to the shoulder. "Frans here can't hold his liquor, can ye, boy?"

The drunk let out a low rumble of a laugh, deeper than Elias would have expected. "Mm doing all right," he slurred. His eyes sparkled with the kind of exuberance too much alcohol could bring. In Elias's experience, that kind of intensity could stay jolly, or turn spiteful. Valeri would choose him, Elias already knew it. His sire would be drawn to the chaos.

The barmaid returned. "Your room's ready, sirs, and the bath as well. I can take you there now if you like, or—"

"Now would be perfect, m'lady," Valeri purred. His gaze flicked to the drunk man and locked tight. "Join us later?" he said quietly, for the drunk's ears alone. He made the compulsion sound like a question rather than the order it was.

Confusion clouded the drunk's gaze even as he nodded. As Elias stood to follow Valeri and the barmaid to their room, he noticed the drunk's eyes on him. A lustful stare. Of course *that* was what he would think Valeri meant. As if Valeri would ever share him. Elias suppressed a shudder. The drunk would be waiting for them when they were ready.

They exited the pub through a small passage next to the bar, emerging into a narrow hall. Dimly lit with a single oil lamp two doors down, the hall smelled of damp wood. The rug beneath their feet was worn thin and frayed at the edges.

"Third door on your left, sirs." The barmaid pointed. "You need anything, just let me know."

"Thank you, m'lady," said Valeri, charming her with a smile.

She blushed and hurried back to the bustling main room.

Valeri led the way and pushed through the indicated door. "A real bath will do us good."

Elias had to agree. After a week of washing with only a cloth and a bin of tepid water, a hot bath would be bliss.

Though the room was small, everything they needed was accounted for. A soaking tub had been brought in and placed before the fire in the wood stove. Steam rose from within. The pail used to fill the tub was atop the stove and not yet boiling, with a rinsing cup beside it. A bed twice the size of the tiny bunk they shared in the ship was pushed into the corner, and fresh towels sat neatly folded on a wooden chair.

"You first," Valeri offered, moving the towels from the chair to the bed. He brought the chair close to the tub and sat, spreading his legs and leaning back. "I want to watch."

Elias stared at the tempting picture he made sprawled on the chair, lips and legs parted, brown eyes dark with anticipation. An idea bloomed. "Take out your cock. I want to watch too."

Valeri's tongue darted out to moisten his upper lip, right over the brown freckle Elias found so charming. Then he obeyed, opening the black leather to reveal the tempting jewels inside. His shaft was still soft, but wouldn't be for long.

Elias stripped without ceremony, eager to get into the water and out of it as well so he could get his hands on his lover. He relished the way Valeri's eyes felt on him as he peeled off the layers, loved the promise of what was to come.

This part of their relationship had always been exquisite. Free of complication. From the first time they'd come together and every time thereafter, they'd fit flawlessly, their bodies in harmony, the give and take of bed-play an uncomplicated delight. Elias couldn't ask for a better lover than Valeri, and he yearned for him and the pleasure of their union.

Climbing into the tub, Elias found the water almost too hot, but he sank in anyway. All the way, dunking his head under to soak his hair. When he surfaced, it was to find Valeri stroking himself to hardness. His dark eyes on Elias, gaze following the water dripping from his skin. Elias kneeled in the tub, hands on the rim, facing Valeri.

"Wash my hair for me while I suck your cock." Elias did not have to ask twice.

Valeri stood before him and reached for the soap. "My pleasure."

Elias opened his mouth and took in the tip with practiced ease. A service that no matter how often he performed, he'd never tire of. Dipping his tongue inside the foreskin to taste the sensitive flesh it contained, he let out a moan and closed his eyes.

Valeri's hands settled on his scalp, urging him forward. Elias let himself be guided, opening his throat in offering, eager to swallow the gift. Hands still clinging to the rim of the tub, he used his mouth alone. Valeri filled him thoroughly, then drew back.

As Elias massaged the cock in his mouth with his tongue, Valeri massaged the soap into his hair. Motions languid, neither of them rushed, both basking in sensation.

Fingers swirled around the base of his skull with the same rhythm Elias set with his mouth. The sound of the water rippling filtered pleasantly to his ears. He sped up. When he gave a good, hard suck, Valeri fisted his hair and tugged.

"That's it," Valeri gasped. "So lovely."

Elias enjoyed the praise almost as much as the hair pulling. He leaned into it, silently asking Valeri to grip harder. But instead, Valeri let him go and pulled out from his mouth, panting and desperate. Such a sexy look on him. Elias swiped spit from his lips with his tongue. Valeri followed the movement with his gaze and then his finger. Elias sucked it into his mouth.

"Shall I let you finish me with your mouth or do you want me to fuck you?"

Elias let go of the tub to grab the backs of Valeri's thighs and yank him closer. "Both. We have all night. Don't be lazy."

A rumble of laughter spilled from smiling lips. "As you

command, my sweet. But first, tip your head back or the soap will get in your eyes."

Elias let his head be guided this way and that as Valeri poured cup after cup of water over his hair until all the soap was rinsed away. When finished, he palmed Elias's cheek, and their eyes locked.

"Use me," Elias ordered. "I need you." He opened his mouth.

Valeri thrust his cock so far into Elias's throat as to nearly choke him.

Groaning in delight at the rough treatment, Elias dug his fingers into the muscles of Valeri's ass and encouraged his pumping. He reached between Valeri's legs to stroke his sac, already tight and drawn, ready to give up its prize.

Elias hummed and moaned around the thick shaft until seed burst down his throat. Valeri held him in place with hands on the back of his neck, not that Elias wanted to be anywhere else, but the desperation in his touch felt amazing.

Smoothing his hands down Valeri's thighs, Elias kept still otherwise. He raised his gaze so Valeri could admire the view, then, ever so slowly, pulled off his cock with a decadent wet sound. He licked his lips and sank farther into the tub. The hot water made his body loose and pliant, except for his cock, which was hard as stone. He left it untouched, enjoying the denial.

Valeri smirked down at him, gaze fond, eyes hazy from lust. "You vixen. You incubus. You darling, clever harlot," he purred, kneeling next to the tub. "Kiss me with that filthy mouth of yours."

With a delighted grin, Elias complied, pressing their lips together with urgent desire. Valeri deepened the kiss, and Elias opened for him, allowing him to lick his own taste from his tongue. When Valeri kissed him like this, he could forget his own name. He sighed his pleasure into Valeri's mouth. This was a wonderful way to ignore all their problems.

"Perhaps you should actually wash?" Valeri suggested, his voice dropping an octave in post-orgasmic bliss. "Turn around, I'll do your back."

Elias let Valeri scrub him down, shivering when he got to the swollen shaft between his legs, but Valeri was perfunctory, cleaning him there as he would anywhere else. Then they switched. Elias dried himself off while Valeri washed.

There was no reason to put his clothes back on. Valeri owed him a good fucking, and he intended to have it. But after Valeri was dry he began to get dressed, much to Elias's dismay.

Elias cleared his throat. "And just what do you think you're doing?"

A wicked sparkle danced in Valeri's deep brown eyes. "I'm going to retrieve our supper. He waits for me in the pub like you'll wait for me here."

Settling in the bed, legs open, Elias gave his length a languid stroke. "Hurry back."

"Hands off that," ordered Valeri. "Save it for me."

Elias formed his mouth to a perfect pout but did as he was bidden. He stretched instead, arching his back then draping his arms overhead and crossed at the wrist. The ploy worked easily. Valeri, still half-dressed, crawled over him on the bed.

"Perhaps a taste before I go then," he said before licking a broad strip from the base of Elias's shaft to the tip and back.

Elias shivered. "Please."

Valeri pressed a kiss to his hipbone. "Be good. Don't touch." He finished dressing and left with a glance over his shoulder that was full of heady anticipation.

Elias's tummy rumbled, craving his dinner. As long as Valeri kept his promise—no killing—this would be a satisfying night indeed. On his belly, his cock twitched in agreement.

7

Four Years Ago

      *F*resh and clean with a set of new, soft clothes against his skin, Elias sat nestled on the lounge and watched as Valeri took his turn at a wash. Elias had offered to step out to give him privacy, but Valeri had declined with a knowing smirk.

You want to watch, so watch, Valeri had said.

Elias wanted to do more than watch, though his desire went without saying; surely Valeri knew that too. The warm air in the cozy, colorful room was thick with it.

Valeri made a show of undressing, stripping off each layer methodically, revealing the smooth pale skin beneath, inch by lovely inch. Elias couldn't drag his gaze away from the demon… the vampire. And what did it say about him that he wanted Valeri even knowing what he was? Maybe because of it. To have a man like that at your side, in your bed, there was a certain pride in that possession Elias found irresistible.

Valeri stood on the bathing tray, wet a cloth and swiped the fabric over his strong shoulders, leaving a trail of water beaded in its wake.

Elias imagined licking the droplets from his skin but stayed perfectly still. He'd only been invited to watch, not touch. A twinge of fear at what might come next, what they were building up to, rattled his chest. Sex with a demon. It was nothing he'd ever dared to consider—why would he—but had quickly become all he could think about.

Blood filled his shaft, and he had to resist the urge to stroke himself.

Valeri seemed to know, turning so Elias could see the evidence of his own arousal. "Go ahead if you want."

The words startled Elias from his staring. "Go ahead, what?"

"Touch yourself," Valeri confirmed. "You want to, don't you?"

Elias considered his next actions carefully. It was one thing to be mouthy in bed-play with another bondslave; it was quite another to order a vampire around. Could he say what he liked to a man such as Valeri?

Trepidation and lust combined to raise the hairs along the back of his neck. He pulled his cock and balls from his breeches and laid his hands at his sides.

"You do it," Elias ordered, his voice projecting a confidence he didn't feel.

Valeri's eyes went very dark as he surveyed Elias like prey. A wicked smile lit his face, teeth gleaming like the metal edge of a dagger's blade.

The vampire stalked forward, abandoning the wash, his naked body a gift and a warning. A low growl rumbled from his throat as he neared. Wet footprints lingered on the carpet.

"It would be my pleasure," purred Valeri, reaching for him.

Elias's heart raced, the thunder of its pounding loud in his own ears. The beat pulsed in his throat where Valeri had bitten him only last night.

Valeri closed his fist around Elias's cock and gave it a firm tug. Elias gripped the armrest of the lounge he sat on in an effort not to writhe right off it. His lips parted on a moan.

"Lovely," Valeri praised. "What else would you like from me, hmm? If you could have anything."

Anything. Anything at all? There was much he desired. Valeri's mouth on his cock, his fangs in his throat, but could he really ask for *anything?*

"I want to fuck you. Can I?"

Elias expected the answer to be no, and honestly, that would be fine. He liked it both ways. If Valeri wanted to take him instead, Elias would gladly turn over and present. The need to merge their bodies overrode higher thought.

Valeri continued to stroke him while watching the war raging in his eyes. Elias let him see it all. The need to claim, to be claimed, to be on the other side of the uncertainty as soon as possible.

Thumb circling the plump head of Elias's cock, Valeri made his decision. "Why not?" He gave a playful shrug and stood.

"Really?" Elias couldn't help the surprise in his voice. Was he going to be granted this? Allowed inside?

As Valeri crossed the room, Elias enjoyed a fantastic view of the ass he planned to plunder. Water dripped along every curve.

"I said *anything*, didn't I?" Valeri opened the top drawer of a chest and retrieved a palm-sized glass jar. He returned, set the jar aside, and pushed Elias's knees together so he could climb onto the lounge and straddle his lap. Valeri's hand landed on Elias's cock and stroked.

Elias sucked in a delighted breath, thrilled with how events were playing out.

Valeri sat back on Elias's thighs. "Touch me."

The command was an easy one to obey. Every part of Valeri was tempting. Touch him where? With free rein like this, Elias hardly knew where to start. His focus shifted to the two pretty pink buds of Valeri's nipples, and he could not resist them. He circled the buds with his fingertips, ran the pads over them lightly, then pinched.

When Valeri leaned into the touch, Elias pinched harder.

Valeri's eyes fluttered closed. His hand hadn't stopped pumping Elias's cock, but he slowed now, as if the twin sensations broke his concentration. Elias counted that as a win, giving the tender buds a gentle tug for good measure.

He liked the feel of Valeri on his lap, the weight on his thighs, Valeri's smooth cock pulsing against the thin fabric covering Elias's abdomen. Such promise between them. And Valeri totally naked while Elias remained almost entirely clothed. He flattened his hands to run his palms over broad shoulders, down the firm mounds of Valeri's biceps then back up.

He should be scared with this lapful of writhing predator in his arms, and part of him was, but he wouldn't be held back by fear. Elias had spent his whole life afraid. This feast boasted new delights, and he wanted a taste of everything on offer.

Elias tilted his head, hoping for a kiss which, when it came, was hard and fast.

Valeri claimed his mouth with zeal, as if only the back of Elias's throat could satiate his hunger.

Gasping as they broke for air, Elias took Valeri's cock in hand and pressed it against his own. Together they stroked both rods, something Elias had done before but the act had never been so arousing as it was this time, with *this* man. Every inch of skin sizzled with arousal.

"Are you always like this?" asked Valeri, startlingly breathless.

Elias leaned in to nip at his bottom lip, daring those deadly teeth to come out and play. "I don't think I've ever been like this. You're impossible to resist."

Valeri laughed. A full belly laugh, deep and joyous, and he squeezed their cocks while he was at it. "Is this you trying to resist me? My god, what will you be like when you've fully given over to your desires?"

Valeri's wide smile was contagious. Elias grinned in return, pleasure coursing through his every nerve. "I suppose we should find out." He reached around Valeri's waist to his spine and followed it down the crack of his ass and pressed, making his meaning clear. "You have oil?"

Valeri let go of their cocks but continued to rock against Elias's belly. He plucked the glass jar from beside them and unscrewed the lid. "Will you be doing the honors?"

"Would you like that?"

"You know, I think I would."

Elias dipped his fingers into the slippery salve as Valeri leaned in, giving him room. "I want to touch you everywhere," said Elias as he began his work.

Valeri sighed into his neck and pressed back onto his finger. "That feeling is mutual."

"Do you want to bite me?"

"All the time," purred Valeri with no hesitation.

Elias tilted his head aside, exposing his neck in offering. "You can."

"I know," Valeri chuckled into his ear, then sucked the lobe into his mouth, but he didn't bite, leaving Elias adrift in anticipation.

With his slick fingers, Elias embarked on the most intimate of massages, loosening muscle and teasing sensitive, hidden flesh. Valeri was a squirming delight in his arms, a pleasure to hold and to touch, and soon...to fuck. Their cocks leaked where they were trapped between them.

"Enough, Elias. Fill me," Valeri ordered, hands gripping his shoulders. He lifted himself to make room, paused for Elias to adjust, then impaled himself with a groan.

Elias resisted the urge to thrust right away, to claim Valeri's body for his own. He clenched his teeth as tight pressure enveloped him completely, hands gripping Valeri's hips and pulling him down until no space was left between them.

Valeri took hold of his jaw and angled him for another bruising kiss, and with that, he began to move.

Matching the rhythm, Elias threw his head back and held on. The ride of his life, and he wasn't even the rider. Valeri was an expert in the saddle, knew how to tug and stretch each drop of pleasure to the fullest. Sweat beaded on Elias's chest.

"Is this what you wanted?" Valeri murmured, lips against his cheek.

Elias rut like a wild dog, panting out his answer. "It's better."

"Next time, I fuck you."

Elias arched his brows. "I'm not entirely sure that isn't what's happening right now."

Both of them laughed even as they strained together, climbing to their peak. Elias reached between them to grasp Valeri's cock. The head was leaking and slippery. He wet his palm and made a slick channel for Valeri to use as he saw fit.

Valeri rocked from Elias's cock to his hand, undulating with graceful ease between fucking and being fucked. Elias met each dip with a thrust, slamming into him hard, knocking the most delightful whimpers from Valeri's throat with each battering push.

It was the sounds that threw him over, free-falling into bliss, his toes curling as he came. Valeri's seed spilled between them, coating his hand and painting his new shirt. His heart thundered in his chest as each tingling shudder of pleasure took hold and released.

As his climax began to release him from its seductive prison, Valeri struck. The bite he'd been waiting for came as a surprise. A welcome and sharp surprise. A sting as fangs pierced flesh, then another sweeping roll of pleasure when Valeri sucked on the wound. Elias's balls drew tight and gave of themselves again, his cock rallied valiantly, and he shook with sheer gluttonous lust.

Elias clung to Valeri as the vampire licked the wounds closed and kissed his neck. It had been perfect and only their first time. What could they build with alchemy such as theirs?

Elias caught his breath enough to ask, "Are you always like this?"

Valeri pulled back to meet his gaze, eyes a fiery chestnut brown. "I've never been like this. I find you impossible to resist."

There was blood on his mouth as he smiled.

Elias should be afraid, but he only wanted more.

Elias, Present, 1432 Common Era

Valeri returned with the drunk from the bar. The man's name was Frans, a fisherman local to Rauma, and he, like many others, had to wait out ship repairs before he got back to work. The storm had done a number on many of the boats in the area.

Elias lay nude atop the covers as they entered. He wasn't shy, and he remembered the flicker of interest Frans had shown before they left. What Frans didn't know was that Valeri would never share what he considered to be his alone. And that was fine by Elias. Frans had one purpose only—to feed them. Afterward he'd be discarded to sleep it off and forget. He'd wake up alone, room paid for, wondering why he'd slept there and who had picked up the tab.

Frans looked Elias over from head to toe, gaze lingering somewhere in the middle, the grin on his face steadily widening.

"He's pretty, isn't he?" Valeri teased.

Frans wobbled on his feet. "Aye, very nice. Like a cherub."

"Wait until you hear the noises he makes, better than tears of the poppy on the tongue and more stimulating too." Valeri slipped his hand to the ties about Frans's collar and began to unlace them.

Elias could smell Frans from where he lay on the bed—still stretched languidly for Valeri's enjoyment—a mix of ale, sweat, fish...and blood. He disobeyed Valeri's order and stroked his cock, eager to feed and then have Valeri to himself.

Valeri ignored the infraction as he tugged Frans's shirt over his head and gave him a little push. "What are you waiting for? Go on."

Frans stumbled forward, lust in his gaze. "What's your name, angel?"

Elias wet his lips before answering. "Elias."

"Turn over, Elias." Frans unfastened his trousers on the way to the bed.

"Not so fast," said Valeri, restraining him with a tug at his elbow.

The movement threw Frans off balance, and Valeri had to catch him or else he'd have fallen.

"The fuck?" spit Frans, pulling from Valeri's grip. "Let me go."

"I don't think so. You're awfully drunk. You might hurt him. Better let me help."

"Don't need help." Frans pushed Valeri out of his way, and Valeri let it happen. Playacting like this amused him.

Elias played his part, eyes half-lidded, hand teasing his shaft enough to keep it full and rigid.

Frans stalked to the bed, tugging his ruddy cock free. "I said turn over."

"Why? So you can pretend I'm a woman?" Elias opened his legs. "I want it like this."

"Better do as he asks," warned Valeri. "He's been known to bite men who don't." He laughed at his own joke.

Elias would have laughed too, but the dark look in Frans's eyes did not sit well with him. The drink had gone to his head. Elias knew a jovial drunk could morph into something more sinister with little notice. Which way would Frans go? It wouldn't matter. Valeri wouldn't let this progress much further.

"If you say so," said Frans, apparently indifferent as long as he got to stick his cock in something. He crawled onto the bed and over Elias.

Valeri struck from behind, knocking Frans off Elias and sinking fangs into his shoulder.

"Wha—"

In a flash, Elias sat up and bit the other shoulder. He sent a wave of calm, and a pleasure so deep as to lull the fright from the drunk's body and turn him to pudding. Valeri wouldn't have bothered. Wouldn't have cared if Frans was terrified or aroused. But Elias didn't think he deserved the fear, so he stole it away as he stole the blood.

Hot, thin from the alcohol, and salty on his tongue, the copper nectar warmed his throat as he swallowed. Valeri's hand had replaced his own on his cock and stroked him as he drank his fill. They sandwiched Frans between them, Elias at his front and Valeri at his back.

Frans melted into the bed, mindlessly thrusting his hips in a lazy rhythm. A pleasured whimper escaped his lips. Between the excess of ale and the blood loss, his cock had softened, but he moaned like he was coming anyway.

With one last swallow, Elias pulled back and licked the punctures closed. Too much more and they risked permanent damage. More still and they could kill him.

The alcohol from Frans's bloodstream went straight to Elias's head. A pleasant wave of dizzy tingles rolled through his limbs. He felt light and content.

And horny.

Valeri still fisted his cock. Elias rocked into the motion, wanting more, wanting it harder. Valeri owed him a fuck and Elias intended to claim it. He reached around Frans to stroke Valeri's flank.

"Lover?" Elias mumbled, his eyes closed, lost in pleasure. "I want you."

The moment stretched like taffy—Elias's need, the soft sucking sound of Valeri still feeding, the slowing *thump thump thump* of Frans's heartbeat.

Elias blinked, forced the drunken stupor aside, and shoved at Valeri's shoulder. "Stop it, you're taking too much!"

Valeri stared at Elias, fangs still embedded in Frans's shoulder, and stubbornly continued. His expression dared Elias to interfere.

"Valeri, don't kill him."

Rolling his eyes, Valeri popped free of Frans's flesh, leaving two open wounds oozing blood. His fangs were covered in red. He let the crimson liquid drip down his chin carelessly. "Why shouldn't I?"

"You promised!" Elias shrieked.

Valeri squeezed his cock in warning. "Shh, you'll wake our hosts."

Elias batted his hand off and pulled away. "Then stop. Close his wounds and let him go."

"I want to finish him." Valeri's eyes darkened with menace. "Who are you to tell me not to?"

Elias's jaw dropped. After four years together, the words stung. "I'm your partner."

"You're my fledgling. You answer to me, not the other way around."

Elias shook his head in disbelief. This argument was endless and exhausting. He left the bed and began to dress.

"What do you think you're doing?"

Elias stepped into his pants. "Leaving."

Valeri tossed Frans off the bed without healing his wounds and crossed the floor to Elias, gripping his wrist to stop his progress. "I didn't say you could leave."

"I don't need your permission." Elias tugged his wrist free and put on his shirt.

Valeri spoke through clenched teeth. "We aren't done here."

"I am." Elias pulled on his boots.

"Elias." Valeri tried a capitulatory tone. He pinched the bridge of his nose and huffed. "Don't go. We have the room all night."

Elias glanced at the drunk slumped on the floor. "Frans is still bleeding. Heal him."

Valeri gave an exasperated sigh. "What do you care?"

"I care!" he said entirely too loudly.

"Shh." Valeri went to take his shoulders, but Elias dodged the touch.

"I don't want to kill people. I don't want *you* to kill people." He jabbed Valeri's sternum with his finger. "It's not necessary, and you promised."

Tipping his head back in frustration, Valeri gave in. "Fine. Fine. Just don't go." He turned to Frans in the corner and propped the man up. He knelt to heal the wounds.

Elias waited long enough to watch Valeri lick the punctures closed, then he left the room, hurried down the hallway, and fled the pub.

8

Elias, Present, 1432 Common Era

*E*lias hoped he had enough of a head start that Valeri wouldn't follow. The cobbled streets passed in a blur and turned to dirt under his feet as he hit the edge of the village. He wouldn't go back to the ship yet, not alone, not since the crew had become suspicious of their nocturnal lifestyle. Plus Valeri would look for him there, and Elias needed some space to think.

Had things been like this for Laurence when he was with Valeri? Elias couldn't imagine the strong, indomitable vampire cowing to their sire's petty demands the way Elias did. And Elias had only been with Valeri for four years. Laurence somehow survived the man for fifteen.

Farmland became forest and the dirt road narrowed. Elias slowed his pace. Branches canopied overhead, not yet boasting full leaves but only the buds of springtime.

Footsteps surged behind him. Elias recognized them—Valeri, announcing himself rather than sneaking up on silent feet.

Resigned to more arguing, Elias rallied. He should have known he wouldn't be allowed the last word.

He stopped and whirled so suddenly Valeri nearly ran into him. "What part of me leaving made you think I wanted to be followed?"

"Didn't you?" Valeri barked with a hint of a sneer. He stepped back and gave Elias an appraising glance from head to toe.

The question stunned Elias. Realization dawned on him; there was an ugly truth in Valeri's words. Yes, he wanted to be alone, but also…he'd expected Valeri to follow. Some part of him wanted it. And if Valeri hadn't come, Elias would have wondered why not. He would have been disappointed.

Damn him.

Valeri cocked his head, an arrogant arch to his brows as if he'd read Elias's mind and knew he'd won. "That's what I thought."

Elias fumed in silence, irritated at having become so transparent. How had that happened?

"He's fine, you know." Valeri offered the knowledge like an olive branch. "Frans. He'll sleep it off. I didn't kill him."

"I suppose you want a medal for that. Did it hurt very much? Keeping your promise?"

"Don't be impertinent."

Elias crossed his arms. "Or what?"

"I won't tolerate disrespect, Elias. I did what you asked of me, then I asked you not to leave, and you refused me the same courtesy."

Elias opened his mouth to say, *I never promised not to leave*, but he had, hadn't he? Not tonight, no, but on a night not so long ago, when Valeri had turned him to a vampire. He'd promised then, and he'd meant it. But now? He wasn't sure if he could stay, not when the tension between them had gotten so suffocating. Though he didn't want to leave either. He was trapped.

Elias searched Valeri's face. "You used to be kinder to me. When it was just the two of us."

Valeri threw his hands in the air. "I'm kind to you now!"

Elias shook his head. "You're not. You're different. You order me around and embarrass me in front of the others. You keep me isolated."

"It's for your own good. I'm protecting you."

"From what? Remy? Laurence? You're the one who insisted we go to Bran Vigny. You knew Laurence worked for The Dozen. You wanted to see him." Elias forced himself to ask the question though he feared the answer. "Did you hope to win him back?"

"What? No!"

A swell of relief eased the worry that threatened.

"Don't be ridiculous," Valeri chided, his face a mask of revulsion. "I've no interest in his pompous ass or his weakling whelp."

The need to defend his new friend hit Elias hard. "Remy is not weak."

"And how do you know that, hmm?" Valeri's gaze turned dark. "Do you think you're keeping him a secret? I know you meet with him, though I asked you not to."

"Not asked," Elias corrected. "Ordered."

"Ordered. Not that it makes a difference to you. You don't listen."

"And you'd have me believe that order was for my benefit, not your own?"

"Of course."

"Horse shit." Elias set his hands on his hips. "You're afraid of what they'll tell me."

Valeri scowled. "Do not speak with Laurence."

"Is that a threat?"

"Does it need to be?"

"What is it you want? My loyalty? You have it. Must I also be miserable to please you? Why are we here?"

"To save Mahu—"

"Not that. I know that." Elias let out a frustrated sigh. "I mean, we know that now; we did not know it then, when this started. Why did we hunt all over Lappland searching for ancient vampires, and when we found them why did we go running to Bran Vigny if not to impress your first fledgling, if not to—"

"Respect!" Valeri shouted, stopping Elias mid-rant. "And not Laurence's, I don't care about him. He shamed me in front of The Dozen, got me exiled, banished to the north. I lost my place at court. I want their respect back. I deserve it!"

"You want what you refuse to give."

"You owe me your respect, not the other way around." Valeri thrust a finger at his chest. "You are my fledgling."

"And that's all I am, isn't it?"

"That's *everything*." Valeri said the word as if it were holy.

"Everything. Then why does it feel like nothing?"

Valeri pinched the bridge of his nose, a habit he had when irritated with Elias. He did it often lately. "You're being dramatic. You must know your value to me."

Elias narrowed his gaze. "My value?"

"Your worth. Your importance. Don't nitpick. You know that I treasure you. If you ever left…" Valeri glanced down as the words trailed off.

For once it didn't sound like a threat. His expression held real fear. The sentiment caused Elias to soften, like he always did in the end.

"I'm not trying to leave you, Valeri. I am trying to *become* me."

Valeri stared at him like he had no idea what that meant.

Perhaps he didn't.

Four Years Ago

Eight nights had passed since Elias's life had changed forever, and he'd begun to accept the idea that this tentative reality could become permanent. His demon lover, a vampire no less, had the means to provide for his every whim and fantasy. Elias had never known wealth, not the comforts money could provide, nor the problems it could solve. He'd never had the freedom to spend each moment basking in a new love, or the free time to pursue whatever they fancied.

Elias sat astride Pavel, racing behind Valeri, who rode the mare they'd named Barley. Next to lovemaking, horse riding had become his favorite pastime. All of the lean muscle he'd earned slaving in the fields was well suited for riding, and Valeri was an indulgent teacher.

Chilly air pinked his cheeks. The first frost had dug her talons into the land and not let go, but Elias had his own warm clothes now. Layers of soft wool with a heavy cloak on top kept the cold at bay. The night smelled of pine and the promise of snow.

Elias had always dreaded the snow. A layer of white meant constant discomfort, the agony of cold bones, and periods of hunger when food became scarce. But everything was different with Valeri at his side, providing for him. For the first time in his life, he need not fear the snow and found himself anticipating the first flakes with joy.

Valeri slowed Barley to a walk as the trail widened. Elias and Pavel followed suit, coming up beside them. They'd explored every wandering path near Valeri's hidden cave-like home in the last week, but tonight Elias had made a special request. They were headed to the nearest village. He wanted to see Valeri hunt.

"You won't hurt anyone? Not really?" asked Elias, feeling the need for reassurance. When he'd made the request from the comfort of their bed, the idea of watching Valeri feed had seemed mysterious and intriguing, but now that the act was imminent, Elias had doubts.

Valeri glanced over to him, his expression amused. "Not if you don't want me to."

"I don't," Elias confirmed. He'd seen what Valeri had done to Maks and had no desire for a repeat performance. But if he was going to spend the rest of his days…or nights rather, with a vampire, he should know how one ate.

They tied the horses not far off trail and continued on foot. The first few houses were scattered far apart, each with a clearing for farming or animals. Folks would still be awake in their homes at this hour.

Self-conscious to be a stranger wandering through their properties, Elias stayed silent. Valeri, who Elias doubted had ever felt a moment of self-consciousness in his life, strut along beside him, whistling. Elias suppressed the urge to shush him.

"Which would you prefer, a man or a woman?" Valeri asked.

Elias hadn't thought of that. Did he have a preference? Not really. "You choose."

"That house," Valeri pointed to a small cabin, "has eight people inside. Better to keep moving."

"Eight people? But how do you know?"

"I can hear their heartbeats. Two of them are young children, already asleep."

"No children," said Elias firmly.

"I wasn't suggesting a child. I'm not that much of a monster."

"Of course, I'm sorry."

Valeri's hand came to rest against the back of his neck, fingers cool on his skin. "You're tense. Calm down. There's nothing to fear."

"Right." Doubt plagued Elias. Why had he wanted to see Valeri drink an innocent person's blood? Now that it was time to choose, he wanted the choice to be no one at all. "Drink from me."

Stopping in his tracks, Valeri turned to face him. "You're scared?"

"Yes."

"Don't be. I've promised not to hurt anyone. And I can't drink from you every night." Valeri tipped his head to the side, hearing something Elias couldn't. "Come. There's a man already outside."

Valeri took his wrist and tugged him along. They scurried past the first house and around the back of a second, larger home. Smoke rose from the chimney and peppered the air with its scent. Valeri thrust his arm in front of Elias's chest, bringing them both to a halt.

"Him," Valeri purred.

At an outbuilding, a large man collected wood into a burlap sack that hung from his broad shoulders. He'd tower over Valeri, tall and wide, a powerful man accustomed to farm work. He would not be easy to subdue.

Elias balked. "Are you sure?"

"I'm sure." Valeri stalked forward before Elias could stop him.

Elias's second thoughts were overrun by third thoughts and then fourth thoughts. He watched as the farmer turned, and suddenly it was too late to take everything back. Valeri would get caught. The farmer would overpower him. Elias would try to help, but he didn't know how to fight. He would fail and—

The bulging sack of wood fell from the farmer's shoulders, forgotten. He had eyes only for Valeri and stood transfixed as the vampire approached.

"Knees," said Valeri, and the farmer knelt without question.

Elias's mouth hung open. When Valeri beckoned for him to come closer, he couldn't help but creep forward.

"Take off your scarf and loosen your shirt." Valeri waited while the farmer complied.

"Is he all right?" asked Elias.

"Perfectly fine. He won't remember a thing. You ready?"

This was it then. Valeri would bite this man, and Elias would watch. He nodded.

Valeri took the farmer by the jaw and tilted his head.

"Wait!" said Elias, a little too loudly. Valeri glowered at him, annoyed. "Sorry, just...don't hurt him."

The vampire turned back to his meal. Elias both regretted asking for this and was appalled by his own fascination. He couldn't tear his eyes away as Valeri bent down and bit the farmer's meaty neck.

The man let out a low moan that sounded all too much like he was enjoying himself. Elias supposed he was. Valeri's bite felt amazing to him, so why should it be any different for the farmer? Would he come like Elias did? Suddenly Elias found himself battling jealousy, which was ridiculous, because Valeri belonged to him.

My demon.

As quick as it had started, the act was done. Valeri closed the punctures with his tongue, pulled back from the farmer, and licked his lips clean.

"Don't forget your scarf," Valeri said to the farmer, who noticed the abandoned garment at his side with a hint of confusion.

Elias remained frozen in thought. So that was how a vampire fed. Valeri had some sort of power over other people. Did he use that power on Elias?

Valeri took Elias's arm and led him away, back in the direction they'd come from. "There. Now you've seen me feed. What do you think?"

I think you do that to me. What would stop you? "He won't tell anyone?"

"He has nothing to tell. I've hazed the memory. He went out for wood and dropped his scarf." Valeri shrugged.

With Valeri's arm looped around his elbow, Elias felt the shrug more than he saw it. They were almost back to the horses by the time he'd collected his thoughts enough to answer.

"I think...it's not so bad. To take only a little and leave them unaware. As long as you don't hurt anyone."

"Elias." Valeri said his name slowly, emphasizing each syllable. "Don't be daft. You must know sometimes I kill them."

Elias did know that. Though he'd never let conversation between them stray too close to the uncomfortable fact. Valeri was a killer. Elias had always known that no matter how much he wished he didn't. Sometimes life was easier lived in ignorance.

"Why?" Elias asked, though he didn't really want that answer either.

"Because I enjoy killing."

Elias tried to hide his shock. Unsuccessfully because Valeri's response was laughter.

"Don't pretend you didn't know that, my sweet," Valeri drawled, voice slow like molasses. "You knew."

Elias hadn't wanted to face the truth, but Valeri wasn't wrong. "I did."

That earned him a smile. The wicked one, wide enough to reveal fangs. "And now, I have a question for you." Valeri tugged him past the horses, farther into the woods and under a dense canopy of evergreens. Their sharp, resinous scent permeated the crisp air.

Valeri stopped, put his hands on Elias's chest and backed him up against a tree. "Do you want it?"

This time, Elias would not play dumb. They'd been dancing their way to this conclusion all week. "How is it done?"

"I take your blood—all of your blood—and you die..." Valeri let the words linger between them.

Elias watched his own breath as the breeze stole it away in wisps and curls until all traces disappeared.

Valeri continued, bright eyes focused on him with singular purpose. "Then I give the blood back. And you wake, reborn. A vampire. Like me."

"Like you." A chill rippled through Elias's chest. "How do you know the transformation will work?"

"I've done it before."

This time, Elias's shock was real. He'd never considered the possibility Valeri had other spawn out there in the world. "You've made another vampire?"

"Once."

Elias knew he must be gawking, but he couldn't help himself. "But where are they?"

"*He* is irrelevant. The transformation worked. Do you want it or not?"

Elias faltered. An owl screeched in the distance. "I don't know."

Valeri hovered, their faces inches apart. "Make a choice."

"Now?"

"Now."

"What if I say no?" Would Valeri kill him? Was this his plan all along?

Valeri leaned in, so their chests pressed together and their cheeks touched. Elias could no longer see his eyes. Couldn't interpret his expression. Somehow this was more frightening. His heart pounded.

"Then I'll give you the money I have on me, and you can take Barley and go south. Pavel is mine. There will be no more between us, and you will never tell a soul about me."

Simple. Take the money, take the horse, find a new life that didn't involve killing people. But it wouldn't involve Valeri either and despite his fear, Elias wanted Valeri above all else.

"I want a companion," Valeri whispered into his ear. "I've chosen you. Will you choose me?"

Thump, thump, thump. Elias listened to his heartbeat for the last time.

"Yes."

9

Elias, Present, 1432 Common Era

$\mathcal{T}$ired of arguing, Elias walked back to the ship with Valeri in silence. Halfway through the journey, Valeri linked their arms. Elias recognized the gesture for what it was. A peace offering, the best Valeri could give. He would receive no apology, but this he could have. He squeezed Valeri's bicep against his side. Whether happy or miserable, they would be together.

They were approaching the ship when the pitter-patter of light footsteps alerted Remy's presence. He trotted in from the board-walk. Next to Elias, Valeri stiffened.

"Best to wait," said Remy.

"What's going on?" Valeri's gaze landed on the vessel.

With an hour's time left before dawn, there was no one about. No obvious reason not to board the ship.

"Aella heard talk amongst the crew. Some of them think we're cursed and no longer want us aboard."

Valeri scowled. "After what we've paid? Of all the ungrateful—"

"Can we help?" Elias cut him off. He stroked the inside of Valeri's wrist in apology.

Remy shook his head. "I don't think so. Aella has a plan. Come, we're just discussing it."

Remy led them farther ashore where the others waited. The air stank of fish, but Elias didn't care. He would enjoy these last moments on land before being forced back onto the ship that made him sick and whose crew had them figured out after all.

Laurence and Aella had their heads together in conversation. Remy went to stand at Laurence's side. Ash greeted them with a nod. At least he didn't seem worried, which was reassuring.

"Good, we're all here," said Aella with a glance to Elias and Valeri. "The crew is split in half as to what action to take concerning our party. One group agrees they're being compensated well enough to tolerate the risk, the other group thinks no amount of money is worth potentially being cursed."

Elias had to stifle a laugh. "So they are all in agreement that we're cursed, just split over what to do about it?"

"Precisely," said Aella.

Laurence's gaze took in the night sky. "We don't have long to decide. We'll either need to be in our cabins, or we'll have to make other arrangements quickly."

'Other arrangements' was a civilized way of saying they'd sleep in the ground, which Elias didn't mind. Though messy, the ability to burrow safely beneath the earth to escape the sun's rays was perhaps his favorite vampire trick. Not all vampires enjoyed the experience. Perhaps Laurence didn't care for it.

"I won't let it come to that." Aella turned to Remy. "I know you aren't familiar with mind manipulation, but if I could draw from you and Laurence to broaden my circle of influence, I should be able to convince most of them you're all harmless."

"Of course," said Remy.

"Most of them?" asked Valeri. "What does that mean?"

"Some humans have a natural resistance to magic of mind

persuasion. Same with vampire compulsion. I could probably lead their thoughts elsewhere in the short term, but they will remember eventually. The rest of the crew will not. The divide could cause trouble. With time, those sailors could be rooted out, but we'll be at sea by then. I can't just throw them off the boat."

Valeri's irritation was clear in his tone. "Why not?"

Laurence looked at Valeri, his expression horrified, but unsurprised. "None of this is their fault."

"And so?" Valeri pushed.

Laurence opened his mouth to speak, but a touch from Remy along with a subtle head shake changed his mind. Apparently Elias wasn't the only one sick of arguments.

Ash spoke calmly to Aella. "I trust you'll take care of it. How long shall we wait before boarding?"

She smiled to him. "You don't need to wait. Most of the crew will be sleeping. Laurence, Remy and I can cast the spell from above deck and send the magic below. We won't really know how well it worked until they wake."

"At which point, it will be too late," Valeri griped. "We'll be trapped in our cabins."

Aella's expression turned serious. "You must trust me. I'll let no harm come to you."

Elias knew trust did not come easy for Valeri. He would not be pleased with this plan, but for once he kept his mouth shut—scowling, but shut.

"Do we have time to go over the spell before we enact it?" asked Remy.

"Yes, if we hurry," Aella answered, and the three of them huddled close. "I'll do the chanting alone, and you and Laurence will add power and resonance like we practiced."

Sensing their dismissal, Elias glanced at Valeri, still frowning, then at Ash. Ash had a presence about him that made him seem perpetually amused, like someone had whispered a bit of gossip into his ear, and he relished knowing a secret those around him didn't. His ice blue eyes hid his mysteries well.

"Did you enjoy your night in town?" asked Elias, in an effort to be polite. And he was genuinely curious. For a diplomat, Ash never had much to say.

"I remained with Aella, who remained near the crew, but it was enjoyable, yes. And you?"

"Yes, thank you," Elias said because he could not say the truth. *Well, I was enjoying my night until Valeri nearly killed our dinner to provoke me, and though he hasn't apologized, here I am, on his arm, pretending all is fine.*

Valeri stayed silent at his side. Elias couldn't guess what he was thinking, only that his anger lingered below the surface.

"We're ready," Aella announced. "I'll go first, Remy and Laurence behind me, the three of you behind them. The spell won't take long, then you may retreat to your cabins."

"Thank you," said Ash. "Lead the way."

Elias and Valeri trailed behind the others back to their dock, then climbed the ramp to board the cog ship. Though Elias was torn about tampering with the crew's memory, he couldn't help but to be excited to see magic right in front of his eyes.

Aella chanted quietly, her words lost to the coastal breeze, while Remy and Laurence walked hand in hand behind her, their free hands raised in front of them. Ash strolled along, unworried. Meanwhile, Valeri remained stiff, his arm clenched around Elias's elbow.

Elias gave Valeri's linked arm a squeeze and caught his gaze. "Everything all right?"

"Splendid." Valeri pursed his lips.

Elias nearly laughed at him then but held back. At times like these, when Valeri was overruled, nothing could appease him. Rather than be annoyed, Elias took a page from Ash's book and chose to be amused.

As they approached the stairwell, a sailor emerged from below deck. Elias froze. It was one thing for magic to work on sleeping crewman, and another to confront a man wide-awake.

"Just what are you lot doing, eh?" asked the sailor, his tone skeptical.

Aella turned her attention on him. "Nothing to see. Nothing out of the ordinary."

His head cocked sideways like a dog struggling to understand his owner's commands. He opened his mouth to say something, but no words followed.

Remy's hand aimed at the man's chest, and though Elias could see nothing coming from his palm, he got the sense magic was flowing.

The sailor took a step toward them. Remy's fingers flexed. The man stopped.

"Go on about your business," said Aella, voice low and almost musical, as if she were singing. "Don't mind us. Nothing to fear."

The fight drained from his eyes. In a daze, the sailor walked past them and set to work organizing the lines.

Elias let out a breath, relieved. Whatever Aella was doing, it was working.

They marched the length of the ship and back, casting the spell. The lone sailor continued to ignore them. Aella stopped her chanting, and Remy's countenance changed from focused to sleepy. His lids drooped. Laurence slid a hand to his waist and pulled him close.

"It's done," said Aella. "I'll keep watch during the day. Rest easy."

Valeri huffed; Elias ignored him.

"Thank you," said Ash with a nod.

Overhead the sky had just begun to lighten. Sunrise would follow shortly. The winds were gentle and the few clouds scattered and light. The weather would allow for the ship's departure, and Elias would sleep through all of it. A melancholy longing for sunshine came and went like the tide. He'd traded his days for nights, and his freedom for Valeri.

"Come," said Valeri, his tone dry. "If we're to be murdered in our sleep we best get on with it."

Elias sent an apologetic glance to the others as he was hauled away.

Four Years Ago

Thump...thump...thump.

Elias's heartbeat dwindled as Valeri drained the last of his blood. He'd struck with a feral fury Elias hadn't expected, biting deeper than the times before this. Not with just the incisors either, but using his entire two rows of teeth, jaws clamped tight, as if he was trying to tear off a chunk of Elias's flesh.

Despite the ferocity of the attack, the pain only lasted a span of heartbeats before it was overwhelmed by the inevitable pleasure of the bite.

Clutching Valeri tight, fingers digging into the flesh of his flanks, Elias sighed and gave into sensation. Squeezed between the trunk of a mighty pine at his back and the steel of his lover's chest at his front, there was nothing to do but feel.

Valeri growled against his skin. Hot blood oozed a sticky trail to Elias's collar bone. The scent of copper hung heavy in the chilled air.

Elias moaned and pressed his hips forward. His cock demanded attention. It always did when Valeri fed, greedy just like his lover.

Valeri met the motion with a thrust of his own, his length hard against Elias's groin.

"Please," Elias mumbled, out of breath. "Please."

A low rumbling groan answered his plea, and without pausing

his feast, Valeri scooped him up and laid him upon the forest floor. He covered Elias with his body, his weight a grounding comfort amongst the tempest. The suckling noise never ceased; it rang loud in Elias's ear, overcoming his fading heartbeat.

Valeri shoved a hand down Elias's breeches and cupped his soft cock in his palm. There wasn't enough blood left in his veins for the shaft to harden, but the touch felt divine all the same. Elias pushed into the caress with what little strength he had left.

Thump... thump... thump...

Elias's muscles failed him. His body went limp, and his head lolled sideways. Dead pine needles crunched beneath his cheek. His vision blurred, so he closed his eyes.

Valeri continued to drink. The weight of him grew heavier by the second. *Still here. Still here. Not dead yet.* Panic threatened to crowd his mind, but he forced the anxiety back. He'd asked for this. He would die and then wake a demon, like Valeri.

Thump... thump...

Thoughts tumbled over each other. Elias couldn't properly grab any of them. The fields on fire, the ash covering the ground, the buds of a new crop breaking through the soil. That life was over now.

Thump...

The world grew silent. Valeri's weight was gone from his chest. Elias floated. In the distance, a soft golden light flickered amid the blackness that engulfed him.

The flicker was dashed away before he could rise and investigate.

Ambrosia exploded on his tongue. Sweet and spicy drops. He arched, seeking more, lips closing to form a seal so he could suck the nectar down his throat in great gasping swallows.

As his strength returned, Elias grabbed at the offered wrist and held it prisoner to his starving mouth. In a haze of gluttony, he drank. The blood filled his stomach, his veins, his cock. He ached with need.

"Very good." Valeri's voice. Extremely close to his face.

Elias opened his eyes to see him, but what he saw was so startling he squeezed them shut again and moaned.

"You're all right," said Valeri, his free hand stroking Elias's short hair. "That's normal. Nothing to fear."

Nothing to fear. Elias would laugh but his mouth was full. He opened his eyes again, carefully this time, just a slit between his lids, but even still color poured in the likes of which he never knew existed. Bright, though it was nighttime, the browns and greens of the forest practically glowing in their vibrancy. Valeri's eyes, acorn brown but shimmering like jewels in their sockets.

And the smells! Beyond the overpowering metallic notes of the blood as it gushed down his throat were the aromas of nature. Soil, rock, pine, dung, livestock, smoke, and grain; all of it jumbled in his nose and fighting for attention. Too much.

Valeri tore his wrist away.

Elias yowled like a feral cat in protest. He needed more.

Lying back, Valeri opened his arms and turned his head to the side, exposing his neck. "Your fangs are ready. Bite me."

Elias ran his tongue along his teeth; the familiar ridges and slopes were interrupted by two deadly daggers protruding from his upper jaw. If he wasn't careful, he'd cut his own tongue. He crawled over Valeri and stared at his throat. Beneath the skin, a web of blue veins sprawled like stria variations in marble. His new preternatural vision could follow each delectable path.

He chose the biggest of them and bit. Valeri's arms closed around his back and held him tight. Blood filled his mouth, and Elias swallowed it eagerly. He ground his hips against Valeri's, cocks hard and trapped between them.

Valeri's hands slid to his ass and encouraged the movement.

Elias rutted like an animal. Teeth in his lover's neck, body between his legs, climax building fast between them. All his senses were overloaded. Too much to taste, too many scents to decipher, the sound of his own desperate feeding pounded in his ears above all else.

"Yes," Valeri growled beneath him. "That's it."

A sudden fear invaded Elias's mind. Could he take too much? He never wanted this to end, but he didn't want to kill Valeri either.

"Take what you need to be strong," said Valeri in that way he had of reading Elias's every thought. "Drain me."

Fears banished, Elias continued with a new zeal. He drank in mindless abandon, thrusting his way to crisis against Valeri's willing body. When Valeri's arms grew weak and fell to the side, Elias grabbed them, yanked them overhead, and pinned them to the ground by the wrists. He liked the feel of his lover helpless and gasping under him.

The flow of blood slowed, but his hips did not. Elias came in his breeches, seed flowing from his shaft in a burst of passionate writhing. Whether or not Valeri came, he didn't know. Maybe he couldn't. His body was pliant as if in slumber.

Licking the last trickle of blood from the vein, Elias attempted to close the wounds as he'd seen Valeri do. He watched the skin knit itself back together by unseen magic.

"Valeri?" Elias's voice sounded different in his own mind. Fuller and more melodious. "Are you all right?"

Valeri didn't open his eyes, but he smiled. "I will be. Don't leave me."

"I would never leave you."

Elias let up on his wrists, but Valeri didn't move them, just let them lie harmless above his head. He looked vulnerable like this, and beautiful. Elias palmed his cheek.

"Do you need to drink from me now? Take some of it back?"

At that, Valeri's lids fluttered open and the golden-brown jewels of his irises focused on Elias. "No. Keep it. I want you to be strong."

"But..."

"Just give me a moment. I'll recover."

Reassured, another thought came to Elias's mind. "Did you come?"

Valeri let out an endearing giggle. "In my pants like a fumbling boy."

Elias grinned. "Me too."

Around them, snow began to fall. Elias stared in wonder. Each flake contained a rainbow of color. Glistening crystals, each one different, falling in silence. He watched a flake land on Valeri's upper lip, right beside the freckle there. He leaned in to kiss it away.

They lay together amongst the pine needles in the snow and said nothing, because nothing needed to be said. Understanding passed between them without words. Demon with demon; together forever.

Elias, Present, 1432 Common Era

They didn't die on the ship that night or any night thereafter. Aella's spell had worked on most of the crew, and those who woke confused, she simply spelled again, with stronger magic. Her magic kept the sailors' suspicions at bay long enough for them to reach their destination eight nights later.

With Remy and Laurence at her back, and Bran Vigny's witches waiting for her magical call at home, Aella had created a portal for the donors to return through. Elias would miss them, but on land the vampires could hunt for themselves. Bringing humans along on the next stretch would slow them down.

This far north, the spring's sunshine hadn't yet completely melted the winter's snowfall. A white blanket greeted them from the forested shore, glittering in the moonlight, slushy and wet. The Bothnian Bay, being the northernmost arm of the Baltic Sea, had thawed enough to allow for vessels to come and go.

For Elias, leaving the ship behind was a huge relief. From here they would follow the Kemijoki River to Rovaniemi, then turn north toward the Arctic Circle in search of the ancients.

The settlement at Kemi had little in the way of amenities. They stopped only to purchase additional food for Aella, then continued on foot.

Valeri led the way. He'd been easily irritated since their argument at Rauma. He'd put a stop to the reading lessons with Remy, insisting on teaching Elias himself, but he'd only picked up the borrowed books to do so once, and they'd spent most of that session bickering. The books sat heavy in Elias's pack now, not that the extra weight mattered to a vampire, but the constant reminder of broken promises niggled at the back of his mind.

Behind them, Remy and Laurence chatted amicably about nothing. Elias wished he could join them. Conversation would pass the time, but Valeri spurned his efforts at small talk, or meaningful talk, or any talk at all really. And he would be furious if Elias walked with Remy and Laurence instead. So Elias was stuck alone in his mind.

Aella and Ash trailed behind the rest of them, but not so far Elias couldn't hear whispers of their conversation. He sighed, staring at the back of Valeri's head with half a dozen questions lingering on his tongue, but none he dared to venture aloud.

What happened between you and Laurence?

Why do you hate each other so?

Did you ever love him like you love me?

What went wrong?

What aren't you telling us about the cure?

Those subjects were all pointless. He'd never gotten a straight answer from Valeri about any of it. Remy might tell him, but asking his friend for his lover's secrets was unfair. Valeri ought to tell him himself.

Elias focused on their journey. The vampires could maintain a fast pace, even trekking on narrow paths through the slush of the remaining snow, but Elias didn't know how Aella was keeping up. He suspected she used her magic, though she wasn't chanting or holding her hand aloft the way Remy and Laurence did when they performed spells.

"Elias." Valeri's call interrupted his runaway thoughts. "I smell reindeer."

Elias stopped and sniffed the air. "You're right."

They would all need to feed. Valeri, Ash, and Laurence had mostly gone without, leaving the donors for Elias and Remy. A herd of reindeer would be ideal, and at this hour, probably sleeping. Easy targets. And much preferable to arguing over another human.

"I'll go. You tell the others," said Valeri before slinking off like a mountain cat to secure their meal.

Waiting for the rest to catch up, Elias leaned against a tree and enjoyed the solid ground beneath his feet. If he never experienced another sea voyage, it would be too soon. Above him, the arctic lights danced green and purple in the sky.

Remy and Laurence approached. They looked as if they'd been laughing. Their eyes glowed bright in the dim light. Elias admired them, for they made such a handsome couple and looked so happy together. So in love.

Remy saw him first. "Is everything all right?"

Laurence's gaze turned suspicious. "Where is Valeri?"

"He's gone for reindeer," Elias explained. "He's very good with compulsion, there's no need for worry." Then he thought, well, Laurence would know that already, wouldn't he? Valeri had probably taught him compulsion as he'd taught Elias in those early nights.

Laurence relaxed, but Remy didn't; he scanned the area, found they were alone, then wrapped Elias in an unexpected embrace.

Elias didn't know what to do, but he returned the hug meanwhile looking to Laurence for clues. Laurence watched with an unreadable expression, which was no help at all.

Remy pulled back enough to catch Elias's gaze. "Are you all right? Valeri keeps you isolated. Neither of you look happy."

Neither of us is happy. "I'm fine. We're fine. He's just…like that. I don't know why."

Remy's assessment didn't let up. His hands held Elias's upper arms and squeezed. "We can help you. When this is over. You don't have to stay with him. You can come with us."

Elias's mouth hung open. He didn't know what to say. His first thought was to defend Valeri, to proclaim his love for his sire, to tell them he didn't want to leave, but was that true? Had he not been thinking it would come to this himself? Would Valeri let him go? Elias didn't know, and somehow the thought made him sad either way.

Laurence stepped in. "There are laws among our kind, Elias. He isn't allowed to control you the way he does. We can protect you."

This information only added to his confusion. His answer came slow and quiet. "I don't need protection from Valeri. He wouldn't hurt me."

Remy's palm cupped his cheek. "There are a lot of ways to hurt someone."

Wasn't that the truth.

Remy continued, "We're your friends, and if you need us, we want to help."

Too stunned to reply, Elias stood there gaping. He grew nervous. Valeri would be back soon, and if he saw Remy touching him, he'd be angry.

As if sensing his distress, Remy released him and went back to Laurence.

Elias was surprised to see Aella and Ash had already joined them and were watching. How much had they heard? Did they think he needed to be protected from Valeri too? All of this made him terribly uncomfortable, and doubly so because Valeri was who he'd always turned to for comfort.

"You'll be safe with Laurence and Remy," said Aella,

confirming they'd heard everything. "Or at Bran Vigny if you prefer. We'll keep you safe from him."

Elias mumbled a soft, "Thank you," but he didn't need their protection. Did he?

The sound of snow crunching signaled Valeri's return.

Relief flooded Elias's veins at the sight of him approaching with two dazed and docile reindeer following along in a trance. He had to suppress the urge to throw himself into Valeri's arms because, even though he knew Remy and the others had a point, the thought of leaving Valeri behind terrified him.

"I've eaten. These are for you," said Valeri.

"Thanks," said Remy, taking the other for himself and Laurence.

"Thank you." Ash took one of the beasts under his sway. "Elias?"

Elias joined Ash and ran a hand down the deer's fuzzy winter coat. The amount they'd take, even together, would not hurt the animals. When they were done, the reindeer would be released from the compulsion and freed to rejoin their herd.

Drinking from an animal was never pleasant. They stank, their fur stuck to your lips, their blood tasted bland compared to a human's. Despite all that, in many ways, Elias preferred it.

At least there would be no argument with Valeri over a reindeer.

Four Years Ago

A terrible thirst woke Elias from slumber. Distressed, he called out to Valeri for help. He wasn't sure he used actual words, but Valeri appeared at his side and offered his wrist.

Elias bit without hesitation, in a blind need so desperate he could do nothing else. The blood hit his throat, and he couldn't swallow fast enough. Gulp after gulp, anything to quench the insufferable thirst.

Valeri petted him with his free hand until Elias came back to his senses. He had Valeri's arm clenched in tight fingers so hard it must hurt, but Valeri didn't complain. Elias loosened his hold and continued to drink. He began to think more clearly.

He was a vampire now and would be dependent on the blood of others for the rest of his life. The sobering thought, as he guzzled blood straight from Valeri's vein, frightened him. What had he done? The feeling wasn't regret, exactly, but the question loomed large in his mind.

"That's enough for now." Valeri's voice broke through the haze of feeding and the impending panic threatening to take hold. "Finish and heal the wounds."

Elias did as he was told, and though his thirst had slaked, the desire for more remained.

Valeri had sat next to him on the bed, and at some point, Elias had practically crawled into his lap. He didn't remember doing that, only the blood. But Valeri's arms felt good around him. He leaned into the touch, considering how to voice his fears.

"We must leave here tonight." Valeri pressed a kiss to the sensitive skin behind his ear, then nuzzled into his hair.

"Leave? But why?"

"The villages nearby don't have populations large enough to support a fledgling vampire. You'll need to feed every night. We must go to Rovaniemi where the dead will not be noticed."

"The dead!" Elias gripped Valeri's shoulders and squeezed. "I don't want to kill anyone. I'll only take a little, like you did from that farmer last night."

Valeri shook his head. "You won't have that kind of control right away. The will to stop feeding before the death of your meal comes with time."

"But you said—" Elias racked his mind. He'd thought to make

sure Valeri didn't have to kill to feed, and he'd assumed he wouldn't have to either, but he'd never actually asked.

"I said, 'I enjoy killing.' Or did you mishear? Perhaps you wanted to."

"Perhaps I did." He searched Valeri's eyes. "I don't want to kill anyone. You must help me. Please."

Valeri softened. "Of course I will help you." He kissed Elias on the mouth. "Pack your things. We'll take the horses and go south to Rovaniemi. I've another house in the city, and there are rumors I want to look into."

"Rumors?"

"I'll tell you later. The journey will take all night. Come along."

Elias got up from bed, washed, and dressed. Packing took only a minute because there was nothing to pack but the clothes Valeri had given him. He looked around their cozy cave-like dwelling. He liked this place. He'd thought they'd be staying and was sorry to leave the comfortable rooms behind.

"Will we come back?"

Valeri gave a shrug, unconcerned. "Maybe? I don't know."

"What about your things?" There was far more in the home than the horses could take with them.

"They're just things. We can get more."

Spoken like a man who'd never worried for resources a day in his life. What must that be like?

Valeri was true to his word. They rode all night, stopping only to allow Elias to feed from a farmer's cow because he didn't want to hurt the farmer himself. Valeri had laughed at him, but in the end, he'd used his compulsion to calm the animal and shown Elias how to drink. The veins in the leg were easiest to get to, close to the surface and under a thinner layer of hide. The taste was awful, but Elias didn't care.

The city of Rovaniemi still slumbered when they arrived in the early morning hours. They left the horses at a barn for boarding. Valeri tossed the sleepy groom an extra coin for the trouble of their early arrival. To Elias's surprise, they continued on to the heart of the town, not some hidden-away cave. They passed by a tavern with colorful banners along the way and finally descended into an underground level of a small shop that sold leather goods.

Valeri fastened a complicated locking system behind them while Elias looked around. Though the rooms were pitch black, with his new vampiric vision he could still see the shape of things. Lounging furniture, carpets, a table and chairs, a hearth under a small fireplace, knick-knacks on the mantle, doors to other chambers. Much larger than the space they'd left behind, but similar in its lush decor. The rug was thick and soft beneath his feet.

Valeri began lighting the oil lamps, and the rich and vibrant color scheme revealed itself. Everything in deep jewel tones. Purple velvet fabric hung from the wall, gold brocade covered the lounge and chairs, the carpet a vivid sapphire blue. Even the brick of the fireplace had color, painted navy with a rich rust-brown wood mantle. He imagined the place in natural light; it would be so bright as to almost be garish, but under the gentle flickering glow of the lamps, the colors were pleasing to the eye.

"Welcome," said his lover, voice pitched low and coming from very close to his back. Valeri's hand landed on his hip. Elias was instantly interested.

He leaned back against Valeri's chest. "It's beautiful."

"I hoped you'd like it." Valeri pressed them together, his cock hard against Elias's backside.

Grinning, Elias turned in his arms. "You have a knack for picking very luxurious carpets. I'd like to see how this one feels against my hands and knees."

Valeri kissed him quickly. "That could be easily arranged, my sweet."

"Light the fire?" Elias began to strip.

"My pleasure."

Perhaps the best way to get comfortable in a new home was to earn a decent rug burn in front of a crackling flame.

Valeri worked him slowly, inch by inch, leaving no part untouched. Elias gave himself over to his lover's whims. Tonight he wanted to be fucked, and he didn't really care how. Besides, Valeri was a master at the how. First on his back, so he could watch. Then on his knees, like he'd requested. And seated in Valeri's lap to finish.

When they were both satiated and sticky, they collapsed together on the pretty blue carpet and stared at the ceiling. Elias threw a leg over Valeri's thigh.

Valeri grasped his hand and laced their fingers. "You approve of the carpet selection, then?"

Elias squeezed. "Wholeheartedly."

The pops and snaps of the fire crackled in the background, and the warm air felt divine on his naked skin. Elias stretched his legs and rolled to his side against Valeri. With his free hand he traced a path from one nipple to the next and back.

Perhaps the mood was right for the question that had been on his mind since he discovered he wasn't the first vampire Valeri had made.

He gathered his courage and asked, "Would you tell me about your first fledgling?"

Valeri's expression hardened as he glared at Elias through half-lowered lids. The mood soured. "I don't want to speak of him."

"Why?" Elias pushed. A part of him really hated to spoil the afterglow between them, but his curiosity wouldn't be denied.

"He's an ass, and the memories are unpleasant. Don't ask me again." The words came out harsh.

Elias fought not to flinch. Valeri didn't usually speak harshly. "Don't be angry with me."

"I'm not angry," said Valeri angrily.

"You are." Elias flattened his hand on Valeri's chest. He'd gotten used to the cool skin, the lack of a heartbeat, the differences between Valeri and former lovers. He adored the thick muscle of Valeri's pecs and below the soft gentle roundness of his stomach.

Not plump, but not trim like Elias either. A body that had never been starved.

"Why do you want to know about him? It isn't a pleasant story."

Elias could think of many reasons, the first of which was to avoid whatever had gone wrong between them. "I want to know everything about you."

"Ask something else."

That wasn't a difficult request. Elias had so many questions. "How did you become what you are? What was your life like before it?"

Shifting, Valeri wrapped an arm around him. Elias adjusted to lay his head on his bicep. Tucked into Valeri's side like this had become one of his favorite positions.

"I was the second son of a lord, my father a Russian Boyar, which is like a nobleman, with land and status and all that entails. We had servants to dress us, cook our food, tend to the gardens. It should have been an easy life."

"It wasn't?"

"Not for me. Though I suppose compared to yours, my childhood was a dream."

Elias had already told Valeri of the orphanage he'd grown up in, the abuse he'd suffered there, and of being purchased like a slave by an overlord at only twelve years of age for farm labor. He'd known nothing but depravation and orders. The idea of regular food was mind-boggling, much less a cook to prepare it. He could only imagine.

"My father favored my older brother, Evgeni. Everyone did. Our tutors, cousins, friends. And not because Evgeni was charming or kind, but because he would inherit, and they wanted powerful and wealthy friends. My father groomed him for the title and left me for the nursemaids. Our mother died giving birth to a stillborn baby girl when I was four. I'd have loved a little sister, but it was not to be."

"I'm sorry."

"It was a long time ago." Valeri sighed. His hand rubbed light circles over the ridges of Elias's spine absently. "After Mother died, I was well and truly friendless. Evgeni was cruel to me, and Father condoned his behavior, so I'd little recourse but to make myself scarce."

"What could you have done as a child? Was he much older, your brother?"

"Not so much, three years, but that was enough. He was always bigger, stronger, taller. I'd no chance against him. He had a pack of local boys who thought he could do no wrong. Even the first boy I ever cared for preferred my brother. In the end, I think he was only with me to be closer to Evgeni, but Evgeni never cared for boys that way. He chose women."

Elias traced Valeri's collarbone with his fingertips as he listened and wondered what it would be like to have a brother who hated him.

"Our father died suddenly when I was nineteen. He fell from his horse and could not be revived. I wasn't sad. I didn't care. He'd never shown me any kindness, and I didn't think it would matter that he'd died. But before his body was even put to ground, Evgeni made noises of throwing me out, leaving me to starve. I'd no doubt he'd follow through with the threats. So I began sneaking about the estate, pocketing jewels and small things of value to exchange for room and board somewhere until I could establish myself at a trade. I enjoyed working with my hands. I thought perhaps I could apprentice at something. Smithing maybe."

Elias could not imagine Valeri as a blacksmith. He was too accustomed to finery. What would he look like covered in soot with grit beneath his fingernails?

"At the funeral, there was a man I'd never seen before. He arrived very late and lingered when others began to depart. My brother yelled at me for some infraction I no longer remember. What I do remember is that the stranger saw his tirade, and I was ashamed to have it witnessed. Afterward, my brother stormed off and the stranger approached to talk with me. Offered condolences. But I was rude. I didn't want to speak to the man who saw my own brother treat me that way. I brushed him off and left.

"The next evening I was in town making preparations to leave before Evgeni had the chance to throw me out. I saw the stranger again. I know now that he'd followed me, but then I thought it a coincidence."

The stranger, thought Elias. That's what he'd called Valeri before learning his name. "He was a vampire?"

Valeri patted his side where his hand had come to rest. "Shh, you. You asked for the story, let me tell it in order."

The tone was teasing, but Elias apologized anyway. He was quite caught up in the tale.

"Yes, he was a vampire, but I didn't know that yet. I thought him just another wealthy lord. He dressed as one. Carried himself as one. It was the obvious assumption. Some associate of my father's who would mourn his passing." At this, Valeri laughed. "Little did I know, he'd shoved my father from that horse."

Elias's eyes blazed open. "What?"

"Not that I cared, remember. I had no love for the man."

"But to murder him? Surely you found that offensive."

"You'd think, wouldn't you? But I've gotten ahead of myself. I knew nothing of him at the time."

"So what happened next?"

"He offered to buy me an ale. I declined, but he insisted. I figured, perhaps a connection to this lord would come in handy when I was on my own, so I let him take me to a pub. We drank and spoke. Or rather, I drank, and he spoke.

"After I'd had perhaps one too many, we went out for fresh air. A walk would do me good. Clear my head.

"'Your brother treats you unfairly,' said Fedor. I could only agree. 'You would make a more suitable heir.' I wasn't going to argue. 'I could help you.' Help me how? I near to laughed in his face. But he didn't speak in jest. His face was perfectly serious. 'I could help you, for a price.'"

"For a price?" asked Elias. "That sounds ominous."

"It was, indeed."

"Was he offering to kill your brother?"

"You catch on faster than I did. I didn't know what he meant. Only that I was drunk and unhappy and about to be homeless. Fedor offered again, 'I can help you.' I asked what he meant, and he told it to me straight. 'I will kill Evgeni. I'm good at making death look like an accident.'"

"Perhaps that's when I should have realized Fedor had killed my father, but it didn't occur to me. What I did realize was Evgeni's death would solve all my problems. And I only half believed Fedor would do it. So I asked how."

"'Never mind how,' said Fedor. 'Do you want it?' Yes. 'It will cost you.' I have money. 'More than money,' he said. 'Ask me to do it.' I looked him dead in the eye and said, 'Kill my brother.'"

This story had taken a turn Elias hadn't expected. He'd never had a family of his own. Valeri was the closest thing he had to family. He couldn't imagine ordering a stranger to kill his own brother. A chill gripped his spine despite the roaring fire.

"The next day, Evgeni was dead. Leapt to his death from the north tower of the family estate. Penned a note first in his own hand. Couldn't bear the grief over our dear father. I had no idea how Fedor finagled that. Evgeni had a strong will, but apparently not strong enough to overcome a master vampire's power of compulsion.

"We had two funerals in the span of a week, and I inherited the lordship, the lands, the staff, and piles of money I didn't know what to do with. Turns out that was not a problem. Fedor had plenty of ideas for what to do with piles of money."

"So he killed your family to have you and your wealth?"

Valeri snorted. "He killed my family for the wealth, alone, Elias. He didn't care one whit for me. He needed a willing pawn, and he had one. I owed him. I wasn't out on the streets thanks to him, and I knew as much. I gave him free rein with the estate for that is what he required. That and he could not kill me because then the family fortune would fall to an uncle who would not be so easy to influence as I. We were stuck together."

"How awful."

"Not really. At least not at first. I had everything I needed. All of Evgeni's old friends wanted to be my friends, of course, since I'd become a lord. Even the boy who'd fucked me to be near my esteemed brother wanted my attentions. I spurned him. I spurned them all. I'd learned by then that I needed no friends. It was safer to keep them at arm's length."

"Did you get along well with Fedor?"

"Well enough while I was still human. He was thrilled to be dripping in jewels once more. His own history was a tale of feast or famine, and he'd a strong preference for feast. Not long there-after I learned he was a vampire. It wasn't enough for him to control the lands and the money, he demanded my blood as well."

"And you complied?"

"What choice did I have? I knew I'd sold my soul to the devil. I pay my debts." Valeri rolled onto his side to look Elias in the eye.

Elias saw a man there he'd only had glimpses of before tonight. A man who knew a loneliness so desperate, he'd kill to escape its depths. He leaned up to kiss his mouth.

"None of it was your fault," Elias said softly, pushing Valeri's curls behind his ear.

"Does it look like I feel guilty?" asked Valeri, his expression open. "Perhaps I should, but I don't. What happened, happened, and three years later, he made me a vampire."

"Why?"

"His motives never changed. Wealth, status, prestige. We had an easy enough relationship, why not cement it in stone?"

"You agreed to it?"

Valeri blinked. "I didn't say no."

"Which is different than agreeing."

"Only in words. I let him turn me. I didn't protest."

"How long were you together?"

"Forty-three years."

Elias let that sink in. Forty-three years was more than twice his own age. "How old are you?"

"One hundred and sixty-something. Three, I think."

Elias's jaw dropped, and his mouth hung open stupidly.

Valeri laughed and kissed his forehead. "And you so young. Do you think me a cradle robber?"

"I suppose you are," Elias teased. "What, were there no other one-hundred-and-sixty-three-year-olds for you to court?"

"Shockingly, no."

"Did you part on good terms? Where is he now?"

"One question at a time. We parted on...good enough terms. He still manages the estate and has done well growing the wealth. I never lack for coin, and that is mostly Fedor's doing."

"Were you lovers?"

"Myself and Fedor? No. Like my brother, he preferred women." Valeri reached down to palm Elias's soft cock where it rested on his thigh. "I'll never understand it."

Elias did the same, finding Valeri's cock already beginning to swell. "You don't like women?"

"I don't like many people."

"But in bed, you've never...?"

"With a woman? No. No interest." Valeri's expression changed; a hint of vulnerability danced in his eyes. "You have though."

Elias nodded. "I have."

"And your preference?"

"My preference"—Elias pushed Valeri onto his back and climbed astride him—"is you."

Elias, Present, 1432 Common Era

*E*lias had thought there would be no argument, but he'd been wrong. Turns out, Valeri could argue over anything.

"I'm gone no more than twenty minutes, and you smell like Laurence's whelp. Why?"

Elias tramped along behind him, their pace frantic in Valeri's rush to distance themselves from the others. Dawn approached, and all six would go to ground. Apparently Elias and Valeri would be doing that as far as possible from the rest of the group. He supposed Valeri wished to scold him in private.

"His name is Remy," said Elias, not for the first time. The thought that Valeri would scent Remy's embrace had not occurred to him, though it should have. He stalled by arguing back. It was a familiar enough pattern. "Why do you continue to speak of him as if he's not a person, same as you?"

"Answer the question, Elias."

"Or what?"

Valeri whirled on him, curls bouncing. "What's gotten into you?"

Elias didn't know. Part of him wondered if Valeri really was as dangerous as the others made him out to be. Could he provoke Valeri to hurt him? That was a stupid thing to do, but nonetheless, the urge to try was there. Something had to give.

He took a breath. Exhaled. "I'm sorry."

Valeri studied his face. "For what?"

"Provoking you. Remy hugged me because he is worried. We both enjoyed the reading lessons you put a stop to, and he wanted to know if I needed help."

"Needed help?" Valeri scoffed.

"Is that so difficult for you to believe? That the fledgling of a vampire who left you would worry for my safety? What does Remy know that I don't? I'm sure Laurence has told him the entire story, where you've only given me bits and excuses."

"I don't want to talk about Laurence."

"You always say that. You know, if you'd just tell me what happened, I wouldn't have to keep asking."

"What did you tell Remy?"

"That I didn't need their help. That you wouldn't hurt me. I lied."

"I would never hurt you," Valeri snapped.

Elias wavered but forced the truth out word by word. "You do. All the time."

Valeri froze. Elias couldn't interpret his expression. Was he angry? Of course he was. Valeri was always angry these days.

But Valeri's face fell. He didn't look angry; he looked miserable. Then he said two words Elias never expected to hear from him.

"I'm sorry."

Stunned, Elias gasped. The urge to soothe rushed in all at once. Elias reached for him. "It's all right." He kissed Valeri's mouth.

Valeri returned the kiss, then pulled away. "It's not. I make you unhappy. I don't mean to. You deserve—"

"Shh." Elias petted his curls. "Kiss me."

Valeri would never refuse him that.

Elias got the kisses he asked for, but next, he wanted the whole damn story. "Take me to bed and tell me what happened between you and Laurence. Even if you don't want to. I know you don't want to, but do it because I want you to."

Valeri gripped his sides, pulled them together. "You're taking advantage of my mood."

"I am." Elias tugged away and lay down on the snow. "Bed and story. Please."

"Fine." Valeri lay on him, his weight a familiar comfort. They relaxed and bid the earth to swallow them whole.

Sleeping in the ground had to be one of the best tricks in a vampire's set. Safe, silent, dark, and always available when needed. The first time they'd slept this way, Elias had been afraid, but the fear didn't last long. Valeri taught him how to push the earth out in an arc over them, forming space between their bodies and the dirt, their own little bubble beneath the surface. This way was less messy, and less claustrophobic than just letting the ground encase them. Once the trick was mastered, Elias never complained about going to ground.

But tonight, Valeri did it for them. Creating their nest, then flipping them over and taking Elias into his arms, Valeri dropped kisses along the crown of his head.

"You won't escape your fate with kisses, Valeri, though I'll take them. Go on. Tell me what happened."

"You're a tyrant." Valeri's hand smoothed down his back and settled on his ass. He squeezed.

Elias bit him on the chest through his clothes, not with his fangs, not for blood, but for the pinch of it. "Start from the beginning. The night you saw him for the first time."

"I'll start before that. There was no specific night it happened, I just came to realize I was lonely and began to pine for a companion."

"How long was this after you'd left Fedor?"

Valeri's expression grew thoughtful. "Ten or eleven years I suppose."

"That's quite a bit of time to be all by yourself."

"I enjoyed the solitude at first. Fedor was naturally domineering, his methods of rearing a young vampire astoundingly cruel. Following his orders grated on me after a while."

"You're also naturally domineering. I can't imagine you with another person like yourself."

Valeri swatted his bottom for that remark, playful. "I am nothing like Fedor. You didn't know him."

"Sorry, sorry. Please continue. You may spank me for it later."

"I just might." With a sigh, Valeri continued the tale. "My gaze began to wander, searching for someone I thought would make a good companion. Someone I could turn."

"How did you settle on Laurence?" Elias had wondered this since the day he first laid eyes on Valeri's first fledgling. He'd always assumed his own body was Valeri's type. Medium height, lean muscle, sleight of build. But he and Laurence looked nothing alike. Laurence was rather huge in comparison. Taller than both himself or Valeri, and bulky, with thick muscles and a barreled chest. Inky black hair, long at the top and short on the sides. Gray eyes. They literally had nothing in common aside from dark hair. Plus Laurence had to have reached forty before he was turned, and Elias had never made it past nineteen. They were different as night and day.

"I liked the look of him," Valeri said, shocking Elias to silence. "He had a gentle way about him, kind eyes, soft spoken and polite. All that weight and yet he never threw it around. I watched him for quite a while before I chose."

"And when you chose?"

"I took him from everything he loved and kept him for myself. That was how it started and why it ended. He isn't one to be kept."

No, Elias could see that in the way Laurence carried himself. He wasn't like Elias, he didn't need rescuing. He had something to love—something to lose.

Cautiously, Elias asked, "What did you take him from?"

"Elias, that's enough, I don't want to—"

"Oh, no you don't! You don't finally agree to tell me this story, the one I've been asking about for four years now, and stop in the middle. Laurence would not have stopped at this point when he told Remy, and you will not stop telling me."

"What do you care what Laurence told Remy?"

"They know more about you than I do! I am your lover, and I want to know what happened between you and Laurence so that it does not happen to us too. You hate him. He hates you. I don't want that for us."

"I killed his wife," Valeri blurted out, "and I made it look like he did it so he'd be run out of town."

Elias was stunned stiff. "You murdered…"

"His pretty wife, yes. So that he would have nothing and be glad when he found me."

"But, Valeri—"

"I'm a monster. Believe me, I know. You want to know if I regret it? I do. But it's done now, and Laurence can hate me all he wants. I'd bring her back if I could, but I can't."

"Have you told him that?"

Valeri choked out a sad trickle of laughter. "Of course not. He doesn't want to hear it. Or anything from me for that matter."

"But if you've never said you were sorry—"

"It doesn't matter that I'm sorry, don't you see? It changes nothing. We were never right for each other to begin with. I don't want him back, and he doesn't want me. Better to leave the past alone."

Elias thought of Maks, his overlord. Valeri had essentially

done the same thing to acquire Elias as he had to acquire Laurence. Killed the person that stood in his way. Only in the first case, he'd killed a person Laurence loved, and in the second, he'd killed a person Elias hated. So his strategy had only slightly improved over all those years. Then again, it's what his own sire had done to acquire him. Killing was what Valeri knew.

"Say something," Valeri whispered.

Elias glanced up and caught the vulnerable expression on his face.

"Do you hate me now?"

"I could never hate you," said Elias truthfully. "But I don't know what you want me to say."

"I've told you I didn't want to talk about it. Now you know why."

"Yes, I understand." Elias hadn't imagined the story would be so awful. "How did he find out?"

"I told him in the heat of an argument. I thought he needed me more than he would hate me. I was wrong."

Elias gave a slow nod, processing his thoughts. "Did you love him?"

"Yes."

"Did he love you?"

"I think so."

"Which would make the betrayal all the worse when he learned the truth."

"And I did not let him go easily. I fought him. I'd have enslaved him if I could, but his friend Livia helped him escape me. The Dozen were consulted and banished me to the north to protect Laurence. I'm not proud of any of it."

"Well, at least that cannot happen to us," said Elias. "I've no one but you that I love." He'd hoped to learn something from this tale that would help solve the tension in their relationship. Only there was nothing to be gained from this knowledge but sorrow.

"I don't want to lose you," said Valeri.

Elias forced a confidence into his voice that he didn't feel. "You won't."

Valeri, Present, 1432 Common Era

Valeri clung to Elias as his beloved slept against his chest. The sun had nearly set; he could feel the night embracing them in their earthen grave. But Elias was young in the blood, and slow to wake, so Valeri took the opportunity to memorize the precious feel of him in his arms. Because one night, despite what Elias had said, he would leave, and Valeri would let him go.

He'd made a solemn vow to that effect, and no matter the pain separation would cause, he'd not go back on his word. Above all, Valeri wanted Elias to be happy, a goal at which he'd failed spectacularly. Instead, he'd squelched Elias's innate sweetness and turned him irritable, anxious, and worse...undeniably miserable. A deep melancholy lingered in Elias's burnt-umber eyes, and Valeri had put it there.

Worse still, he could not seem to stop. Relentless driving anger prickled constantly beneath the surface. When the fury became too much to contain, it was Elias who bore the lash's sting. Cruel words, careless touches, little betrayals. Valeri failed to control them, thus he hurt the one he loved most. Not once or twice, but nightly. A habit, and one he could not break.

Elias stirred at his side.

No, not yet. Do not wake yet. Only a few minutes longer.

Valeri stroked his spine, easing him back to slumber.

Elias used to fall asleep with his fingers tangled in Valeri's hair, just behind his ear. Then, Valeri had snapped at him for it, called him childish of all things. He regretted the words the moment they left his lips but was too proud to take them back. Elias hadn't curled his hair since, and Valeri missed the gentle affection more than he missed the sun's warmth on his shoulders.

Letting his mind wander, Valeri suppressed a chuckle at the dichotomy his fledgling presented. Elias would fuck him like a wildcat then snuggle into his side like a kitten and twirl his hair. Effortlessly charming. Valeri couldn't bear to share him with anyone, so he'd kept Elias's sweetness all to himself.

But Valeri had ruined him, like he ruined everything he touched.

Laurence had been a kind man before Valeri sank his claws in. He'd turned Laurence into an angry and untrusting soul driven to escape him by any means necessary. Because that is what Valeri did to people. He deserved to be alone.

Though he wasn't alone quite yet.

Elias lifted his head and pressed a kiss to Valeri's throat. "Good evening."

Valeri cupped the back of his head. "Go ahead."

Neatly piercing a vein, Elias sealed his lips over the punctures and drank. Valeri basked in the sensation, holding Elias close. He wished to have this every night for the rest of his life, but the rumblings of the end already threatened.

Would Elias look at him differently now that he knew what Valeri had done to Laurence? Would he side with them if it came to that? Perhaps he should tell Elias all he knew...

Elias licked the wounds closed and kissed the wet spot, sending a pleasant shiver down Valeri's spine. "Thank you."

"Always." Valeri didn't loosen his embrace.

Elias laid his head upon his chest. "The others will be waiting on us."

"Fuck the others." Valeri knew Elias was all too conscious of his status as the weakest among them, and he hated that it bothered him. Though Remy was younger in the blood, he'd been made uncommonly strong thanks to Mahu. The ancient vampire had helped Laurence turn him, and without that help, the whelp would have died. But there were no ancients dawdling about when Valeri had turned Elias.

"I don't want to waste any more of their time," said Elias. "They must wait long enough on me as it is, Valeri. I don't want to be a burden."

Valeri stroked the delicate arch of his lower back. "You could never be a burden."

"You cannot expect me to believe that," Elias mumbled into his chest.

Have I failed at this too? Have I made you feel like a burden? I'm sorry. Valeri often had apologies in his head for Elias that he couldn't bring himself to voice aloud. Yet another flaw of his nature.

"All right." Valeri gave in. "I suppose we should rise, but I'd keep you to myself all night if I could."

"Of that, I'm well aware," said Elias, his voice flat.

His lover had been awake only minutes, and already Valeri had made him sad. With a sigh of regret, he bid the earth to release them, and they rose together above the ground.

Mahu, 1432 Common Era, Bran Vigny

Tossing and turning in fevered sleep, Mahu dreamed of his lost love. His devil-halfling with eyes like the starry dusk sky. His best and worst kept secret. His biggest regret.

Dakarai answered Mahu's call, appearing from the ether, his tail wrapped around his torso as if he needed the comfort of an embrace, even if it was his own.

Relief expanded Mahu's chest at the sight of his lover, hale and hearty after all these years—after centuries. Though Daka looked out of place at Bran Vigny. When Mahu closed his eyes and dreamed of the incubus, he was radiant in the sunshine, out and about in the ancient lands of Kemet, laughter in his eyes. Golden. But here it was dark, and Daka's melancholy expression turned his face into a stranger's.

Confusion tangled Mahu's thoughts. "Are you really here?"

"I am and I'm not." Daka's voice, a gentle tenor, sounded the same as it always had. A balm to Mahu's soul.

Mahu released a shuddering breath. "I've missed you."

"And I, you."

"Am I dying?"

The image of Daka wavered, flickering away, then back again, closer, right next to his bed. He frowned. "You are."

Mahu's heart sank. "I'm sorry."

Daka reached for his hand. "So am I."

Elias, Three Years Ago

"*W*hy can't she play?" Elias asked the group of men at Rovaniemi's local tavern. "Are you afraid she'll beat you?"

His jeer worked perfectly. The men laughed at the idea, and the ringleader responded by raising his mug. "Aye, you can let her try. Just see she don't loose the arrow at one of us!"

Elias rolled his eyes and turned back to the serving lass. Valeri was upstairs meeting with another vampire, Lajos, about the whispered rumors of a court of ancient beings near the city. Valeri was obsessed with the possibility and never let Elias tag along on these rendezvous. So Elias was left to his own devices in the tavern below.

A game of targeting skill had sprung up among the men, and they'd invited him to join. An empty wine barrel had been over-turned, hauled onto a table, and the bottom used as the target. The little arrows were shortened and weighted, with feathers at the end, and the objective was to throw them so they stuck closest to the center of the barrel.

Already Elias had learned he was not very good at the game, sending arrows both to the floor and the wall. But with some practice, he managed to hit the target, though never very close to the center.

The woman serving their drinks had cheered them on, then asked to try herself. After the men had a good laugh, Elias collected the arrows and set about showing her how, but the group put a prompt stop to it.

"Women don't play arrows," said a man who stank of ale and hadn't hit the target all night.

"What's your name?" asked Elias, ignoring the men.

The pretty blonde gave a smiling nod. "Jemma, and you? I've seen you here before."

"Elias." He handed her an arrow. "And don't listen to them. It's not that hard."

"Speak for yourself," a rowdy drunk quipped from the side. Elias glanced in time to see him palm his crotch. "Some of us are plenty hard."

"Go stick it in the snow then, Ralphie," cried Jemma. "Ain't no one here interested in your prick."

Rousing laughter sounded from the other men. Elias thought Jemma a spitfire and wouldn't want to get on her bad side. He'd seen her escort more than one man too deep in his cups out of this tavern by the ear.

"Come stand here," said Elias.

Jemma took her spot. "Throw the pointy end at the barrel, yeah? Anything else I need to know?"

"You've got the right of it." Elias took her shoulders and squared them up. "Just look where you're aiming and let it fly."

Hand poised in the air, arrow clenched between thumb and fingers, Jemma concentrated, then threw.

The arrow hit with a solid *thwack* damn near center of the barrel, earning her a round of shocked cheers from the gathered men.

"Well fuck me running," said Ralphie.

Jemma's grin was wide as whales. "I did it!"

"And better than any of us," said Elias, handing her the next arrow. "Have another go."

Jemma threw the whole slew of arrows. None hit the ground or the wall, and one stuck near to the center. "You were right. It's not hard."

Being sober probably helped. Not that it had helped him, but it seemed to do wonders for Jemma. Or perhaps she was a natural. In any case, the game of arrows was the most fun he'd had in ages.

"I'd better get this lot their refills." Jemma turned her winning smile on Elias. "Thanks for this." She wrapped him in a hug and smacked a kiss on his cheek.

Elias had to stand still and grit his teeth to bear it. Not that he didn't welcome a hug and kiss from Jemma—he did—but he could smell the luscious scent of her blood when they were this close, thrumming below her skin, and though he'd fed once already this evening, the allure was difficult to resist.

Valeri's hard grip at his elbow knocked the sense back into him as he was yanked from Jemma's arms.

"He's all yours," said Jemma to Valeri with a hint of a defensive edge to her voice. They'd been there before, and Valeri wasn't shy about their relationship. She knew Elias and Valeri were a couple. "I was just leaving."

"What was that about?" whispered Valeri against his ear, his tone harsh.

"Ease up on my arm. Everything's fine," said Elias, and the pinch of Valeri's fingers relented. "The men taught me to play arrows, and then I showed Jemma. Turns out she's better than all of us."

Valeri scowled. "Since when do you know the serving lass by name?"

Elias's eyes went wide. Was this jealousy? Over a woman? He

was tempted to laugh, but Valeri's dark mood made him think twice. "Since tonight, Valeri. Are you all right?"

"Fine. Let's get out of here." Valeri made to drag Elias from the room.

Elias shrugged out of his grip. "My cloak." He had to cross in front of the group of players to grab his cloak from the hook on the wall. One of them made a clicking sound with his tongue.

"In trouble with your fellow?"

Elias hadn't thought to be embarrassed until that moment. Then he realized what they'd just seen, and what they must think. Not that he cared for their opinions, but he'd been having fun, and now he wasn't. And Valeri was to blame.

Elias glowered at the man. "Mind your business." He threw the cloak over his shoulders and exited the tavern with Valeri at his heels.

"What did you do that for?" Elias hissed. "You embarrassed me."

"I could ask you the same. I leave you alone for not even half of an hour and find you in the arms of a bar wench?"

They tromped through the snow in the direction of their underground home. The road wasn't busy at this hour, but nor was it vacant. Elias kept his voice down. "Jemma was happy to have gotten the better of the men. The hug was in thanks because I invited her to the game. That's all."

"Oh, that's all." Valeri sneered.

"Yes, Valeri. What did you think? That I was flirting with her? Do you think I want Jemma?"

"Do you?" asked Valeri through clenched teeth.

"Of course not!" Elias said too loudly, then reined himself in. "You are being ridiculous. Jemma only wanted to join the game—"

"Oh, shut up."

Elias did.

Not because Valeri had told him to, but because he was so stunned by the harsh words. By Valeri's glare. By his actions.

Valeri had never spoken down to him like this before. They didn't fight. What was happening?

"I am being realistic," said Valeri amid Elias's shocked silence. "You slept with women before me. Do you miss it? Do you want a woman? Because letting her that close was dangerous, Elias. You nearly lost control of the bloodlust."

Was that what Valeri was angry about? Nearly blowing their cover? Elias sensed the triggered bloodlust was the smaller infraction and what really had Valeri hot was seeing Elias with Jemma in a moment of happiness.

Elias took Valeri's wrist and stopped them walking. "I don't want a woman, Valeri. I don't want anyone else. I have you. I love you."

Valeri searched Elias's face and must have seen the truth there. His fury began to visibly melt. He took Elias's hand. "Let's go home."

Hand in hand, they continued toward their rooms. Their pace slowed to normal from the frantic, angry stride Valeri had set from the tavern.

"Did your meeting go well?" asked Elias, hoping for a change of subject, anything to ease the new tension between them.

"No," snapped Valeri. "It did not."

Perhaps that accounted for his ill temper. "I'm sorry to hear that. I'm sure you'll have more success next time." He knew better than to pick for details. Valeri would tell him when he was ready. Or he wouldn't. But questions might only aggravate him further.

"Rovaniemi is a dead end," Valeri huffed. "There will be no next time."

Good. Perhaps we can move on from this fruitless search for a court of the ancients. He suspected the rumors were only myth, but Valeri couldn't let the mystery go. Elias wished he knew what drove him, but Valeri didn't like to talk about it.

"We must leave for Kuusamo and speak with the Breodun

nomads there. It's said they harbor a keeper of records who could aid in my search."

"Leave Rovaniemi?" asked Elias. He'd grown accustomed to the villages and people in the year since they'd arrived. "But I like it here."

"You will like Kuusamo too."

Elias hoped so. "Will you tell me more about what you're looking for? Perhaps I could help."

"It's dangerous, my sweet, and I don't need your help."

Elias didn't want to start another argument so soon after their first, but he couldn't help but add, "Everyone needs help sometimes, Valeri. Even you."

Elias, Present, 1432 Common Era

The journey from Kemi took them four days, following east along the river to reach the villages of Rovaniemi. The town hadn't changed much since Elias last saw it. Situated between hillsides just an hour's walk from the Arctic Circle, their old set of rooms would serve as home base for the remainder of the mission.

Elias walked the familiar streets, eager to return to the underground house they'd shared when Valeri first brought them there, only this time, Laurence, Remy, Aella, and Ash would be joining them. Perhaps he'd have a chance to show them around. Elias hoped the others would like the local tavern as much as he did, though Valeri would no doubt disapprove of the distraction.

The court of the ancients. Everything had always centered on them. And the mysterious court had been nearby all along.

Valeri had been denied entry once already, but he thought having a delegation sent by The Dozen would gain him entrance. Ash was a known diplomat, and Valeri assumed the ancients would speak with him. Elias wasn't so sure. He remembered earlier attempts and failures, but with Mahu's life on the line, he could only hope they'd be successful.

"Here we are," said Valeri, leading them to their dwelling beneath the leather shop just before dawn.

Everyone filed in. The rooms had been kept clean, aired, and free from dust by a service Valeri hired with his seemingly endless supply of funds. The colors were as Elias remembered. Bright jewel tones, textured fabric, scented candles. He'd learned this was the kind of luxury Valeri always curated for himself if given enough time.

"This is lovely," said Remy. "Did you live here long?"

"No." Valeri set his bag on the hearth and gestured for the others to do so as well. "Off and on for nearly a decade."

Elias thought that was a long time, but he was the youngest of the group and still measured his life in months and years rather than decades and centuries.

These rooms had once seemed spacious for two people, and Elias supposed they were compared to the tiny compartments on the ship, but with a group of six the den felt no bigger than a mouse hole.

"Make yourselves at home." Valeri set about lighting a fire.

Laurence and Remy took the chairs by the table.

"Gladly," said Aella, flopping onto the lounge with her bag in her lap. She dug through the contents and retrieved a hunk of jerky wrapped in paper. "I'm starving."

Ash sat next to her. "You should have said something. We would have stopped for you to eat."

"No, we were cutting the timing too close as it was." She held up the dried meat. "I'll enjoy this more knowing we have a safe place to sleep for the day. I'm exhausted."

Aella had used her magic throughout their trek to keep pace with a group of vampires. She'd also needed her powers to stay warm while underground during daylight. In addition to that, she'd gotten less sleep than the rest of them throughout the journey overseas because of her duty to be their eyes and ears when the vampires were forced to take cover from the sun.

"We should rest here until Aella has recovered," said Ash. "Perhaps a few nights before we reestablish contact with your sources."

Elias chimed in before Valeri could argue. He'd hoped to avoid more arguments. He was sick of bickering. "Of course. That's a good idea. Tomorrow night I could take you to the tavern down the street. They have card tables and sometimes a targeting game of arrows."

"That sounds fun," said Remy. Elias had no doubt Remy was also heading off potential arguments from Valeri. Their gazes locked in a moment of understanding. "A rest would do us all good. Leave us fresh for what's to come."

Valeri had a scowl on his face but remained quiet. Thank the demons for small favors.

"There are three other rooms." Elias gestured to the hall. "A small study and two bedrooms."

"Laurence and I will take the study. We don't mind sleeping on the floor." Remy looked to Laurence, who nodded his confirmation. "That will leave the bedrooms for the rest of you."

"If you're certain. I'll fetch the extra bedding." Elias headed to the room he'd shared with Valeri to gather extra blankets and pillows.

Rolling his shoulders to ease the tension, Elias opened the door. The charming bedroom looked untouched since last he'd seen it, everything in its place. Emerald coverlet, four poster bed, a thick, white rug, and lush tapestries on the walls. A small room, but richly decorated in Valeri's taste and homey in a way that made Elias's chest ache for better times.

He opened the great wooden chest at the foot of the bed and dug out the spare wool quilts.

Behind him, Valeri cleared his throat. "Would you like some help?"

Elias dropped the blankets back into the chest and spun around. Replies went through his mind, but the house was small and the others had excellent hearing, so saying something to the effect of *yes, please take me to bed and remind me of how it used to be between us*, was out of the question. Instead, he lunged at Valeri and climbed him like a squirrel up a tree. An eager squirrel, but a silent one.

To his credit, Valeri didn't drop him, and kissed like he'd had the same idea as Elias. This room brought back fond memories for them both.

When they broke apart, Elias forced his voice to remain even. "Yes, please. I'd welcome your help."

Valeri set him down, laughter in his eyes. He bent to pick up the abandoned bedding. "Come, let's prepare these for our guests, then get some sleep."

"Ah, yes, sleep." Elias winked then grabbed the pillows and followed Valeri down the hall.

In that moment, he could pretend everything was well between them, and that disaster did not loom large after they procured help for Mahu.

13

Valeri, Present, 1432 Common Era

*V*aleri couldn't stand by idly while Aella recovered her strength, not when he was so close to his goal. Let the others waste time at the tavern. Meanwhile, he'd set the cogs turning on acquiring an audience with the court of the ancients, and for that, he'd need to speak with that silver-tongued liar, Lajos.

The Dozen had underestimated him in the past, but if Valeri brought them the secrets of the ancients—if he provided a cure for the aging sickness whether they approved of the means or not —they would be forced to respect him. He and Elias could have a place at Bran Vigny. Valeri would be honored a hero rather than ridiculed as nothing more than an abusive sire. Finally, he would be appreciated.

Valeri would succeed no matter the cost. He had to trust that the others would see things his way in the end.

Lajos was an artist, though Valeri suspected he played a greater role than that. He'd misled Valeri, stalled him, and ultimately thrown him off the ancient's trail. Valeri owed the vampire a piece of his mind, and Lajos owed him answers. Though he'd rather feed on the blood of a rabid opossum than have another conversation with the swine, Lajos was his best chance at securing an audience quickly.

Valeri would normally go through a solicitor to request a meeting with Lajos, but he didn't have time for the official route, and he knew where Lajos painted. He would risk being rude and simply show up.

A moment's doubt had him wishing he'd left Elias behind at Bran Vigny, out of harm's way, but he couldn't bring himself to be parted from his fledgling. What would he have returned to, if he'd let Elias remain? The vampires at Bran Vigny would have cautioned Elias against him. Elias might leave Valeri for someone new. He wouldn't take that risk, so he'd dragged Elias along, and now whatever danger lay ahead, Elias faced it too. If Valeri regretted anything, it was that.

There was no sense in worrying over what could not be changed. Elias would be fine. Valeri would protect him at any cost.

Rapping on the door to Lajos's private studio, Valeri shifted from foot to foot with impatience.

For a vampire he suspected worked directly for the court of the ancients, Lajos had a cover story that was remarkably convincing. Lajos primarily used oils for his paintings, and his imagery was impossibly realistic down to the last detail. Not limited to one style, Lajos painted portraits, still lifes, landscapes, and even massive depictions from mythology. His talent knew no limit, and was wasted on a vampire stuck in the Arctic Circle compelled to do the bidding of others.

Valeri despised him.

Not for his wasted talent, but for the lies he'd told which had stalled Valeri's progress finding the court of ancients in the first place.

Lajos swung open the door and scowled upon seeing Valeri at his threshold. Valeri met the scowl with one of his own.

"Back so soon?" Reddish-blond eyebrows arched to twin points on Lajos's pale forehead. He wore a muslin shift covered head to toe in dried paint. A rainbow of stains scattered across the garment but concentrated on his right thigh where he had an obvious habit of wiping the brush. "I suppose I should have suspected as much. Of all the seekers, you're the most persistent, Valeri. But where is your darling fledgling? Don't tell me you've come without Elias."

"Never mind Elias," Valeri huffed and pushed his way inside. "I need a favor."

"By all means, do come in." Sarcasm laced Lajos's tone. He shut the door behind them.

Valeri inhaled the nutty scent of the linseed oil used to mix paints. Lit brighter than a Hallows' Eve pumpkin, the studio was massive, but there was nowhere to sit. Canvases in various stages of completion lay on every surface. Probably for the best, Valeri didn't intend to stay long.

Standing with a hand on a cocked hip, Lajos pursed his lips. With a svelte frame, and delicate, feminine features, his stature wasn't intimidating, but his glare was. He waved his free hand as he spoke, paintbrush dangling from his fingers. "Whatever can I do for you? In the market for a portrait, maybe? Elias is always welcome to come sit for me, with those angelic cheekbones and cupid's bow lips, that button of a nose... Painting your lover would be my pleasure—"

"Enough. You know I'm not here for a painting." Although the idea of an image of Elias that would be his forever, something to keep when the real Elias had finally had his fill of Valeri, well, it was tempting. But not what Valeri came for.

"Of course you aren't." Lajos gave an overly dramatic sigh. "A shame really, because a painting would be possible, and what you're about to ask me for...is not."

Valeri glowered. "You don't know what I'm here to ask for."

Lajos glanced up at him through lowered lashes. "Try me."

"I need an audience with the court of the ancients, and this time I will not take no for an answer."

Lajos yawned as if he were bored. "You really think I didn't know that? You're quite predictable in your demands. The answer continues to be no."

"I expected as much. Now for the part you don't know. I've brought a delegate from The Dozen who wishes to plead our case. Surely they won't turn away the magnanimous Ash. Such an act would be intolerably rude and provoke the ire of the vampires of Bran Vigny." Valeri was banking on the politics of vampire hospitality, that the ancients wouldn't flout the tradition.

Lajos narrowed his gaze. He stood so still as to take on the presence of a statue and not a living, breathing being.

Valeri fought the urge to step back and put more space between them. He wasn't easy to intimidate, but there was a warning in Lajos's posture. In his glower. Something primal in Valeri reacted to the threat Lajos posed, the hidden power in his petite, girlish frame.

"Let me be sure I have you correct," Lajos drawled, enunciating each word. "You've taken the information you learned in part from my help, that the court of the ancients is indeed nearby, and, having failed to gain an audience for yourself, you've run home to The Dozen. The Dozen. Who banished you to my realm in the first place. With your tail between your legs, you ran to them, and what? Told them there are vampires here older than them by millennia? I wonder what lies you spouted to convince them to loan you a precious delegate. Have you made promises you can't keep, Valeri? Hmm?"

Valeri's back hit the wall. He hadn't realized he was moving until the jolt of it stopped him.

Lajos hadn't budged. He held the tip of the paintbrush's handle to his lips, waiting for Valeri to fill the silence.

"I didn't have to resort to lies. I discovered the truth in my time with the Breodun people whom *you* sent me to see. Their keeper of records knew more than you thought. The truth was enough to warrant the delegate."

"And what, pray tell, is this truth you claim to have uncovered?"

"That the ancients possess a cure for the aging sickness." Valeri would not let slip what he thought that cure was. "That they haven't shared such a secret is criminal. We would have this cure. A vampire suffers as we speak. Mahu."

"One vampire's suffering doesn't justify the price you ask us to pay. There is a reason that information is kept secret. Surely even you can parse out some theories as to why. Knowledge in the wrong hands is dangerous. You've caught a lion in a squirrel's trap. He roars with fury. He'll chew off his own leg to get his revenge. You should turn around and go home before he breaks free. Forget what you think you know."

"I will not. You speak in riddles, but let me speak plainly. I demand an audience with the ancients. If this is in your power to grant, I expect you to do so. If it's not, which is what I'm guessing, I expect you to seek clearance from one who can. Without delay."

Lajos considered, his expression dour. "Your demands are unwise. This won't go how you think it will. I'll give you one last warning, though you don't deserve the courtesy. Take your fledging and your delegate and run while you still can."

"I've given you my answer," Valeri huffed. "I won't be intimidated any further. Do your job."

"If you insist, but Valeri." Lajos's entire demeanor changed. Gone was the hardness and barely contained power. Vanished were the intense gazes and threats. His face softened, his expression turned pleading, his amber eyes earnest. "Leave Elias with me."

Valeri's gut revolted at the thought. "Never!"

"You must," Lajos insisted. "He's an innocent in this and does not deserve the consequences you would thrust upon him."

"Elias stays with me." Valeri pounded a fist to his chest.

"Even if that means he dies with you?"

"No one is going to die!" Valeri would have loved to tell Lajos about Aella. About the powers Laurence and his whelp had cultivated. That his group was much stronger than Lajos realized, but he would not be provoked into tipping his hand. He had the advantage and intended to keep it.

"You're always so sure of yourself," Lajos countered. "Your arrogance will be your undoing. And your child's. Please consider my offer. I will protect Elias from you."

"Not for me? *From* me." Valeri scoffed and strode past him to the exit. "Just get us an audience. And keep your filthy hands off my fledgling."

"You'll regret this. Leave him where he'll be sa—"

"Elias is mine." Valeri slammed the door behind him.

Elias, Two Years Ago

Over the following year, Elias tagged along as Valeri dragged them from Rovaniemi to Kuusamo to Kitka and back on no less than four occasions. At one point over the summer they spent six weeks endlessly hopping from one nomadic Breodun tribe to another. Elias learned to sleep in the ground, in caves, and at abandoned farmsteads. How to track horses that had wandered off during the day, even how to speak a little of the Breodun language. Part adventure, part drudgery, the constant wandering had begun to wear on his nerves.

When Valeri first told Elias about his search for a group of ancient vampires, Elias had thought the quest intimidating. At one hundred and sixty-three years old, Elias thought Valeri was ancient enough already and had trouble wrapping his mind around vampires who'd seen a millennia or more come and go. He wasn't sure tracking them down was a good idea, especially since they didn't seem to want to be found, but he'd learned not to pick that particular battle with Valeri.

Besides, Elias had been so caught up in discovering the world around him with his new vampiric senses and with Valeri's seemingly unlimited supply of wealth, he couldn't bring himself to care much about a stuffy old court of ancients. If the quest made Valeri happy, then Elias would endure it.

But he was beginning to think the pursuit was hopeless, and worse, it wasn't making Valeri happy anymore, quite the opposite. His sire's frustration increased with each dead end, and Elias bore the brunt of his bad moods.

They sat together in a small clearing in the middle of the forest outside the village of Kuusamo. Under the glimmering greens and purples of the arctic lights and beside a fire Valeri had made for them, Elias felt the mood might be right for the conversation he'd been hesitant to start.

He watched Valeri closely. Valeri was leaning against a fallen tree trunk, his legs stretched in front of him and crossed at the ankle, expression open, content, shoulders relaxed. This was as good a time as any.

"Valeri," Elias began.

Valeri turned his affectionate gaze on him, a fondness present in his stare with something deeper underneath, a lust that could be awoken with even the most subtle of hints. Elias loved that about him. How easy it was to go from sitting by the fire fully clothed to naked and writhing if either of them had so much as a whim. But tonight, Elias was after answers.

He knew rumors had led Valeri to Lappland, and that those rumors had been confirmed by Lajos. Valeri suspected these vampires to be twice the age of the oldest southern vampire, and he thought the ancients held some secret that allowed them to live so long without going mad. Valeri sought this secret and coveted the respect such a discovery would bring.

But when Elias pressed for further detail, Valeri became evasive. If this endless search was to be his life, Elias deserved the entire truth.

"Why did you leave the other vampires? What made you come here?" These were questions he'd asked before, but tonight he wouldn't allow for Valeri's excuses.

Valeri sighed, probably annoyed at the prospect of this conversation again. "You already know these answers. I left to seek a cure."

This was where Elias had spotted the lie, though he'd never called Valeri on it before. "No. You've told me of hearing rumors that ancient vampires lived here, but you heard those rumors in Turku. You'd already fled north. You didn't come here to find a cure, you came here and then discovered a purpose. Why did you leave to begin with?"

Crossing his arms over his chest, Valeri began to close off. Before he could stop the line of inquiry entirely, Elias crawled to him and put a hand on his knee.

"Please, Valeri. I know there is something you aren't telling me. It hurts that you keep such secrets."

Valeri dropped a hand on top of Elias's. "It's impossible to refuse you when you say it like that."

Elias squeezed his knee gently. "Then don't refuse me."

A sigh marked Valeri's irritation, but he relented. "I didn't leave of my own free will. I was banished by a group of vampires called The Dozen."

"Banished?" Elias tried to keep the shock from his tone. "What for?"

"The vampire I made before you turned them against me."

Elias flipped his hand so he could lace their fingers together. "Am I never to know his name?"

"Why do you care about his name?"

134

"I care that you won't tell me. Do you loathe him so much it vexes you to say it out loud?"

"His name is Laurence, and you can stop your questions there. I do not wish to speak of him."

Laurence, thought Elias. *Finally.* It certainly didn't sound like the name of a monster, but Laurence must be awful if Valeri hated him so.

"What did he say to The Dozen to get them to banish you?" Elias phrased the question carefully. Valeri would never entertain a question like, *what did you do to get yourself banished?* Though with what he'd seen of Valeri's questionable morals, Elias could think of a number of ways the circumstances might be his own fault.

"So you took 'stop your questions' to mean 'change your line of questioning'?" Valeri smiled as he spoke, so Elias knew he hadn't provoked any anger. Yet.

"Indeed." Elias grinned. "Will you answer?"

"Laurence wished to be separated from me and wasn't about to allow me the last word on the matter. He'd made friends in high places." Valeri shrugged this off. "He used those contacts to get what he wanted and succeeded in having me exiled. The end."

That was so far from the whole story as to be laughable. It contained no parts of the beginning, only an iota of information from the middle, and of the end, nothing at all. At best it was a fragment, but Elias had become good at parsing out information with little to go on.

"So when you learned about the ancients, you thought, if you could acquire their secrets and bring them to The Dozen, you'd be allowed back. Is that what you're after?" *Or are you trying to get to Laurence?* Elias knew better than to ask that bit.

"I deserve to be respected. I want their gratitude and a place at court worthy of my status. Is that so much to ask?"

"I don't really know," answered Elias honestly. "I don't know any of those vampires or how they make their rules and laws. Why would you want to return when we could go anywhere?"

"Enough." Valeri's tone indicated he meant it.

Elias switched tactics. "Then tell me more of what you know of the court of the ancients. Why are we here, and what can I do to help?"

"I don't need your help, I need your company. You are already doing everything I require from you. I won't risk putting you in danger."

"But aren't you in danger when you leave me to hunt for secrets?" Elias had always worried about this, but getting a straight answer from Valeri was like asking for blood from a stone. "If something happened to you, how would I know? What would I do without you?"

"Nothing is going to happen to me. I'm careful. I'm stronger than you. It's safer for both of us if you stay out of it."

"All right, fine. I will stay *physically* out of it. I won't nag you to come along creeping through campsites under the cover of darkness for whatever it is you're looking for. But tell me what you're after. Tell me what you've learned and what you're still trying to decipher. Let me in because this is my life too."

Valeri gave a put upon sigh. "You're exhausting sometimes, you know that?"

"You're no cinnamon baked apple either."

With a chuckle, Valeri drew him close. "Come here, let me hold you, and I will update you on my efforts."

The request was an easy one to grant; Elias enjoyed cuddling. He curled into Valeri's side and tangled their legs.

"I've begun to suspect Lajos knows more than he's letting on," Valeri started.

Elias cringed. He didn't care for Lajos. The older vampire looked at him with a hunger in his gaze that made Elias wish for a bath. He spoke of Elias as if he were a prize to be won and not a person with his own thoughts and opinions.

"His lead sent me to Kuusamo, but he only wanted me out of his city. I think the ancients are closer to Rovaniemi than he lets on. He might even work for them. I will soon find out."

"How?"

"The Breodun people we've been following have lived on these lands for millennia, just like the ancients. Lajos mentioned the possibility that they might have passed down legends of the vampires over the generations. He thinks he's sent me on a goose chase, but he's actually pointed me toward the most solid evidence yet. He didn't know that beyond passing down stories by mouth, the Breodun have a keeper of records in every generation. The position is secret, along with her location, but she guards written legends on physical scrolls. The answers lie with the keeper; I need only to find her."

"She will let you see their scrolls?"

"Once I find her, she will have no choice."

That sounded more like a threat than Elias was comfortable with. "But the Breodun have been kind to us. You won't hurt them, will you?"

"I'll try not to."

"Valeri, you must promise."

"You and your promises. Did you not hear what I just told you? I'm a breath away from the information I seek. The keeper of records is somewhere between here and Kitka. I'm certain I'll find her soon."

"Of course," said Elias, though he wasn't sure what to make of this. Stealing scrolls seemed like a bad idea, but Valeri wouldn't be easily dissuaded. If Elias could just keep his lover peaceful, that would be enough for him. "Promise me. Please? Don't hurt anyone."

Valeri tangled fingers in Elias's short hair and gave a gentle tug to angle his face for a kiss. "You have a soft heart. All right, I promise."

Elias returned the kiss with a sense of relief.

14

Elias, Present, 1432 Common Era

$\mathcal{E}$lias laughed so hard he had to clutch his stomach. Grinning from ear to ear, he stepped in to collect all the arrows so Aella could try again. He thought no beginner could be worse at the game than he had been when he'd first learned, but Aella proved him wrong.

Arrows littered the wall, the floor, and remarkably, the ceiling, but none were to be found on the target. Elias wouldn't have laughed at her, except Aella was nearly howling at her own ineptitude, so he figured joining in would be all right.

He glanced straight up. How was he supposed to retrieve the arrow in the rafters?

Jemma took Aella by the shoulders, squaring them to the barrel. "It's simple, really. Just look at the center of the barrel, keep your wrist nice and straight, and let her fly. Nothing to it."

Elias handed over the arrows. He and Jemma scurried well out of the way as Aella took aim. Jemma had fussed at him for leaving without saying goodbye, but after she'd given his shoulder a good shove for the offense, she'd welcomed him back with a hug.

"'Look at the center,' she says. 'Nothing to it,' she says." More laughter rang in Aella's voice.

She could use her magic to win the game, and Elias liked her all the more that she didn't.

Laurence and Remy had taken a table, each with a mug of something they couldn't actually drink. They watched the game only half interested, their heads together in their own conversation, grinning at each other while they shared their secrets.

Ash had mastered the game on his first try. He was a natural, like Jemma. Now he stood behind Aella, cheering her on. That is, if you could call his sedate style of clapping and the sly grin on his face cheering.

Aella loosed the first arrow.

Thunk.

Right in the wall, but closer to the target this time.

"That's progress," said Ash. "A little to the left this time, yes?"

"A little to the left," Aella repeated and drew back her arm.

Thunk.

She hit the barrel! A resounding cheer rose from the onlookers, Elias included. He knew she'd get it. The game had taken him quite a bit of practice to master, and he'd never be as good as Jemma, but he'd turned into a decent player.

Aella didn't stop to celebrate.

Thunk, thunk, thunk.

Three arrows and three hits to the barrel. None of them quite centered, but she'd gotten the hang of aiming. Perhaps they could play a real game and even keep score. Elias didn't stand a chance against Jemma, but with her as his teammate they'd make good opponents for Aella and Ash.

Elias went to collect the arrows again but stopped as he noticed Jemma stiffen. Her grin vanished and was replaced by a frown.

"Uh-oh." Her gaze flit back to Elias. "You're man is here, and he looks madder than a wet cat."

Elias's stomach sank. What could have made Valeri angry this time? Was there nothing Elias could do that wouldn't raise his ire? Valeri had known they were coming to the tavern; if he was going to throw a tantrum, why not have it out before they were all having a good time for a change?

Elias didn't turn to see Valeri for himself. Rather, he watched the faces of his companions as they took him in. Aella's grin morphed to a scowl. Ash carried the amused expression he often wore, though tinged with annoyance. Remy and Laurence glanced at the approaching storm, then to each other as if preparing to act on Elias's behalf.

Elias exhaled.

Valeri grabbed him by the arm and spun him so they were face to face, toe to toe.

Laurence stood from his table, but Remy took hold of his wrist so he didn't approach. Yet.

Elias registered he'd only have a moment to appease him before the others intervened.

"Come. We're leaving," Valeri demanded.

Elias put his hand between them, over Valeri's still heart. "Everyone is watching, Valeri."

"I don't care." Valeri didn't spare the others a glance; he looked only at Elias. "I need you home. Now."

"I'm enjoying myself. With our friends. I don't want to leave."

"It's not a request."

"Then tell me why," Elias pleaded. "Calmly. Or ask me to leave with you nicely."

"I'll tell you when we're home." Valeri squeezed his arm hard enough Elias flinched.

"You're hurting me."

Valeri loosened his grip. Opened his mouth. Closed it. Finally his gaze swept the tavern, which had grown quiet, because not only were their own number staring, but the other patrons had noticed the drama too.

Laurence's stance had become outright threatening. Only Remy held him back, but if Elias beckoned, he'd unleash his mate. Elias got the feeling Laurence wouldn't waste such an opportunity to lash out at their sire.

"I'm sorry. I didn't intend to hurt you." Valeri's expression turned desperate. "Please."

Something in his tone caught Elias. This wasn't Valeri's normal brand of jealousy. He was upset, and not because Elias was having a nice time without him; there was more to it.

"Where have you been?" asked Elias.

"With Lajos."

"Are you all right?"

"Fine," Valeri huffed. "He got under my skin. I want you where I know you'll be safe."

Shocked Valeri had told him the truth so easily, Elias was tempted to give in and go home with him. But if he didn't learn to stand his ground, the toxic dynamic between them would never change.

Glaring at the fingers around his bicep, Elias said, "Let go of my arm."

Valeri released his grip without argument. The defeated expression didn't sit well on his features.

Elias moved his free hand to Valeri's cheek. "You're here now, and you can see that I'm safe and sound among friends. I don't want to leave, but I'd love it if you stayed. Play arrows with us. I'll bet you're good at it." He'd never been able to convince Valeri to play with him before, but one more invitation was worth a try.

As the crowd realized there would be no fight, the ambient noise in the tavern began to rise. Only their group remained on edge, waiting to see what Valeri would do.

"None of them want me here," said Valeri.

The urge to say, *of course they do*, came and went. The platitude would be a lie. Valeri hadn't made himself an easy man to like. "I want you here. Since when have you cared what others think?"

LEE COLGIN

"I care too much what others think," Valeri whispered, his voice set low for Elias alone.

"So you do." Elias took his hand and tugged him closer to the game. "Then here is your chance to beat us all at arrows."

"Elias—"

"Please?"

Valeri pinched the bridge of his nose and sighed. "As you wish."

"Thank you. It will be fun. You'll see."

Laurence reclaimed his seat, but both he and Remy continued to watch the proceedings closely. Though it felt nice to have allies, Elias had never wanted to be aligned against his own sire. He wanted to be safe on Valeri's side.

Jemma gave Valeri a handful of darts. "Pointy end at the target. S'about time you learned to play."

Valeri took them and graced her with a thin smile. "Thank you for the tip."

"You'll do fine," Jemma said.

"I'll do my best, but I've seen you at this game." Valeri tipped his head. "There's no beating you at arrows."

Muscles deep in Elias's chest unclenched and relaxed. With any luck, Valeri would hit the damn target.

Elias, One Year Ago

Elias concentrated, catching the doe's gaze and pressing his will upon her. If he could calm her long enough to approach, to slide his teeth carefully into her vein, he could feed on his own.

Creeping forward step by careful step, Elias inched closer to the cautious animal. Gorgeous, with big brown eyes and a fluffy winter coat, she huffed and stamped a foot.

"Easy," said Elias, his voice soft. He focused a soothing calm in her direction, willing her to relax and allow him the access he needed.

Valeri would do this for him any time he requested the favor, but Elias wished to learn the compulsion for himself. What came easy on humans was more difficult in animals. Their instincts were finely honed to alert them to danger, and they recognized vampires for the predators they were. Since Elias preferred to feed from animals, this was a skill that would serve him well, if only he could master it.

And frankly, what else was there to do? With Valeri off scroll-hunting more often than not, Elias had all the time in the world to perfect this particular art.

The deer stiffened, but before she could startle and race away, Elias renewed his efforts.

Calm, relax, peace.

They stood maybe four paces apart. This much Elias had achieved before, but no farther. He took a long slow breath. The air smelled of the spruce trees that surrounded them, spicy and sweet.

Calm, relax, peace.

Another step forward.

She watched him with eerie stillness. Her ears twitched, but the spell remained unbroken. Another step. Elias reached out his hand, allowing her to sniff. Another step.

Calm, relax, peace. I mean you no harm.

Elias ran a hand down her soft neck, scratched behind her ear, and made soft cooing noises. "Good girl. Thank you."

He took the last step and bent down, bringing their faces together. "That's it, easy. This won't hurt at all, I promise."

Delicately, Elias bit through her thick coat and into the vein beneath her pelt, all the while ensuring she felt at peace. Her powerful heartbeat sent surge after surge of blood for Elias to feast on. He didn't need much. When he'd drunk his fill, he carefully closed the wounds and petted her flank.

"Thank you, sweet girl," he crooned, backing away as slowly as he'd approached. He didn't want this doe to experience a moment's fear on his account. He intended to hold the compulsion for as long as it took to clear her line of sight.

"Well done!" said Valeri loudly from some distance away, breaking his concentration and sending the deer galloping off, fleeing for her life.

Elias let out a huff. His shoulders sank. Oh well. At least he'd tried. He would have been successful too, he'd felt his skill working, if only Valeri had stayed gone a bit longer.

Shoving his irritation aside, Elias turned to greet his lover. What he saw revealed a pleasant surprise. Valeri looked...happy. Truly glowing in a way that had become rare lately. More often Valeri appeared brooding or distant, frustrated by his obsessive dead-end search, but the wide smile on his face spoke for itself.

Elias forgot about the deer and grinned back. "Thank you. I think I'm finally getting the hang of it."

"You're young still to be mastering compulsion over animals. I'm impressed."

"You look well." Elias hesitated to ask in case he was wrong, but he had to know. "Have you found what you were hunting for?"

Valeri stepped in and nuzzled his neck, peppering his throat with kisses. "I have indeed, and it's better than I could have ever imagined."

Elias angled his head to give Valeri better access. He could barely contain his hope that maybe this quest was coming to its conclusion. "I'm glad for you. After all these years."

"I know. This will make the trouble worth it." Valeri's tongue swiped from shoulder to ear. "May I?"

Leaning into the touch, Elias murmured, "Mmm, please do."

Valeri slid his palm over Elias's ass as he slid fangs into his flesh. His other hand held Elias's lower back. A low growl rumbled in his chest. Valeri's happiness was contagious. Elias swayed in his embrace, pressed himself tight to Valeri, and dared to dream that maybe their lives could be filled with something other than the pursuit of ancient secrets.

With a satisfied sigh, Valeri pulled his mouth from the wound and licked the punctures closed. He'd only taken a taste. He kissed Elias's cheeks and the tip of his nose, then met his mouth. Elias returned the kiss, licking at the freckle he loved so much on Valeri's upper lip, all the while a grin still spread on his own face. Kissing and smiling at once was such a lovely feeling.

"It's good to see you like this," said Elias against his jaw.

"It's good to feel like this," Valeri confirmed. "We must leave for Rovaniemi at once. That bastard Lajos lied to me, and now I have the proof I need."

Elias's mood drooped at the mention of Lajos. "Why go back if he lied to you? Tell me what you've found. Do you know how they've evaded the aging sickness yet? Or where they are? What's happened tonight?"

The entire crux of Valeri's self-appointed mission was to bring this knowledge south to the vampires of The Dozen. Elias had been dreaming of the day they could leave. He'd lived in the lands of ice and snow for the entirety of his twenty-two years, and the draw of hot summer nights and foreign lands beckoned to him.

Valeri laughed, bent down, wrapped arms about Elias's thighs, and scooped him up like he weighed no more than a house cat. Elias parted his legs and clung to Valeri's hips.

"So many questions! My goodness, one at a time, please." Valeri carried him in the direction of their camp.

Clenching Valeri's shoulders, Elias joined in the laughter. "I hope you plan to bed me because otherwise this is quite a lot of teasing for a conversation about some stuffy old people."

"Not old people, the court of the ancients, my sweet. Better than the holy grail, and I have finally found them." Valeri planted a sloppy kiss to Elias's mouth. "And yes, I plan to bed you."

"Good. Then start explaining on the way. Why must we see Lajos when neither of us even like him?"

Valeri covered the ground quickly, returning them to one of their makeshift camps. "Lajos works for them. I've suspected as much for some time, but tonight I found the evidence to prove it. I think he can secure me an audience, and even if he can't, their court lies on the east bank of a lake not an hour's walk due north of Rovaniemi at the Arctic Circle. I'll find them myself."

Fear bloomed in Elias's chest. "But, Valeri, won't that be dangerous? These vampires don't want to be found. If you go there alone…"

"I only need to confirm what I've learned, then we can sail south with this knowledge and request aid from The Dozen. There are witches and vampires among their ranks who'd rival the ancients in power, I'm sure."

How can you be sure when you know nothing of their power? Elias thought to ask, but he didn't want to sour the mood. It was such a treat to have Valeri like this, giddy and spirited. First he'd take advantage of Valeri's success, then he would question it.

"How shall we celebrate?" asked Elias, pressing his groin against Valeri's. Already he'd begun to go stiff in his breeches. Apparently being jostled and carried through the forest by his lover turned him on. They couldn't get to camp quick enough.

"Naked." Valeri smirked and picked up speed.

Though the temperatures were easily below freezing, the night air felt invigorating on Elias's cheeks. As a vampire, the cold couldn't hurt him as it once had when he was human, but that didn't mean he had to like the frozen north. What would it be like to make love to Valeri on a green patch of spring meadow, warm earth under his skin, rather than the familiar prick of pine needles and crunch of snow?

They'd made a temporary camp amongst the ruins of an old farmstead. Overgrown now, the old rock walls and dug out foundation created a barrier from the wind and was an easy place for a firepit. They slept beneath the earth, but in the wee early morning hours before sunrise, often enjoyed each other's company there in the open air before a crackling fire. About a night's ride south, they had a small place not unlike the first cave-house Valeri had brought him to in Kuusamo, but near Kitka, life was as primitive as it got.

Valeri set him down and pushed his cloak off his shoulders. "Did you track that doe yourself, or get lucky?"

Elias returned the favor, shoving Valeri's cloak to the ground. "I tracked her."

Valeri's smile revealed glistening fangs. "Good boy. I'm proud."

"What shall I have as my reward?"

"Anything you like. Name it, and it's yours."

Taking a step back, Elias pulled his cock from his breeches. He stroked it with one hand and signaled Valeri down with the other. "Your mouth then. Open up."

Valeri went to his knees without protest, staring up at Elias, brown eyes sparkling. He moistened his lips with his tongue and opened his mouth.

The view alone had Elias's balls tight with need. How Valeri could go from triumphant to positively sinful in the span of seconds boggled his mind. He leaned in and fed Valeri the tip, watching as his lips stretched to accept the offering.

"Now I want your throat." Elias took Valeri's head in his hands and encouraged this next bit of submission. He loved Valeri's wildly open nature when it came to sex. He'd found nothing off limits, and even the tried-and-true options, like the cock sucking he was reveling in, never grew stale.

Valeri grabbed Elias by the hips and yanked him forward, humming around the length in his throat. The vibration sent arousal flaring in Elias as he tangled his fingers in Valeri's curly hair.

"Greedy," Elias huffed. "Don't make me come, I want to be hard when you fuck me."

The words pulled a moan from Valeri, who tugged Elias's trousers from his hips and pushed them down around his ankles.

"My boots," said Elias, eager to be naked.

Valeri pulled off his cock. "They can wait. Come here." He tugged Elias to the ground with him. They landed in a laughing joyous heap on their cloaks.

Arranging Elias on his side, Valeri spooned behind him, cock out and leaking between Elias's cheeks.

"Oh, yes." Elias pushed his ass back. "Excellent idea. Just like this."

"Glad you approve."

Apparently they wouldn't be getting naked after all, but Elias couldn't find it in himself to be bothered. He liked the restriction of being trapped by his own pants tangled around his ankles. He liked the idea of Valeri, fully clothed behind him, only his cock out and exposed to the night air until he buried it inside Elias. He liked the pretty picture he knew they must make in this position.

Valeri shoved his length between Elias's closed thighs and thrust. With no oil, he kept his motion shallow, the drag of skin on skin just shy of painful. Not that Elias would say no to pain. Valeri's cock nudged his balls, pushing a moan from between parted lips.

"Oil? Spit? Blood?" asked Elias. "I don't care, just put it in me."

Snarling against the back of his neck, Valeri brought fingers to Elias's mouth. Spit then, that would be fine. He sucked and licked Valeri's fingers, soaking them with saliva while Valeri continued to fuck his thighs.

By the time Valeri reached between them to prepare, Elias's every nerve ending was on fire. His dick ached with need. He pressed back for more pressure, babbling his consent. "Ready. Now, Valeri, now."

Soft laughter tickled the shell of his ear. "You certain? Might hurt."

"Want to feel it," Elias answered on a breath, so pent up he'd have said yes to a dry fuck at this point. He healed so fast, nothing Valeri did would really hurt him, and he liked the intensity of the burn this way.

"Then feel it, you shall," Valeri said against his ear as he pushed in.

Elias relaxed into the movement, surrendering to the stretch and the fullness, melting against Valeri's chest. "Yes."

Valeri shuffled as he thrust, wrapping Elias in a tight embrace, trapping his arms against his chest and holding them prisoner so Elias could do nothing but take it.

And Elias loved to take it. "Harder."

Valeri obeyed, rocking Elias in his grip, biceps flexing as he pulled them as close as they could get, his soft belly filling the curve of Elias's lower back. Valeri's breath came in heavy pants against the nape of Elias's neck.

If Elias could only touch his own dick, he'd burst, but he couldn't move his arms an inch. He whined. "Valeri."

"What, love?" Valeri purred against his skin. "What do you need?"

"Touch me."

Valeri found a nipple and pinched it between his fingers. "Like this?"

"Touch my cock."

"You can come like this." Valeri massaged the nub hard, then flicked it.

The tweak sent fire to Elias's leaking shaft. He squeezed his eyes shut, which only intensified the sensations. "Is that what you want?"

"Yes. I want you desperate for it."

"I am," Elias admitted with a grunt.

"Good."

Valeri continued his assault on Elias's nipple even as he pounded into his ass. The urge to spill built steadily, his cock pulsing against his abdomen. With his free hand, Valeri pressed his wrist to Elias's lips, an offering he would be crazy to turn down. Elias tongued the sensitive flesh. When he bit, he would explode, and he wanted them to come at the same time.

"Tell me when," said Elias, his lips on Valeri's skin.

Valeri acknowledged him with a low groan of pleasure. He was close. His dick swelled, stretching Elias to the maximum and rubbing his insides just right.

"Now," Valeri cried.

Elias sank his fangs into Valeri's wrist. As the blood burst on his tongue, so did the seed from his body. Euphoria claimed him in waves. Valeri pumped into him, shaking with the pleasure of it. Together they writhed as they rode out their bliss.

What came on fast and hard left in a slow, sensuous slide. Each sensation another one to savor before the next took its place. Teeth sliding from skin, flesh sliding from flesh, Valeri's iron grip relaxing into a gentle hold.

Taking a deep lungful of cool air, Elias stretched like a cat then turned in Valeri's arms, a little awkwardly as he was still stuck in his own pants, but he managed. Face to face with his love, basking in satisfaction, Elias snuggled in.

Valeri rubbed his back. "Well done, my sweet."

Elias chuckled. "Why, thank you, it's been a very successful night."

"It has indeed."

Elias had learned that times like these were generally best for pulling bits of information from Valeri that he might not otherwise reveal.

In light of that, Elias asked, "Tell me what you found tonight?"

If it was possible, Valeri's eyes glowed even brighter.

"Everything."

15

Elias, One Year Ago

"I'll go with you," Elias offered, unwilling to be stuck in their underground rooms alone again. Plus he wasn't convinced Valeri should go by himself.

"You'll stay here." Valeri tucked a knife into its sheath on his belt, then shrugged on his leather doublet. "Where I know you're safe."

Elias batted Valeri's hands off his laces. "Let me." He threaded the cord from the bottom and weaved them upward through each grommet. Valeri stood still to allow his fussing. "I'm worried. You shouldn't go. These vampires have declined to meet with you. Lajos says they're dangerous. Let's go south for help."

"You fret too much. I'm going to confirm their location, and then we'll leave for the Baltic. You must be patient a little longer."

Elias tugged the lacing rougher than was precisely necessary. "I'm not being impatient. I'm being practical. One less-than-ancient vampire against a court of ancient vampires is doomed to failure."

"Not against," said Valeri, snatching the laces from Elias and backing out of his reach. "I'm not charging into battle, I'm gathering information."

"By yourself."

Valeri tied the laces off. "I'll be fine."

With a sigh, Elias capitulated. "Be careful. Please."

"Of course." Stepping in, Valeri dotted the tip of Elias's nose with his finger. "And you, stay put."

Elias turned his head to avoid the offending finger. "If I'm not here, I'll be at the tavern."

"No, not tonight. Don't go out, stay—"

"What?" Anger rose. "That's ridiculous. You intend to leave me alone all night and forbid me from walking down the street? I'm going to go and say goodbye to Jemma before we leave."

Valeri set his jaw. "I said no, Elias."

"She's my friend. I'll see her if I like."

"You're a vampire. Humans aren't your friends, they're your dinner. Stay put where I know you're safe."

"Or what?"

"Or I'll feed from your precious Jemma."

Elias balled his fists. Rage burned hot behind his eyes. "Don't you dare."

"Do not presume to tell me what I do and do not dare. One night in these rooms where you're safe, and then we sail south. Don't pretend it's so much to ask."

Elias had been beaten, for he would not risk Jemma's safety to say farewell. And he could not trust Valeri to feed without killing. Inside, he fumed, but niggling worry for Valeri's safety wouldn't be quelled by anger alone. He took a breath.

"Fine. I'll stay here. Take care and hurry back to me."

"I will." Valeri leaned in for a kiss, which Elias granted, then he left.

Elias stared at the closed door and the four walls that were to be his prison for the rest of the night. Would he ever be allowed to have friends that weren't called Valeri? Was this why his first fledgling, Laurence, had left?

Valeri, One Year Ago

Alone, slinking up the stairs and out onto the dark village street, Valeri rolled his shoulders and attempted to shove thoughts of Elias from his mind. He must focus on the task at hand, not on his stubborn, ungrateful, fool of a fledgling who'd put himself at risk for the sake of a silly bar wench. Valeri scoffed as he passed the tavern on his way out of town.

If Elias would only listen the first time, they could avoid these petty arguments and enjoy peace. But no. Everything Valeri asked was met with resistance, bickering, and back talk as if they were equals and not sire and fledgling.

Perhaps it was his own fault. Valeri didn't have the heart for the kind of punishments his own sire had doled out for this sort of infraction. The kind of punishments that had kept Valeri in line for decades. He couldn't starve Elias, or withhold his blood. Couldn't chain him up in the dark. Couldn't imagine his beautiful, spirited lover imprisoned for his little rebellions.

And so the little rebellions had grown teeth. They'd morphed into fully fledged arguments and stubborn insolence. Yet still, Valeri couldn't bring himself to mete out the proper discipline.

Fedor would call him soft. He'd have laughed when Valeri lost Laurence, and he'd be laughing now as Elias sassed him in his own home. But Valeri refused to turn into Fedor, even if it meant he'd lose Elias someday. The thought broke his heart, but he would not be cruel to Elias. He loved him too much to consider the betrayals that would ensure proper loyalty.

Valeri left the villages of Rovaniemi behind to head north through the woods toward the Arctic Circle. In his inane musings, he'd neglected to pay close attention to his progress as he tromped through the snowy midnight forest.

Close now, he could sense the lake ahead. A massive body of water, Norvajarvi sprawled across thousands of acres. Circling the perimeter would take most of the evening. Valeri estimated the distance at nearly twenty miles, but if he could pinpoint the location of the court of ancients before he left, he was sure The Dozen would send him back with a team.

Arriving at the bank of the lake revealed a stunning light show in the sky. Bright green and purple flares danced to the heavens and back. A pang of longing burst soul-deep. If only Elias was by his side, they could witness the beautiful display together. Elias always loved the night sky's lights. Valeri closed his eyes and saw the awed expression on Elias's face.

With a sigh, he let the silly reverie fade and focused on his mission. He chose a direction, northwest, and began his trek around the lake.

He'd walked for hours before cresting the tip of the water's edge and circling back south along the other side. The shores were nearly uninhabited, he'd only passed two small settlements with primitive dwellings on his journey. No sign of vampires at all.

Valeri wouldn't be discouraged so easily. His information came from a reliable source, and he'd tracked it down himself. He knew the ancients were close, and he'd find them tonight. He could practically taste the victory.

Though it had taken Valeri years to find the keeper of records, when he'd finally succeeded, he hadn't been disappointed. An older woman by the name of Marta guarded chests of scrolls and drawings, mostly the legends of her own people, but also the history of his—vampires.

The Breodun had lived alongside the region's vampires before the ancients cut themselves off from the rest of the world, and they'd seen strange half-breed vampires with powers Valeri hadn't known existed. Gates at the Arctic Circle that led to another world but hadn't appeared in centuries. The phenomenon had been right there by the banks of the Norvajarvi.

As he continued his moonlight trek, Valeri saw the telltale sign of civilized habitation in the distance. Straight lines and right angles. Nature didn't create those, people did.

There, rising up from the ground, a stone wall beckoned like flame, and Valeri was the moth. He made straight for it. Still some ways off, the wall appeared no taller than an average adult. Not built for defense then, as it would keep no one out.

Drawing near, Valeri's senses were on high alert. He didn't want to be detected if he could help it. Find the ancients, get the hell out. That was his plan. He wouldn't be able to acquire the cure by himself; he'd need The Dozen's help for that.

A low stone building loomed behind the wall, shrouded by an immense spruce forest and for its size, well concealed along the landscape. This had to be what Valeri searched for. He crept closer and snuck onto the wall for a better look.

Perched perfectly still on the balls of his feet, Valeri scanned the area. Dark stones made up the squat structure, but though the building rose no higher than maybe ten feet, it sprawled to cover a large swath of ground. Valeri suspected an underground complex, perhaps running beneath this very wall. He listened, focusing his hearing beneath the earth herself, and confirmed the presence of vampires—they were breathing but had no heartbeats.

And if Valeri could hear them, then they could hear him.

Light on his feet, he fled the grounds inland as fast as he could. Though he heard no sounds of pursuit, the need to put distance between himself and this enthralling mystery drove him to run.

The farther he got from the ancients, the more his success sank in.

He'd found them. He'd done it. The location of the court of ancients was secure. Valeri had exactly what he needed to return to The Dozen with an offering they couldn't resist.

Triumph expanded his chest and sent blood thrumming through his veins. His cock swelled in his breeches. His only thought was to share this success with Elias as soon as possible.

Directly in his path, a woman appeared out of nowhere.

Valeri skidded to a halt, a wave of unease rising in his throat like bile. "Who are you?"

She said nothing, merely looked him over with an intensity that made Valeri feel naked, as if she could see inside his soul. Her eyes had an odd, sunny yellow glow, and her skin had an otherworldly iridescent sheen. Bare arms went uncovered in her flowing sea-green satin shift, though it was cold as ice outside. She appeared perhaps twenty-five years old, though her true age was impossible to tell.

"I am Isla," she said, voice musical and light. "You must be Valeri."

He narrowed his gaze. Fear danced along his nerves, but he would not be intimidated. He'd done nothing wrong. "How do you know my name?"

Her expression turned thoughtful. She pushed a lock of long white-blonde hair behind her ear and stepped closer. Though she barely came up to his shoulder, Valeri had to fight the urge to step out of her reach.

"I know your name because you've made yourself a nuisance to us. Surely you're aware of that, after all these years."

Us, thought Valeri. She was one of them. An ancient! Maybe even one of the half-breeds.

"I bring you a warning," said Isla. "One you must regard carefully. This is the end of your quest, Valeri, one way or another. Leave us in peace. Take your lover and go. Think no more of ancient secrets."

Valeri opened his mouth to argue but found he was incapable of speech. His voice wouldn't come. He wrapped his hand around his throat.

"I mean you no harm, but I could rain down upon you the ultimate harm if you choose not to heed my words."

Isla didn't move an inch, but she didn't need to. She unleashed a burst of power, silent and invisible, though Valeri felt it rattle his bones. A wave of rippling ill-intent rumbled through his chest. Overhead, the evergreens swayed and pinecones plummeted from their branches to the forest floor en masse. The display left Valeri unharmed but wary.

When Valeri glanced from the treetops back to Isla, she'd vanished. He searched the landscape, but there was no sign of her. He let his hand drop from his throat and tried his voice.

"I'm going," he said to no one, because Valeri was alone.

Though relieved he could speak, the experience had shaken him. These vampires had powers he'd never witnessed in the species. A passing thought of giving up, taking Elias and heading somewhere safe, rose and evaporated. He was too close to quit now. Bran Vigny had powerful witches with magic like Isla's. That's who he'd need on his side in order to confront them. The Dozen wouldn't send him back empty-handed. Meeting Isla gave him an idea of what they'd be up against.

With fresh resolve, Valeri raced home to his lover.

Elias, One Year Ago

Elias—bored to tears and struggling to ignore his anger at Valeri as much as possible—startled when a soft knock sounded at the door.

No one but the owner of the leather shop knew they lived here, and Horsten was fast asleep on the ground floor. Elias heard his steady breathing and the occasional bellowing snore.

Who could possibly be at the door at this hour?

The knock sounded again, quietly, as if the knocker knew Elias would hear him. He listened carefully. Slow and steady breathing, but no heartbeat. It must be another vampire, but the only one Elias knew was Lajos. And Valeri had been impossibly cautious to be sure Lajos didn't find their den, sometimes dragging Elias dozens of blocks in the wrong direction to lay a false trail.

Elias rose, drew close, and whispered, "Who's there?"

"Elias, it's Lajos," the vampire murmured on the other side of the wood. "I must speak with you."

Jitters coursed through Elias's veins. Already his nerves were on edge, worried for Valeri, and now he must deal with Lajos as well? Something about the other vampire had rubbed him the wrong way from the start.

Valeri would probably be angry if Elias let Lajos in. But it would be rude to ask him to go away. He stared at the lock, willing the hardware to make the decision for him.

"I mean you no harm," said Lajos. Which, Elias thought, was exactly the sort of thing someone who meant him harm might say. "I know where your sire is, and what he's doing. Open the door, someone must warn you. Let it be me."

With a reluctant sigh, Elias turned the lock, gripped the knob, and hoped he wasn't making a mistake.

Lajos stood at the threshold, his carrot-colored hair loose around his shoulders, expression pleased, green eyes glittering like jewels. His appearance held a certain sort of ethereal beauty, and his petite stature made him deceptively approachable. Elias wasn't fooled: his exquisite charm concealed a viper whose bite had the power to poison.

"Thank you," Lajos said with a nod in greeting. "May I come in?"

Though Elias feared he would regret it, he stepped aside and allowed Lajos to enter. "To what do I owe the pleasure?"

Lajos let out a twinkling laugh. "Oh stop, Elias dear, please. I know you detest me."

Elias opened his mouth to protest, then thought better of it.

"Well then, what is it you want? Valeri won't be pleased you're here."

"Afraid he'll punish you?"

"What? No! But you'll understand if I don't want to provoke him with visitors I don't even like." Elias shrugged. It was rude, but Lajos already knew the truth. Why hide his disdain?

Lajos shook his head sadly. "What a pity. Your sire doesn't deserve you. If you ever tire of him, you're welcome to come to me. I would appreciate you." Lajos's lazy green gaze drifted from Elias's head to his toes. "*All* of you."

Elias cringed. "Stop that. I'm not interested. Get to the point or get out."

Lajos sauntered to the lounge and dropped onto it in a cozy sprawl. His burnt ochre tunic stood out against the gold brocade. So this would not be a quick visit, then. Elias sat in the chair opposite, crossed his legs, and waited for Lajos to fill the strained silence.

"Valeri courts danger with this foolish campaign of his."

"You think I don't know that?"

Lajos's lips curled to a sly grin. "My apologies. Perhaps I've underestimated you. Tell me, Elias, what are your thoughts on your sire's pursuits?"

It sounded like a trick question. Tell the truth, and risk Lajos thinking Elias was on his side and not Valeri's. Lie, and he'd believe Elias supported Valeri's endless quest.

Elias kept his tone even and decided not to answer at all. "Have *you* tried talking him out of it? Tell me, how did that go?"

The jingle of Lajos's laughter bounced around the small room.

Elias found no humor in their situation. "Is my lover in danger?"

Lajos's expression grew serious. "Yes."

Confirmation of his fear sat heavy on Elias's shoulders. "And what would you have me do?"

"Persuade him to give up. He is pathetically enamored with

you. Put your significant charms to good use for a change, and get the both of you out of here. As far as you can. Never come back."

Though things were perhaps even less funny with this dire warning, Elias had to suppress a sad chuckle. "Enamored with me? Surely you jest. He can hardly stand me some nights. Tonight for instance. And your presence will only make that worse."

"For that, I'm truly sorry, but you're a fool if you don't realize his devotion. Valeri may be shit at expressing it, but his love for you can surely be seen from the moon." Lajos studied his nails as if the next bit were of no importance. "I've offered for you on several occasions—no small sum either, for you are worth your weight in gold—and he won't hear any of it."

Elias hid his revulsion. "Valeri is rich. He doesn't need your money."

Moistening his lips, Lajos lowered his voice. "I've offered him more than money."

"What else is there?"

Lajos caught his gaze with glowing emerald irises. "Power."

"I'm surprised he turned you down." Elias wasn't sure how Lajos was doing it, but a thrumming pulse radiated from the other vampire, enough to raise the small hairs on his neck. "I'm not a thing to be bought and sold."

"Good for you for believing you have choices." Lajos gave an indolent shrug. "Perhaps I'm wrong. Perhaps you do. He may love you enough to let you go one day, if that's what you decide, but I wouldn't bet my ponies on it."

Crossing his arms over his chest, Elias leaned back. "I'm still waiting for your point."

"I've already made it." Lajos pursed his lips, gave Elias a long, slow glance. "Use your charms to get him to leave. There's nothing for Valeri here. The vampires he seeks won't tolerate his poking around much longer. If he won't go, you should. Perhaps that's the better idea. Go, and I guarantee, he'll give chase. That will get you both out of harm's way."

What Lajos didn't know was that he and Valeri had already planned to sail south. Elias wouldn't tell him. He'd let Lajos think his warning had been heeded. When Lajos discovered their absence, he could feel smug for all Elias cared.

"Why are you here, Lajos? Not in these rooms with me now, but in Rovaniemi. I've seen your paintings. You could take your art somewhere it would be appreciated. Rome. Paris. Yet you remain in this land of ice and snow. Why?"

Lajos's casual sprawl had stiffened. "You really are smarter than he is."

Elias would not be fooled by flattery, and he didn't believe it anyway. "Will you answer?"

Instead of looking at Elias, Lajos took in the room, eyes roaming the colorful decor and settling on a mediocre painting of a sunset done in bright yellows and vibrant oranges. They sat together in sullen silence long enough for Elias to conclude that the answer was no, Lajos wouldn't explain why he stayed in Rovaniemi.

Then, while still staring at the subpar painting, his voice came soft and singsong,

"I'm not allowed to leave here yet.

I am here to pay a debt.

We must take what we can get.

And you should cut your losses."

Unsure how to reply, Elias considered his words. "You owe a debt to the ancients?"

Lajos grinned, revealing his fangs to be as petite as their owner —and just as deadly. "The ancients." He rolled his eyes. "I suppose it's a fitting enough term, but that's not what they call themselves. How pretentious. No wonder Valeri calls them that."

"What do they call themselves?"

"They are The Vartija, the wardens of the gate."

Curiosity flared. "What gate?"

"It doesn't matter," Lajos drawled slowly, now that he had

Elias's full attention. "The gate hasn't opened in millennia. It's dormant."

"Were you here last it opened?"

More laughter, as if Lajos thought him particularly amusing. "Buttercup, I'm not *that* old."

Elias scowled. "How old are you then?"

"That I'll keep to myself. An artist must have some secrets, if only to keep the air of mystery we so painstakingly curate about ourselves."

"All right," said Elias, switching tactics, "then if the gate hasn't opened in millennia, as you say, why do they stay to guard it?"

Lajos gave a flippant shrug. "They cannot leave. The gate is their obligation as they are my obligation. If it should open, they must protect it."

"Protect it from what?"

"You overestimate my knowledge of the subject. I'd say you should ask them yourself except I prefer you living to dead."

Elias wasn't ready to give up his line of questioning. "Well, do you know where the gate leads?"

Lajos tutted. "No more teasing bits of information from me. No matter how irresistible I find you."

"I'm taken."

"I know. I don't so much care, but believe me, I know. Your sire has made that abundantly clear."

"If you won't answer any more questions, and you've said what you came here to say, I'd appreciate it if you left."

"It won't go well for you when your master finds out I've been here, will it?"

"No," Elias answered honestly. There would be an argument for certain.

Lajos sighed with more drama than even Valeri could muster.

Vampires, thought Elias. Were they all like this? He hoped The Dozen would be different.

"I'll intercept." Lajos stood from the lounge and smoothed his

ACROSS THE SAPPHIRE SEA

hands over his fitted tunic. "I'll take all the blame. Don't say I never did anything for you."

Elias didn't know what he meant by 'intercept,' and he didn't care. He just wanted him gone. He stood to show Lajos out.

"You'll try though?" asked Lajos, his tone serious. "To persuade him to leave."

Elias opened the door for him. "Yes. I'll try my best."

"There's a good lad." Lajos leaned in to kiss his cheek. He had to stand on tiptoes to do it.

Elias endured the gesture, but didn't return it. "Good luck with your debt."

Before departing, Lajos cast him a shrewd glance. "Smarter than your sire indeed."

16

Elias, Present, 1432 Common Era

*A*n anxious quivering had settled in Elias's gut.

Lajos had taken two nights to secure their group an audience with the ancients. Elias had half thought Lajos wouldn't agree to arrange the meeting, or if he did, that he wouldn't be successful. When word came the audience would actually happen, the announcement held a note of surprise.

Valeri had been elated.

Elias couldn't help but wonder if this was a bad omen, that they'd agreed so easily. Before he and Valeri had left Rovaniemi for Bran Vigny nearly a year ago, Lajos had been adamant a meeting was impossible. What had changed? Was a delegate from The Dozen really all it took?

As the least experienced of their group, Elias thought his opinions wouldn't count for much. Not with Valeri at the helm, a witch of Aella's caliber, and esteemed vampires like Ash and Laurence. Even Remy, freshly turned, held more sway.

What did Elias know? So he kept his concerns to himself and

followed their lead, even though the circumstances sparked suspicion.

They trekked north through towering evergreens to Lake Norvajarvi to meet what fate had in store. Lajos wasn't among their number—another detail that pinged Elias's warning bells. Not that he wanted more of Lajos's company, but at least the vampire was a familiar menace…the ancients, however, were shrouded in mystery.

"Not much farther," said Valeri from the front of their line.

They crossed through a young forest, one that had probably experienced a serious burn two or three decades prior. Few mature trees had survived the fire, and what had grown back was dense underbrush and skinny trees spaced tightly together, all fighting for the same rays of sunshine. Difficult to walk through.

"Do you think they'll send a delegate out to greet us?" asked Remy, his tone laced with hope.

Elias thought of Valeri's return from his trek last year. He'd encountered a woman called Isla, but hadn't volunteered this detail to their group, so Elias had stayed silent. Valeri knew, because Elias had told him, that these vampires called themselves *The Vartija* and not *the ancients*, but Valeri hadn't shared that either. Elias wished he'd said something. To mention it now would be suspect, and they would wonder what else Valeri held back—because that was what Elias wondered.

Valeri either didn't realize Remy had been talking to him, or he didn't care.

So Ash answered instead. "At Bran Vigny, when new guests arrive, we greet them in the courtyard. But as I recall, Valeri said the ancients' location has no courtyard."

"No," said Valeri. "Their residence is low to the ground and unassuming, built close to the lake amongst the trees with no clearing around the structure. Keep an eye out for a stone wall to our left."

"Perhaps I should join you at the front." Aella shuffled up from her place at the rear.

"If you like." Valeri's tone was grudging.

Elias moved aside to let her pass. Though they weren't expecting hostility—The Vartija had agreed to this meeting after all—it was only wise for their most powerful member to take the lead. When the time came for greeting, Ash would take over. His experience as delegate made him the obvious choice to speak for the group. Even Valeri had agreed.

A low thrumming vibration tickled the soles of Elias's feet. "Do you feel that?"

"Feel what?" asked Laurence.

Elias didn't know how to explain it. "Like the ground is...pulsing?"

"I feel it too," said Remy. "It's almost warm."

Aella stopped and thrust an arm in front of Valeri so he had to halt too. They all froze in their tracks. She tilted her head as if listening. "There's a beat to it, isn't there? A certain rhythm? Feels similar to magic, but not a spell I'm familiar with."

Elias looked from face to face, each one wary. "Do you all feel it now?"

Nods all around, including Laurence.

"We must be close," said Valeri.

Bending to lay a hand upon the earth, Aella asked, "Did you sense this last time?"

Valeri mimicked her, touching the ground. "No, not at all. But I circled the lake and approached from the north before. We're approaching from the south."

"I think they are directly beneath us," Aella concluded.

A tremor of nerves coiled tight in Elias's stomach. After four years of tagging along on a search he once thought would never end, they were literally on top of Valeri's precious ancients. He thought of Mahu and hoped for his sake they'd return to Bran

Vigny triumphant. Beyond that, he longed for a life without obsession. A chance to make friends and to mend the tattered remains of his relationship with Valeri—or to cut the cord.

Aella stood. "Let's go."

Small, lean trees gave way to older, mature giants with thick branches towering over their heads. The tangled underbrush was replaced by a carpet of soft, wet pine needles peeking through the last of the melting snow.

Elias could walk shoulder to shoulder with Valeri. "Are you happy?"

Valeri gave a tight-lipped reply. "I will be."

"We've made it." Aella pointed ahead. "The wall, it's through there."

Sure enough, a short, dark stone wall stood visible in the distance. Not like how Elias had pictured it in his mind, but smaller, unobtrusive. What waited for them behind the wall stirred his nerves. Elias took a deep breath and told himself to relax. He was safe amongst their number.

No one came out to greet them, and they could find no gate in the wall. In the end, they scaled the rocks in order to approach the building's lone door. Nothing like Bran Vigny, no fancy entrance, no glorious towers, nothing pretentious or ornamental. Just a squat stone dwelling without windows stretching a vast distance to either side, perhaps an acre long and wide, with a plain brown wooden door.

Ash stepped forward and knocked, Aella at his side. Elias and Valeri stood behind them, Remy and Laurence bringing up the rear. Their group seemed small now that they stood waiting for entry outside the massive complex. Elias wondered how big the underground portion sprawled.

He slipped his palm against Valeri's and laced their fingers. Valeri squeezed his hand gently.

The door opened to reveal a petite woman, young in appearance, with eyes yellow as a cat's. Waves of white hair flowed over slim shoulders and contrasted beautifully with her green gown. Her oval face revealed nothing, her expression neither welcoming nor hostile. She waited for them to speak first.

Ash bowed low, and the rest of their group followed suit.

"Greetings, my lady," he began formally, his tone conveying respect. "It is our honor to meet you tonight. My name is Ash. I've been sent by The Dozen to speak with your people. My companions are Aella, Valeri, Elias, Laurence, and Remegius. We bring well wishes from Bran Vigny's inhabitants to yours." He repeated the bow.

Elias felt he was being inspected and found unworthy. Not exactly a novel feeling, but unwelcome all the same.

"I am Isla," she said, her voice sparkling like moonlight on a snowflake. "You've had a long journey. Come inside."

Noting the lack of welcome, Elias filed in with the rest of them.

"Valeri," said Isla. "I hadn't expected to see you again."

"My lady." Valeri's voice somehow remained smooth though now the others would know he'd held information back. "The pleasure is all mine, I'm sure."

Elias would have sworn he could feel Laurence's anger that Valeri hadn't told them about this woman and their past exchange. His grip tightened around Remy's waist. Aella, as well, sent a scowling glance in Valeri's direction, which he ignored, his false smile securely in place.

"This way." Isla guided them farther inside.

Glowing wall sconces lit the wide entryway. The interior walls were the same dark stone as the exterior. With no windows the place reminded him of a crypt, though tapestries hung along the hallway to add a touch of life.

Clutching Valeri's hand, Elias followed down a long hall to a broad staircase that led below the earth.

"You'll have to excuse me," said Isla. "It isn't often we entertain guests. As a result, my hostess skills are a bit rusty." Her feet were absolutely silent on the stone steps.

Elias felt sure there were others in this dwelling, but he couldn't hear them, which was odd. The low thrumming he'd sensed earlier grew stronger as they descended and masked other sound.

"You're entering the Warden's Hall to meet with our assembly. They await your presence." Isla stopped and gestured to a set of plain double doors. "Through there."

"Thank you, Lady Isla," said Ash. "Shall I knock or simply enter?"

Elias was glad Ash was in charge. He wouldn't have known what to do in a situation where the rules of engagement were as obscure as The Vartija themselves.

"Call me Isla." She tipped her head. "Your group may enter. They're expecting you."

Ash opened the door and led their group inside. Isla followed along behind them.

The spacious room was brightly lit with lamps strung from a high, vaulted ceiling. The claustrophobia Elias had begun to feel vanished in the open space.

A group of five sat in a close half circle in the center of the room, chatting amongst themselves. How Elias hadn't heard their conversation from outside was a mystery. Perhaps the room was charmed.

An enormous painting took up the far wall, depicting men on galloping horses under blue skies. Aside from its scale, the painting was ordinary. No ancient secrets, no hidden gate. The only thing strange about the art was its location in the underground world of vampires who hadn't seen blue skies in millennia.

Heads turned as they entered. The group stood to greet them.

Ash went through the introductions once more. "Thank you

for welcoming us into your home. We are honored to make your acquaintance."

Elias suppressed a mirthless laugh. They weren't welcome here, that much was obvious. None of these people were happy to see them. No one appeared openly hostile, but this greeting was reluctant at best.

Another round of bows followed.

Elias scanned their faces. Three men, two women, and one vampire so androgynous he couldn't distinguish their sex. All with various expressions ranging from curiosity to irritation.

His gaze settled on the second woman, her face the most open of them all. Petite, like Isla, and with the same iridescent glow to her skin, only her hair was dark brown, like Elias's, and her green eyes shone bright as damp moss in the sunlight. She caught his stare, and to Elias's surprise, she smiled.

Elias returned the smile with a shy one of his own, then lowered his gaze out of respect.

A tall, thin man with sharp features and straw-colored short hair stepped forward. "Greetings to all of you." His eyes lingered on Valeri, and his scrutiny intensified before moving on. "We prefer to keep our location secret. However, since Lajos informed us you already knew where we reside, we've decided to hear your request. Have a seat." He gestured to the empty chairs.

In Bran Vigny, The Dozen had sat in a straight line behind a looming table while petitioners stood before them. This circular setting was far less formal. More cooperative. Yet it was the only welcoming aspect thus far.

The green-eyed vampiress beckoned to Elias, indicated he should sit in the chair next to hers. Elias tugged Valeri in her direction.

"Thank you," he said softly as everyone found their seats. "I'm Elias."

"Sachi," she said, extending her hand.

"Nice to meet you." Elias went to take her hand, but she

reached farther to take his wrist instead. So he took hers as well. Their eyes met, hers twinkling with a glow not unlike Remy's and Laurence's. She must be very old or very powerful. Or both. But her bare wrist was soft beneath his fingers, and if she meant him harm, Elias couldn't tell.

"Nice to meet you too." Sachi gave a nod and resumed her seat.

On Elias's other side, Valeri sat stiff and silent. The wooden chairs had maroon velvet cushions, plush and comfortable. Sitting in a wide circle like this, they could all see one another's faces. If he wasn't so nervous about what was about to happen, he'd have called this setting cozy.

Ash filled the silence before it could turn uncomfortable. "You have my humble apologies for intruding upon your solitude. Shall I proceed directly to the point?"

"Please," said Isla.

"We're here to beg your wisdom. It's come to our attention that many among your number have lived well past the two millennia mark without succumbing to the aging sickness that plagues our kind in the south."

Ash paused, inviting a representative from their number to speak if they wished, but all remained closed-lipped. Elias would have bet *all* of these vampires to be past the two millennia mark. They slipped into a stillness so deep they could be mistaken for statues. Only their clothes looked real, long tunics, loosely flowing in solid colors, and none dressed for the weather. Perhaps they always stayed indoors. But how did they feed?

Ash continued, "Where I'm from, there is a madness that takes hold of older vampires. They suffer. Moments of lucidity come and go. Often their past returns in their minds with such force it's as if they're reliving old times. Some pleasant, and some quite the opposite. Nothing we've tried has helped. No herbs, no medicines, or no magic have made a difference. At length, death comes to put an end to their suffering."

Sachi frowned. Among them, she was the only vampire to

appear concerned. Sachi, Isla, and the androgynous vampire seemed different somehow, but Elias couldn't put his finger on it. Aside from the sheen to their skin and their twinkling cat-like eyes, they looked like young people. Mind-boggling to think they might have witnessed the turning of tens—or hundreds—of centuries between them.

Ash glanced from face to face. "A vampire suffers as we speak. A sweet and gentle man, called Mahu, who hails from the ancient lands of Egypt. I've known him my entire life. Mahu has a generous soul and a kind word for all who cross his path. We don't know how much time he has left."

Elias glanced to Remy, who would be dead now if not for Mahu's selfless donation of blood during his transformation. Remy watched the proceedings with a cautious expression, his body leaning toward Laurence. Perhaps out of all of them, Remy had the most reason to wish a cure for Mahu.

When met with their continued silence, Ash had no choice but to put their case bluntly. "Do you possess a cure for this aging sickness? Is there something we can do, something you could tell us, or give us, or teach us, to save our friend Mahu, and vampires like him, who have yet to develop the sickness but inevitably will?"

There. A poignant plea followed by a resounding silence. Surely one of them must reply.

The answering voice belonged to Isla. "We denied Valeri's first request for an audience. We sent a warning via our agent. I personally told Valeri to leave and not to come back or he risked his death, and yet here he is with an entire delegation." She scanned their number with cold eyes.

"I beg your forgiveness," said Ash, who had to be irate inside that Valeri withheld that crucial piece of information. If the others hadn't wondered what else Valeri was hiding before this, surely they were wondering now. "We've been horribly rude to bother you so. But we're in desperate need of your help. If you could look past our trespass and teach us what we need to know, we'd be in your debt. Perhaps there's something you want that The Dozen could provide in return."

"We need nothing from you," said the tall man who had not given his name. "I'm sorry your Mahu is sick. We aren't monsters, but one man's suffering won't justify the consequences of our exposure."

Something in his tone sparked Elias's anxiety. Aella sat stiffly and glanced to Laurence and Remy. The three of them were here to protect all six, and it looked as if they were preparing to do so.

"We would never expose you," said Ash. "We've only found you thanks to Valeri's sleuthing, and he has only told our people. The ring of knowledge need not extend any further."

"That is already too far," said Isla, her tone firm.

Valeri's hand reached out to clench Elias's, his grip nearly painful.

"If you could advise us what to do for Mahu," said Ash calmly, "we'll be on our way and will never disturb you again."

"You don't understand," said the tall man. "We cannot allow you to leave with the knowledge of our location, much less our secret of longevity."

Fear spiked in Elias's chest. His gaze found Sachi's. She met his frightened expression with a sad one.

The tall man continued, "Our options are limited and will be put to a vote. We wipe your memories, transport you to Russia, and leave you to pick up your lives with a blank slate."

Elias failed to repress a shudder.

"We keep you here, as prisoners until you can be trusted."

Another horrible option.

"Or, we kill you as we have those before you who sought secrets that weren't theirs for the taking."

"You assume we are defenseless," said Valeri. "We're not."

Elias wished Valeri would stay quiet, just this once.

But Valeri kept talking, "None of your proposed solutions will do you any good. Every vampire in The Dozen knows your location, and they will not suffer our deaths, disappearance, or imprisonment lightly."

Ash quickly added, "None of The Dozen wish you harm. None intend to share your secrets. We do not come to you with threats, but with pleas. We wish peace between our people, and help for Mahu."

"What you wish is irrelevant," said Isla. "You cause us great damage. Relocating The Vartija is no easy task, but when your people come looking, I assure you, they will not find us."

Valeri stood. "I found you."

Elias grabbed him and jerked him back to his seat, pinching the skin on his flank harshly. Valeri would get them all murdered.

"And you will die for it," said Isla.

Valeri turned sharply to Aella. "We need one of them." He pointed to Isla and Sachi. "One of the glowing ones. They're half-breeds. Their blood is the cure."

Elias blinked, his mind reluctant to process Valeri's words. He'd kept this secret the entire time? "What?"

Valeri's gaze flit to Elias. If he felt guilty, it didn't show in his hardened expression.

"You knew what the cure was and didn't tell us?" Rage flamed hot, constricting Elias's chest. "But we can't steal a person!"

The words were out before Elias could think better of them. He slammed both hands over his stupid mouth. Everyone had turned his way. Shock and anger painted the faces of The Vartija.

"Of course we can," said Valeri. "Aella." He looked at her as if he fully expected her to obey. Pop open a portal, steal a living being, and rush them all to safety.

Elias had never been so disgusted. "I'm going to be sick."

Aella's muscular frame held the coiled energy of a wolf about to strike, but she kept it in check and looked to Ash for guidance. Remy and Laurence were on the edge of their seats. The Vartija were equally stiff and stone-faced.

"No one is stealing anyone, Valeri," said Ash, though he wasn't looking at Valeri. His gaze remained directly on Isla. "He does not speak for our group. We wish you no harm, but nor do we intend to sacrifice ourselves to your extreme version of justice."

The tall man stood. "Ash, you seem a reasonable man, but we've been threatened in our own inner sanctum—"

Isla stood with him and finished his thought. "Actions have consequences." She raised her hand toward Valeri.

Elias lunged to put his body in front of his sire's. He was furious with Valeri, but he didn't want him dead.

"Remy," said Aella.

Power radiated from Isla's outstretched hand, barely visible, an iridescent wave headed straight for them. Valeri grabbed Elias and made to reverse their positions, but it was too late.

Or it would have been.

The shimmering wave hit a barrier and dispersed in a wild glow of light that fizzled and died out without causing harm.

Valeri tugged Elias out of the way.

Remy was standing now, arms outstretched, Laurence at his back with a hand on the nape of his neck, Aella at his side. "Come," he ordered.

Elias released the breath he'd been holding. They moved to stand behind Remy. In front of him, an opalescent barrier stood between their group and The Vartija.

The six Vartija watched with varying levels of intensity. None seemed in a hurry to retaliate. Elias sought out Sachi and mouthed, *I'm sorry. I didn't know.* He felt he'd somehow betrayed her when Valeri suggested she be kidnapped.

Sachi gave a subtle smile, her soft features shining with an unearthly glow.

"Again, Isla," ordered the tall man.

Isla raised her hand.

"Don't bother," said Remy, maintaining the barrier. "This is the one bit of magic I'm rather good at."

Sachi spoke, "Stand down, Isla."

The tall man whirled to glare at Sachi.

"You too, Bannos." Sachi stood to approach Remy's shield, her posture unthreatening.

The tall man, Bannos, stepped aside to allow her to pass, his face a mask of resentment.

"Remegius, how does your barrier work? Will it allow one to pass who means no harm?"

"It will, my lady, but be certain of your intentions." Remy spoke as if this were an ordinary conversation, and he hadn't just cast a magical arc around their group to prevent execution. "If you think we ought to have our memories wiped or be otherwise punished harshly for a crime we didn't know we were committing, my barrier will cause you injury."

Sachi nodded. "Thank you for the warning." She casually stepped through to join them with no ill consequences. "Marvelous!"

Elias held tight to Valeri's hand as Sachi approached. Her glowing green eyes focused solely on Elias.

"I would like to speak with you alone—"

"No!" Valeri snapped.

Sachi ignored him. "I promise no harm will come to your fellows in our absence. Would you come?"

Would you come?

The last time Elias heard those words was four years ago when he'd been a bondslave in a barley field. A handsome demon wielding a whip had asked that same question. *Would you come?* And he'd said—

Elias straightened his back. "I'll come."

Valeri jerked his arm. "No, Elias, absolutely not. You cannot leave the protection of our witches."

"We shouldn't let ourselves be separated." Ash's voice.

Elias hardened his tone. "I want to talk to her. She won't harm me."

"You don't know that," Valeri hissed. "Don't take the risk!"

Elias tugged his hand free and tried to ignore the hurt the insult caused. He turned to Sachi. "They'll be safe?"

"You have my word," Sachi promised.

"Then I'll come with you."

"No." Valeri reached for him, but Elias dodged his grasp.

Sachi glared at Valeri. "Elias has made his decision. I won't allow you to overrule him." She offered her hand to Elias, and he took it. "Remegius, I will look out for your friend and return him to you safely. May we pass?"

Remy glanced to Ash.

"Why do you wish to speak with Elias?" asked Ash. "I am the delegate, and the risk should be mine. Elias is young and inexperienced. I would protect him."

"He is the only one among your number that I can trust to answer my questions honestly," Sachi explained. "No harm will come to him while he is under my protection."

Ash searched her face, then nodded to Remy.

"You may pass," said Remy.

"Thank you." Sachi glanced to Laurence. "Please keep his lover from following."

Laurence took Valeri's shoulders firmly in hand. Valeri struggled, but Sachi pulled Elias through Remy's arc before he could break free.

She addressed the other Vartija. "Show our guests to the east wing and leave them in peace so that Remegius does not tire himself out."

"Elias," cried Valeri from the other side of Remy's barrier. His face was the picture of panic.

"I'll be fine. Behave yourself." Elias would probably pay for that admonishment later, but he couldn't bring himself to care at the moment. All of this was Valeri's fault and could have been avoided if he'd been honest. Their group would never have agreed to steal a person, and that Valeri believed they would proved how out of touch he was with whatever was left of his tattered humanity.

Elias wasn't sure what he could say to Sachi to plead their case, but he wanted the chance to try.

Sachi's elegant brows arched. "Shall we?"

"Please," said Elias.

17

Valeri, Present, 1432 Common Era

$\mathcal{F}$uming and more frightened than he'd been in his entire life—which was saying something as he'd lived through the likes of Fedor as a sire—Valeri paced the salon from one end to the other.

"Please," said Ash. "You must sit down and speak with us. This tantrum you're throwing will not help our situation or get Elias back."

"I can't believe you let her take him," Valeri snarled. "I gave you the answer and you threw it away!"

"I believe he is safe with the woman. Come, sit." Ash gestured to the chair across from his.

They'd been put in a parlor-style room, perhaps one used for gatherings—that is if these beings, *The Vartija*, ever used to have gatherings before they went absolutely insane and started killing visitors.

With thick stone walls and the incessant thrumming noise, they could speak quietly without much risk of being overheard.

Furniture arranged in a circle dominated the center of the room. Tables with art and vases nearly as tall as a grown man decorated the corners. Tapestries hung on the walls.

Valeri ignored all of it as he stormed angrily back and forth.

"Leave him," said Laurence. "He's useless. We must come up with a solution between us."

"Useless," Valeri growled. "We wouldn't be here if it weren't for me!"

"Precisely," said Remy from his place at Laurence's side. "And Elias would be safe. But you withheld vital information and now we are prisoners. Instead of making allies, we've made adversaries. If anyone is hurt or killed, you're to blame."

Ash held up his hands, fingers spread wide. "Stop this. With any luck there will be time to argue later. We need to go over our options, and for that, we need Valeri's cooperation. He still knows more than the rest of us, starting with, what did you mean when you called the women half-breeds?"

Valeri stopped his pacing, crossed his arms over his chest, and resigned to tell them everything. "Mixed bloods. I wasn't certain the legends were true until I laid eyes on Isla for the first time. You've seen them for yourselves. Surely you can tell they're something else. Something beyond vampire."

Aella nodded. "Yes, they're different. All three of the women possess some sort of magic I'm unfamiliar with. What else do you know?"

"During my time with the nomadic tribes, the Breodun, I found their keeper of records. Their scrolls said—"

"They let you read their scrolls?" asked Laurence, his tone skeptical.

Valeri's gaze snapped to Laurence. "Do you want to know or not?"

"Quiet, both of you." Ash raised his voice. "I've had enough of your bickering. Valeri, make your point."

"Their scrolls said that in this place, thousands of years ago, a gate to another world would open on the solstices. Creatures from our side could cross to theirs, and vice versa. The vampires here mated with fae folk from another realm, and thus produced a hybrid. Drinking the blood of a half-breed heals ailments and grants immortality of the kind the ancients enjoy. Without a half-breed of their own, The Dozen will continue to fall victim to the aging sickness, and Mahu will surely die."

"But we cannot simply take a person against their will," said Ash. "What on earth made you think we'd agree to that?"

"He didn't think we'd agree." Laurence. Of course. "That's why he didn't tell us. He knows it's wrong and thought that, in the moment, we would betray our morals. Easy for someone with no morals to think others would so willingly give up their own."

"You didn't even tell Elias," said Remy. "He was so shocked as to scorn you in front of everyone."

"Shut your mouth," said Valeri, his head full of menace. He'd had enough of Remy's lip this journey to last an entire lifetime. He had no idea how Laurence could stand the runt.

"Don't speak to him that way." Laurence scowled, gray eyes glowing. Valeri would never get used to the unnatural hue.

Aella stood and also began to pace. "What if you've overcomplicated this? What if we don't need an entire person, but merely a small offering of their blood to take back to Mahu? Perhaps we could work out a trade."

"Do these people seem open to a trade to you?" Valeri scoffed. Asking for a handout would never work. They needed a prisoner, that was all there was to it. But first, they must get Elias back from wherever Sachi had taken him. If there was one thing Valeri regretted, it was his decision to bring Elias along. He should have left him at Bran Vigny where he would have been safe until this mission was complete. Once he had Elias back, he'd never let him out of his sight again.

"We won't know if we don't ask," said Aella as she walked. "What is Elias likely to say to her?"

"How should I know?" Valeri snapped.

"It's a valid question," said Ash. "You control his every movement. He obviously didn't know you intended us to kidnap a halfling, but what else have you told him?"

Valeri didn't see the importance of this line of inquiry. "I've kept him out of it." Though Elias knew about the gate, didn't he? Lajos had mentioned it, along with another name for the ancients. Valeri had told him of Isla. But the rest he'd kept secret. Perhaps he shouldn't have.

Oh Elias, don't get yourself in any trouble. I'm so sorry.

How mad would Elias be when he returned? He'd been furious with Valeri when he left, but Elias never stayed mad long. Valeri could count on that. Elias's good nature had eased them through many arguments. He would charm that half-breed, then come back to Valeri safe and sound, and Aella could portal everyone out of there.

Aella's gaze flitted from Valeri to the others. She dropped back into her chair. "We must at least try to pursue a trade. Convince them their secret is safe with us and offer something of value in return for a sample of blood for Mahu. Do any of you have other ideas?"

"The Dozen are wealthy. We could offer to pay," Laurence suggested.

"These vampires don't seem to lack for resources," said Ash. "My instinct says to appeal to their empathy, but they've rejected that plea once already."

Aella scowled. "Rejected then threatened severe retaliation. If it weren't for Remy's barrier…"

She didn't have to finish that sentence. They all knew Valeri or Elias both might be dead without the magical shield. The thought grated on Valeri like sandpaper.

"Do you think they operate by committee?" asked Ash. "They

mentioned a vote. But then Sachi spoke as if she were the leader and commanded the others in the face of opposition."

"Perhaps we have only to win her good opinion, and the others will follow," said Remy. "Hopefully, Elias will bring us some useful information."

Valeri glowered at the four of them, with their heads all turned together, effectively excluding him from the conversation. They wouldn't even know about these vampires or the cure if it weren't for him. And as far as he was concerned, they were focusing on the wrong thing.

"We ought to go after him." Valeri glared at Aella. "Use the magic we brought you along for, get us out of this blasted room, take Elias and the woman, and go."

"You aren't listening," said Laurence. "None of us, nor The Dozen, would ever agree to your criminal plan. Think of something else or be quiet."

Inside, Valeri fumed. He opened his mouth to argue but closed it as the door swung wide to reveal one of the half-breeds. Not Sachi or Isla, but the other one. The third one.

Their group was on their feet in an instant, Remy's hands twitching at his sides. Valeri had to admit, having a witch around who could produce a barricade came in handy. He turned his attention to the newcomer.

Skin glowing brighter than the full moon's rays over freshly fallen snow, their ethereal appearance confused the eyes. Was this a man or a woman? Valeri couldn't be sure. He also didn't think it mattered. What mattered was where Sachi had taken Elias and what was she doing with him.

"Where is my fledgling?" Valeri demanded none too tactfully.

Golden eyes settled on him, the weight of their stare pushing him back a step. The purple tunic flowed about their ankles as the halfling came to a stop. "Elias is safe with Sachi. She is gentle. Have no fear."

Even their voice seemed to shimmer, if such a thing was possible, the twinkling notes of it echoing through the large salon before fading to silence. Or, not silence, but thrumming.

"What is that constant pulsing noise?" asked Valeri on impulse. "It never stops."

The creature's pink lips curled to a smug smile. "Ah, apparently you do not know all our secrets after all. Some things aren't meant for you to understand, seeker."

"I apologize for Valeri's rash nature," said Ash, much to Valeri's annoyance. "What can we do for you?"

"Actually, it is I who came to offer something to you."

Ash's brows lifted. "And that is?"

"Myself."

Elias, Present 1432 Common Era

Elias lay on his back in the boat, body bobbing with the current of the water beneath them, marveling at the stars overhead. The sky was crystal clear. How had he gone so long without simply enjoying the majesty of the night sky?

Sachi lay next to him, her head by his, but her body stretched the other way, so that her feet were at one end of the boat and his were at the other.

Valeri must be going mad. Elias had been gone for hours. But his conversation with Sachi showed no sign of slowing, and it would do Valeri good to think on what he'd done. What he'd thought they all would do.

"This is my favorite place to dream," said Sachi, her voice quiet.

They drifted along in the big rowboat somewhere in the middle of Lake Norvajarvi. Sachi had taken him from the underground compound and down a little trail in the woods to procure it. They'd shoved off from shore and simply rowed away. She'd been quiet in the beginning, as if she knew he needed to sort his own thoughts, then she'd begun a line of questioning that had absolutely nothing to do with ancients, or cures, or secrets. Elias found her refreshing.

Sachi asked after his journeys. What did the lands to the south look like? Were their mountains? Had he seen a whale from the ship? Did warm summers melt the snowcaps? Were the plants different? The flowers? The people? What other languages were spoken? Had he seen a person with brown skin? How tall was Bran Vigny? Did it really pierce the clouds?

When her curiosity proved endless, Elias began asking questions of his own. Why have you never left Lappland? What is it like to live forever? Aren't you cold in your sleeveless gown? Do you ever miss real food?

There was such relief in these questions, in this conversation that ignored all the danger and uncertainty of his reality. Sachi was easy to like, with her friendly, inquisitive nature and bright intelligent eyes. Elias was ashamed of Valeri for demanding either she or her friend be kidnapped.

As much as he enjoyed the lighthearted chatter, Elias had to ask the question he'd been asking himself for a while. "Should I leave my selfish lover?"

Sachi rolled her head to the side to look at him, but Elias kept his eyes on the stars. Though he'd asked for it, he couldn't face her scrutiny yet.

"Ah, Elias, only you can answer that question. Ask me something I can actually help you with."

"What should we do, Sachi? My group and I. We've traveled here under Valeri's false pretenses, angered your people, suggested a crime, and failed in our mission. Mahu will die. The Dozen will mourn him. My friend Remy, whom he saved, will be sad. And Laurence. There are times I wish..."

When he didn't finish, Sachi asked, "What do you wish, Elias?"

"Nothing." Elias shut his eyes. "I don't really mean it. I shouldn't say things I don't mean."

"You can tell me."

"Sometimes I wish I'd never met Valeri." The admission tugged painfully on his heart. "But that isn't really true. He can be good. I think he wants to be good, he just, well, he isn't good at it." Elias gave a sad chuckle and opened his eyes. "That sounds stupid, but it's accurate. He saved me from a life of hard labor and an early death from exhaustion. He's given me everything I have: shelter, warmth, nourishment, clothes…this life. I must sound ungrateful."

"You don't. You sound honest." Sachi sighed; Elias watched the silver swirling mists of her breath disappear on the breeze. "Life is complicated. Love is complicated. Choosing the right thing isn't always straightforward or easy. Sometimes we get it wrong."

"I don't want to leave him," Elias admitted, perhaps more to himself than to Sachi.

"Perhaps you won't have to, but Elias." Sachi rolled to her side and propped her head on her hand. Elias couldn't avoid her eye contact now. Her expression turned serious. "You must learn to advocate for yourself. No one will do it for you."

"And you?" Elias asked, sensing she needed the same advice she was doling out to him. "What is it you want?"

"Many, many things." Sachi's voice thickened with longing. "Perhaps too many to count."

"Tell me one then," Elias probed.

Her gaze grew distant. "I'd like my life to have meaning again."

"Of course your life has meaning."

"It used to," she said wistfully.

Elias didn't know what to make of that. Her words brought sorrow. He sensed she'd said all she would on the topic.

The water rippled softly against the boat. The gentle bobbing didn't upset his stomach like the big cog ship had done. He'd liked learning how to row, the feel of the wooden oars in his hands, his muscles working to push the water aside and propel the boat forward. He liked lying there now, enjoying the fruits of their labor. The peaceful lake, the chirps of night birds overhead, the occasional flop of a fish leaping for bugs and falling back into the water.

Another question jostled in his mind for attention. "Would your people really execute us?"

"No. I won't allow it. Isla wasn't going to kill your sire, just restrain him. We've killed in the past to protect our secrets, but I'm done with such archaic punishment. It takes a unanimous vote to kill, and I won't give mine. But they will not let you go. And I'm not powerful enough to free you myself."

Elias desperately wanted to tell her about Aella, about her ability to portal, especially when the destination was home and witches waited on the other side to help. They could leave whenever they wanted, but would they leave without the cure? It didn't seem they'd have a choice. Though he felt with all his soul he could trust Sachi with this knowledge, he knew Valeri would order him to stay silent.

He knew it, and he rejected it.

"Sachi, there is much that I should tell you."

"I am here to listen," she said as she lay back down.

Elias was a bit relieved. It would be easier to spill these secrets as he gazed upon the stars rather than her sweet, open face.

Elias told her everything. Of Laurence, Valeri's other fledging, and of his fledgling Remy and how Mahu had helped them survive Remy's transition. Of the witch Remy had been before, and of the vampire-witch he'd become. How Laurence had also developed the power under Aella's tutelage. Of portals and magic and their inevitable departure despite whatever punishment The Vartija sentenced them to.

Sachi listened in perfect stillness. Only when Elias finished with an apology that they would leave, with or without a cure, did she stir.

"With, Elias," said Sachi, her tone determined, "you shall leave *with* the cure."

Hope fluttered in his chest. "But what do you mean?"

Jaw set, she met his gaze, green eyes shining with intensity. "I mean, I am coming with you."

18

Valeri, Present, 1432 Common Era

"What do you mean, you're offering yourself?" asked Ash.

The halfling's catlike stare made Valeri uneasy. This had to be a trick. He wouldn't trust this creature for a second.

"My blood," they answered. "It's what you came here for, isn't it? I won't leave my home for you, but I'll allow you each to drink."

"You offer your blood, but not your name?" asked Valeri. He could think of no good reason for such an offer. Drinking their blood must benefit The Vartija somehow. *Mind control?* He'd heard of such, though he'd never known it to be true.

Their gaze flitted back to Valeri, pinning him in place. "I offer both. My name is Finley."

"We aren't the ones who need your blood, Finley," said Ash, rather calmly for the circumstance, Valeri thought. "It is our friend Mahu who suffers. He is far too sick to make the journey."

"You've misunderstood," said Finley, their voice as musical as Isla's had been. "There will be no help for Mahu. I'm sorry for your loss, but you must see our dilemma."

"I'm afraid I don't." Ash gestured to the chairs. "Not completely. Perhaps you could sit with us and explain your position more clearly."

"If you wish, but I'm afraid there are no words that will change the outcome in your favor."

"Nonetheless, what else have we to do while we await our fate?"

They resumed their seats, though Valeri found it nearly impossible to be still when Elias was off with some half-breed, god knows where. His chest constricted with worry. His anger simmered below the surface.

Finley sat primly in the chair across from Ash, next to Remy. They crossed their legs and arranged the lavender smoothly over slim thighs, hands clasped in their lap. "You're awfully calm about the possibility of your own executions."

"Would you have us panic instead?" asked Laurence.

"Of course not. Most of us hope it will not come to such a regrettable conclusion, especially since there are better options. It's why I offer my blood."

"I fail to see the connection," said Ash.

"If you drink from me, you'll get a taste of what it's like to be a vampire of The Vartija. Perhaps you'll want to stay."

Vartija. That was the title Elias had learned, and Valeri had promptly forgotten. He'd been so angry that Lajos had snuck behind his back to speak with Elias, he'd barely registered what Elias told him.

"What is that word, Vartija?" asked Ash, "I'm unfamiliar with it."

"It means 'wardens.' The Vartija is what we call ourselves."

Aella's expression grew curious. "Wardens of what?"

Finley cast their otherworldly gaze on the witch. "Perhaps one night in the future, I will tell you. Once you've proven yourselves loyal."

"We don't belong here, Finley," said Remy. "You must realize that. We need to return home, with or without the cure for Mahu. We were always meant to return home."

"You're Remegius, correct?"

Remy nodded. "Yes, but you may call me Remy as my friends do."

"Remy, then." Finley smiled. Their cherubic features surely charmed everyone else in the room, though Valeri would have none of it. One of these half-breeds had Elias. As far as he was concerned, they were the enemy.

Finley continued, "How did you cast that shield? I've never seen magic quite like that, and other than ourselves in The Vartija, I've never known a vampire to have magic."

"I was a witch before I was turned," Remy explained. "I know that most witches lose their power after the transition, but I didn't. At least not completely. As to how I cast that spell, I can't tell you."

"Of course not, no. I suppose you cannot trust me, can you?"

"It's not that, though you're right. I don't trust you. I can't tell you because I don't really know. I've always been fairly decent at spells that manipulate the ether, but I've never taught the skill to another."

Then how did Laurence learn magic? Valeri wondered, then he realized Remy may be hiding the truth from Finley. The vampires here had yet to see either Laurence or Aella perform magic, though surely they knew Aella to be a witch.

Aella shared a glance with Ash, who nodded before she spoke. "I am a decent instructor. I could teach you and your people that spell, and others like it."

"Let me guess," said Finley. "For a price? An offering of my blood and promise of safe passage home, I assume. I'm afraid it's out of the question. No one learns our secrets and goes free."

Valeri huffed. "The Breodun people know, yet they roam free. So you stop at the wholesale slaughter of thousands of innocents, at least."

"Is that how you learned of us?" asked Finley pointedly.

Valeri narrowed his gaze. "Why should I tell you?"

Finley leaned forward. "To take the suspicion off Lajos for one, and for two, because I suspect it's the truth."

"I learned from their keeper of records, but there is no reason for you to kill her if you aren't going to kill all of them. Another will just be installed in her place."

"We won't kill the Breodun. They've never betrayed us the way you've just betrayed them."

Valeri changed tactics. "What about Lajos? He knows your secret, yet he is free."

Finley shook their head. "Lajos is not free. You make too many assumptions."

"That's enough, Valeri," said Ash. "Be polite, we're guests here."

Guests! That was laughable. They were prisoners at the moment, and Elias was a hostage.

"Will none of you take me up on my offer?" asked Finley as they rose from their chair. They held their bare arms out straight, wrists exposed. "You came all this way for our blood."

Ash stood to meet them. He towered over the diminutive Finley, but he didn't use his height to intimidate. That wasn't Ash's style. "Only Valeri knew that's what we would need. The rest of us hoped the cure would be something simple—a tonic you could share, or a potion you could teach us to make."

"I see." Finley clasped their hands together. "I am sorry the answer isn't so simple. I will leave you in peace while we wait for Sachi to finish speaking with Elias."

"I want him back," Valeri snapped.

"And you shall have him. When Sachi has finished," said Finley before leaving on silent feet.

Elias, Present, 1432 Common Era

"You're coming with us?" asked Elias, full of hope.

Sachi leaned in. "That is how we solve this. Your witch Aella creates this incredible portal you speak of. Fae magic could never accomplish such a feat. I'll come to Bran Vigny with you, and Mahu will drink my blood. No one will have to die this way."

Elias couldn't believe what he was hearing, but the stars were their witness. "Your people, though. Will they be angry with you?"

Her head tilted. "Furious, I imagine."

If that bothered her, Elias couldn't tell. He must warn her. "The journey back home for you will not be simple. Aella can portal home, but she cannot portal from Bran Vigny to Lappland. It's too far, she doesn't know the land well enough, and there is no one to help her on this side."

"I don't want to come back." Sachi sounded quite sure of herself.

Elias's eyes widened. "You don't?"

"No," she answered without hesitation. "This is the opportunity I've been waiting for. I'm tired of protecting a gate that no longer exists. I grow weary of wishing for a realm we lost access to ages ago. We waste away here, longing for what was, and we do not enjoy what is. I wish to know what *is*."

Elias followed along as her words came faster and faster, and her eyes sparkled like emeralds.

"I'd like to see other lands and feel the warmth of a southern summer. I want to explore the continents. I've heard of big cities where people trade from all over the world. Constantinople. Rome. I'd love to see Egypt. To see pyramids and ancient writings unlike our own. To lie on the bank of the Nile. To uncover civilization's secrets rather than protect them. Do you understand?"

Elias laughed. He couldn't help it. "Sachi, I am twenty-three years old. My wishes are much simpler than yours. I'd like to make a friend. Perhaps go a week with my lover without argument. Your list makes mine seem ridiculous."

"Oh no!" She sat up, grabbed his hand, and held it in her lap. "You don't seem ridiculous to me at all. You're pure. Innocent."

Elias shook his head. "Not innocent."

Sachi studied him. "Perhaps not, no. But you're good. And that matters. Your wishes matter too, and making a friend is a worthy goal. I'd like us to be friends."

"I would like that too." Friendship was the thing he desired most in the world.

"So it's settled." Sachi squeezed his hand. "I shall come with you. That solves most of the problems."

Elias shuffled to sit as well. "The one it leaves behind is huge."

"Yes," she agreed reluctantly. "The rest of The Vartija will not be happy their secret is out."

"Not that," said Elias, though her point was valid.

"What then?"

"Well, Sachi...you *are* the secret, correct? Yourself and the other faeborn. What happens when word spreads? The reasons The Vartija have been so protective are still valid. Every vampire community across the globe will want your blood for themselves. Aren't you worried about that?"

"No, I'm not. Why would I be? They can have it. I want my life to mean something again. If I can save aging vampires from going mad, then I want to. And I'll start with Mahu."

"But what if not every group is like The Dozen? What if they are like Valeri? The Dozen would never agree to kidnap you and use your blood against your will, but Valeri was obviously willing to stoop to it. What if others are like him?"

Sachi's gaze turned to the horizon. On one side of their boat, the water seemed endless. On the other, the shore grew closer and closer. The current was pulling them back to The Vartija one ripple at a time.

She held her chin high. "No one can steal what I offer willingly."

Elias's caution wouldn't budge. "But there is only one of you, Sachi. How many vampires are there in the world?"

Sachi shrugged. The motion looked incongruous on her, like she was too elegant for a casual shrug. "I have no idea."

"Me either, but you see the problem?"

"I see the problem."

"Maybe we should try to keep the secret. For your own good," Elias suggested. "Right now, besides your people, only The Dozen know. The knowledge should end with them. You cannot save the world's vampires." He said the words, but he didn't really know what they meant. *The world's vampires.* How many was that? A thousand? Ten thousand? Elias had no idea.

"You're wise for your twenty-three years, Elias. And already you seek to protect your new friend. But let's leave that problem for later and concentrate on the one we have now. The Vartija will never allow me to go. We must have a plan."

Elias's shoulders slumped. "I'm no good at plans."

"I am," said Sachi, her eyes twinkling brighter than any of the stars.

19

Valeri, Present, 1432 Common Era

𝓗 ours had passed. Hours! And Elias had not been returned to him. This worthless group seemed content to stew in this pit of a waiting room while the ancients toyed with them, deciding their futures as if they had no say in it themselves.

When pacing failed to calm Valeri's nerves, he'd argued to break the locks and storm the complex until Elias was recovered. Met with a united front from the others to simply wait until closer to dawn before they did anything rash, Valeri was forced to fume in silence. Or act alone.

Without their magic, Valeri's efforts would be useless. But doing nothing while Elias could be in danger was taking its toll. He'd been stupid to bring Elias. Valeri vowed then and there to never put him at risk again. When he got Elias back, he'd protect him at all costs. If they had to disappear to be safe, they'd do it. He no longer cared for The Dozen's opinion. For a place at their court. For the respect of his peers. Only Elias mattered.

"Valeri, he's all right," said Laurence, the most unlikely source of comfort to ever exist. "You'd know if he weren't, your bond would alert you."

Valeri bit back the urge to tell him to mind his own business, though he did have a point. Valeri would know if his fledgling were hurt or afraid. Wherever Elias was, he wasn't upset. But the thought gave little comfort when Elias wasn't by Valeri's side where he belonged.

"We won't leave without him," said Remy.

What did they want? His thanks for pointing out the obvious? They would get nothing from Valeri but a glower.

The click of the lock sounded, and Valeri's gaze darted to the door. Hope surged in his chest. He leapt to his feet.

The door swung open.

Elias walked in. Whole, safe, and from his expression as their eyes met, possibly quite cross with Valeri.

The world righted itself. Valeri lunged for him.

Sidestepping his reach, Elias glared. "Don't."

Sachi stood at the threshold, watching the exchange without comment. Valeri's blood boiled at the sight of her, that she had the audacity to take Elias from him. To turn Elias against him. But no…he'd done that himself, hadn't he? Valeri seethed and made another attempt to collect Elias into his arms, if only to be certain Elias was unharmed.

Elias dodged and made for Remy. "I said don't."

Valeri followed. He'd apologize, beg if he had to, admit his solution had been terrible, but Laurence stepped between them, all bulky and barrel-chested and immovable, and if Valeri could go back in time and unmake him a vampire he absolutely would.

Thwarted, Valeri turned his hurt on Sachi. "What have you done to him?"

Her unnatural green eyes flared bright, and her serene appearance took on a feral quality that set the hairs on his neck on edge. Without meaning to, Valeri took a step back.

"Elias makes his own choices." Sachi's voice hurtled as a

dagger. "It's you that must learn to respect him, not I." She turned on heel and departed. The click of the lock engaged.

Valeri whirled back to find Laurence's stupid chest in his way. Behind him, Elias whispered to Remy.

"You know he's safe," said Laurence. "You'll have to be content with that for now. Leave him be."

"Elias," cried Valeri, his voice unrecognizable to his own ears in its pathetic whimper.

Elias glanced his way. Their eyes locked. Valeri's soul twinged for the hurt he saw there. The hurt he'd put there.

"If you think I can easily forgive you for lying to me—to all of us—for suggesting we kidnap an innocent person and for putting us all in danger, you're gravely mistaken."

Valeri opened his mouth to beg forgiveness anyway, but Elias shook his head.

"Hold your tongue. We have vital information to discuss. Your wishes no longer rule this mission."

Valeri closed his mouth. His chest constricted. He'd seen Elias mad with him plenty of times, but something about this was different. Had he finally pushed Elias over the edge?

The door opened again. Valeri hadn't even heard the lock.

Finley entered alone.

Valeri had the passing thought that this could be their opportunity to finish the mission. There stood a half-breed, unprotected. With Elias back, their group was whole again. Aella could make the portal, they could grab Finley and be done with this. But he knew now the others would never agree. He began to think about why.

Valeri studied Finley, their gentle eyes and open expression. They'd been kind, even offered blood, though to what end Valeri didn't know.

Regardless, Finley had done nothing to harm them and was living here in peace. Who was Valeri to trample that serenity?

Nobody. The others already knew that. Elias knew it. *But the mission—*

"My apologies for the delay," said Finley in their melodious tenor. "We need more time to come to a decision. We must hear from Sachi and consider all she has learned. As dawn approaches, we offer you the comfort of private bedchambers."

They want to divide us, thought Valeri, alarmed. Would Elias even agree to stay with him? Valeri couldn't bear to be parted from him again. They'd never slept a day apart since they'd met. His heart ached at the possibility. His hands itched to shove Laurence out of his way so he could hold Elias.

Ash stood and gave a quick bow to Finley. "Thank you for your hospitality, but we'd prefer to stay together. This room is perfectly adequate."

Valeri sighed in relief.

Finley nodded. "Understood. Can I bring you anything? Do your young ones need to feed?"

"No," said Laurence, possibly too forcefully. "Thank you, no."

These people were far too eager to get them to drink their blood. Whether from genuine generosity or ulterior motives, he couldn't be certain. Valeri would feed Elias himself. Laurence would feed Remy. They could manage a few nights this way before the situation grew dire. Hopefully they'd be long gone by then.

Finley opened their hands, uncurling elegant fingers. "Then, if there's nothing else, I'll leave you be."

"There is nothing else," said Ash.

Finley bowed and left the room.

Valeri sighed his displeasure, exhausted by all the polite courtesies. The bows and the nods, as if they were friends when really they were prisoners. He ignored the guilt threatening to creep through newly formed raw patches.

"We should go," said Valeri. If they weren't going to get what they came here for, they had no reason to linger.

Elias shook his head and whispered quietly to the group. "I have something to tell you. We may not have failed after all."

Elias, Present, 1432 Common Era

Sleeping without Valeri at his side proved impossible. Elias had grown too accustomed to curling up with him, and no matter how mad he got, he still ached for the weight of Valeri's arm over his back, the familiar pattern of his breathing under his cheek.

With his entire soul, Elias didn't want to leave Valeri, but they couldn't go on as they had been. Not with both of them miserable. Something would need to change. He let out a long, melancholy sigh, feeling quite sorry for himself and the work that lay ahead if he stayed. Maybe he should leave Valeri after all.

The sun was high in the sky; Elias could feel it in his bones. Exhausted, he leaned against the wall, too frustrated to continue to try to sleep on his own.

Around him, the others slumbered on the floor. Remy nestled against Laurence, Aella the little spoon to Ash's big one. But Valeri, like him, was wide awake. He lay on his back, knees up, eyes staring at the ceiling. Elias let his gaze linger, roaming Valeri's chestnut curls, his arching cheekbones, and that little freckle on his upper lip. He loved to kiss that freckle.

Elias blew a breath through clenched teeth and climbed to his feet. Valeri's gaze turned to his with such longing as to melt the meager resolve Elias had mustered. *I don't want to leave you.* Heart heavy, Elias sank to the floor to sit beside him.

"Elias," Valeri whispered on a breath, tone reverent, saying his name as if in worship.

"You are an absolute ass," said Elias, glowering.

"I'm sorry." Valeri's fingers twitched where they lay on his abdomen, as if he wanted to reach for Elias, but knew better than to try.

The words surprised Elias. Apologies from Valeri were rare and seldom genuine. But this one was wrapped in sincerity. Elias could see the emotion in Valeri's expression, the regret, the longing. The combination disarmed him, his anger fading to a deep sadness. Elias gave in and lay down next to him like he'd longed to do for hours.

"This does not mean I forgive you," said Elias, pulling Valeri's arm around him just how he liked it.

"Of course not," Valeri murmured against the crown of his head.

"You cannot go on treating me as if I belong to you."

"I know."

Elias snuggled into his spot. "I'm still mad at you."

"I understand." Valeri held him close.

"I don't know that this can be fixed," said Elias honestly. "Don't get your hopes up."

Valeri's chest rumbled as he spoke. "I shall remain hopeless until you tell me otherwise."

Elias's lips curled to a smile against his will. "Be quiet. Go to sleep."

Elias, Six Months Ago

Bran Vigny Castle gleamed with a splendor Elias had never dared to imagine. After the long sea voyage, and an overland trek to get there, the rising towers and sprawling gardens exceeded his every expectation. The castle truly reached the clouds, tickling their wispy white tendrils with its spires. Astounding.

The interior proved even more magnificent. A veritable museum of treasures strewn about everywhere he looked. Sculptures, paintings, tapestries. Every piece of furniture a work of art. His senses were inundated by the beauty of it all, the richness, the culture contained within these walls. Elias had seen nothing like this in Lappland.

He had a passing thought of Lajos. Though he detested the vampire, Elias couldn't help but think the artist would be more at home at a place like this than in cold and dark Rovaniemi. He wished the plan wasn't to return. Already Elias knew he'd prefer to stay in the castle, where vampires, witches, and humans roamed freely through the sparkling hallways and warm courtyards.

Valeri had petitioned The Dozen for an audience through letters, so when they arrived, an apartment had already been prepared for them. Though Elias longed to explore, Valeri insisted they keep mostly to their rooms.

Not even a week after they'd settled in, Elias was enjoying a bath by himself when Valeri stormed into their apartment, his expression furious. While the water cooled and the bubbles popped one by one, Valeri ranted about Laurence's arrival. And not only that, but Laurence had brought a lover, a runt of a witch called Remy. The Dozen wanted this witch to be on the team sent with them back to the ancients.

Elias listened, for that was all that was required of him; Valeri didn't leave space for him to get a word in during his raving. All he could think was finally, *finally*, he would get to see this Laurence for himself. This other vampire Valeri had made who'd abandoned him. Maybe something he learned from Laurence would help him fix whatever was breaking between him and Valeri. He clung to hope.

Before they could meet, all hell broke loose. They awoke early one evening—too early for them to rise as the sun still shone outside—to loud booms that shook the castle walls.

Elias clung to Valeri until it ended, and though Valeri held him, he'd no answers to offer. They only found out what had happened afterward, and Elias was never sure Valeri told him the entire story. A battle had raged. Bran Vigny's witches had triumphed. And Laurence had turned his witchborn partner to a vampire.

Valeri's response was one of relief. If the witch had been turned, then he'd lost his magic and would be no help on their mission. Relief soon shattered like icicles in springtime, because not only had Remy retained his powers, but Laurence had gained them, and both were slated to journey with them to Lappland.

Valeri became impossible, and Elias bore the brunt of his frustration. He'd yet to lay eyes on this mysterious and loathed Laurence or his new fledgling, Remy. Valeri kept him locked away in their rooms so much that Elias grew restless.

With boredom came boldness, for what did he have to lose? Valeri lived in a constant state of irritation, why not give him something to be irritated about?

Elias ventured from his room. He began to meet people. First the donors, who were available to any vampire in the castle upon request. Then other vampires. A woman called Livia who had harsh words for Valeri, but was very kind to Elias.

And finally, Laurence.

Well, he didn't meet Laurence, not really, but he saw the man. Elias wouldn't have known who he was if a smaller, younger vampire with long yellow hair hadn't called out his name.

"Laurence, wait for me."

The big vampire stopped in his tracks, turned, and his handsome face lit up with a welcoming smile, gray eyes glowing silver. "Remy! You're early. We have an hour before we must meet Aella."

Elias stared from where he'd frozen in the corridor, hoping to blend in with the wall as he ogled the pair.

Laurence was huge. Well, maybe not huge per se, but tall and broad with brawny muscles and a rounded chest and eyes only for Remy, which was good because it meant he did not catch Elias staring.

Remy, by contrast, was a petite beauty. Short of stature, thin like Elias, with a lean frame and a youthful face. His blond hair hung in loose waves around his shoulders, and despite their size difference, he fit perfectly in Laurence's embrace as they greeted one another not ten feet from where Elias stood.

"An hour you say?" said Remy with a twinkle in his eyes. "I can think of a number of ways to spend an hour with you."

Laurence gave an indulgent grin. "Well, let's see how many we can check off your list, shall we?"

The pair hurried past Elias, who ducked to avoid notice.

So this was Laurence? This was who Valeri had chosen first?

Laurence must have been Valeri's type. But Elias was nothing like Laurence. Not proud or strong or handsome. Not muscular or imposing. He was just Elias. Rather scrawny—though not as small as Remy had been, but still—he was nothing compared to a man like Laurence.

What had Valeri ever seen in him?

2 0

Elias, Present, 1432 Common Era

The Vartija were already gathered at Warden's Hall when Isla brought Elias and his party to meet their fate. The same group from last night—the three halflings: Isla, Finley, and Sachi; Bannos, the tall vampire who'd ordered Isla to attack Valeri; and two other men who'd still not been introduced—sat in a half circle as if they were about to play cards and not sentence six souls to death or imprisonment.

Though he was still furious with Valeri, Elias had drunk from him upon waking and stood at his side now. He wasn't sure what awaited them when they were out of this catastrophe, but he wouldn't abandon his sire yet.

Bannos stood as they entered and gestured to the empty chairs. So polite. So civil. Their apathy made Elias sick to his stomach, a familiar feeling he was eager to be rid of.

Elias risked a glance at Sachi, and she met his gaze with a brave face and subtle nod. They had a plan. Their group knew the details, and the seven of them were ready to see it through. With a bit of luck, they'd be back in Bran Vigny by sunup. Without it, well, Elias didn't want to think about what could happen.

Everyone sat. The old wooden chairs, probably ancient themselves, squeaked in protest.

Bannos addressed the group, but his eyes were trained on Remy. "Your vampire-witch has made coming to a solution difficult."

Laurence sat stiff in his chair.

Did they expect an apology for not being easier to dispatch?

"So long as your solution is within reason," began Ash, playing his part, "it's not out of the realm of possibility that we could be convinced to cooperate. What have you decided?"

"The decision was not unanimous, therefore, it's only temporary. You benefit from our long-rooted desire to move away from executions. We'll allow you to choose. You may remain under our supervision until you either prove yourselves worthy, or until such time as you make such a nuisance of yourselves as to warrant further action. Because of you, we'll need to abandon this location and secure another."

Ash sat forward in his chair. "Or?"

"Or you may submit your minds to our magic. We'll wipe all knowledge of our existence and deposit you someplace safe where you can begin anew. The process isn't exact, and many of your memories will be lost, up to and including vital pieces of what makes you *you*."

Ash frowned. "That is not much of a choice."

Bannos narrowed his gaze. "It's better than the alternative."

"Obviously, we want to keep our minds intact," said Ash.

"There is more." Isla's voice, as musical as Finley's or Sachi's, but not nearly as friendly. "Whereas the five of you are not at fault for what's happened," her gaze drifted over each of them to land squarely on Valeri, "Valeri had been warned to stay away. He knew the consequences of his return. His actions warrant punishment."

Though Elias had suspected as much, his muscles stiffened, and his jaw clenched upon hearing it. He didn't entirely disagree, yet he wouldn't allow harm to come to his sire if he could prevent it.

Beside him, Valeri remained perfectly still, lips pressed in a thin line, eyes narrowed. He looked for all the world like a man itching to fire back.

Isla squared her shoulders, chin jutted forward. "Valeri will be relegated to a gaole cell where he will be starved of blood."

Elias failed to contain a horrified gasp.

"In his weakened state, he'll be given an option to beg our forgiveness upon the winter solstice. If he fails to earn that forgiveness, he'll starve until the spring equinox at which time he'll receive another opportunity. And so on until he earns his place in polite society. His only visitor will be Elias, and that is a courtesy to Elias because he is young in the blood. Visits will be at Elias's discretion, not Valeri's."

Elias let out a breath. He didn't have to pretend to be terrified, his fear was genuine and would be obvious on his face. Oh gods, they really had to get out of there. Valeri would go mad in custody, and Elias might too.

"And if I refuse?" asked Valeri, his voice pitched low in quiet fury.

"The choice isn't yours to make." Isla turned her carping gaze to Ash.

It now fell on Ash and Aella to make their capitulation look convincing. For his part, Elias had only to take Valeri's hand and act scared, which was easy, because he was terrified. Just as The Vartija didn't know their full strength, their group didn't know The Vartija's either. Success was no guarantee. He hoped Sachi knew what she was doing.

"Starving a vampire is an extreme punishment," said Ash at length. "We admit to frustration with Valeri ourselves, but your suggestion is cruel beyond our limits."

"Wait. Before we discuss *him*," Aella cast an irritated glance at Valeri, "define what you mean by 'remain under your supervision,' because it sounds like Valeri isn't the only one who'll be imprisoned."

Isla's brows arched. "It's not imprisonment. You'll be allowed certain freedoms."

Aella raised her voice. "'Allowed certain freedoms' implies we'll be denied others. I have done nothing wrong—"

Sachi stood. "Before this conversation continues, Valeri's punishment isn't up for debate. Only yours. Keep your memories and stay, or lose them and go. It's really that simple. I'll escort him to his cell while you think on your choices."

At her approach, Valeri scooted back in his chair, the legs screeching against the stone floor.

"Please don't take him," begged Elias as she neared. His gaze flitted to Aella. The witch's fingers twitched at her sides.

Remy sat on edge, and Laurence already had a hand touching the back of his neck. They'd need to act fast while Sachi stood close enough.

A knock sounded at the door, startling a flinch from Elias.

Everyone's heads turned at the interruption.

Bannos, irritation written across his face, gestured to one of the men. "Gauss, see what that is."

The burly vampire, Gauss, rose to go to the door, striding through the middle of their group to do it, and putting himself at their backs.

Remy cast a worried glance to Aella.

Sachi grasped Valeri by the arm, landing herself firmly within their circle. "You must come with me. It will go easier for you if you cooperate."

Valeri scowled and remained seated.

Elias clung to his other arm. He refused to let go. "You can't take him. I need him. Please."

Aella exhaled, closed her eyes, and began to chant. In front of her, Remy raised his arms.

"You'll be able to visit him." Sachi's voice rung hollow, her playacting no longer convincing. Her worried eyes found Finley.

"What are they doing?" asked Isla, alarm threaded through her tone.

"Wait!" cried Gauss from the door. "Sachi's maid has found a note!"

"Now, now!" cried Sachi.

Remy's opalescent arc began to form around them.

Finley jumped up from their seat. "What's happening? What note? Sachi?"

"The maid says Sachi has pledged to go back with them," said Gauss. "That she is leaving us through a portal their witch can summon."

Aella's soft chanting beat like a metronome in the background. With each repetition Elias's fear ticked up a notch.

Finley lifted a hand, and a wave of magic slammed Remy's shield.

Remy staggered, but Laurence held firm behind him.

"Grab hold of Sachi." Finley shouted the order to Gauss as Remy's barrier blocked them from reaching her themselves. "We can't let her leave!"

Isla joined Finley in the onslaught on the protective arc. Together they directed a swirling rainbow of energy against it. The opal sheen faded, flickering ominously, but the shield held.

Bannos and the other man only watched, frustration evident on their faces. Apparently they had no magic of their own.

Gauss circled, took a running dive, and slid under the backside of the pulsing magical dome before it could close completely, leaving the eight of them crowded beneath.

Ash tackled him, grabbing him around the middle and halting his effort to claim Sachi.

Gauss growled as he struggled to his feet despite Ash's hold.

The two of them began to brawl. Ash spun them, taking hit after hit as he placed himself between Gauss and Sachi.

Feeling helpless as Aella went through the motions to open a portal, Elias clung to Valeri and locked gazes with Sachi. "Are you sure?"

Tears had formed in her eyes, but she nodded. "I'm sure. Hurry! Isla and Finley are very powerful when they work together."

Gauss managed a swipe at Laurence, but Laurence's concentration never broke. He focused completely on Remy, ignoring the chaos erupting around them.

Ash tumbled Gauss to the stone floor with a loud grunt, though the fight was far from even. Gauss had the advantage, his strength already overpowering their leader.

Elias panicked. "Valeri, we must help Ash."

"I'll do it. You stay close."

Letting go of Valeri's arm was one of the hardest things Elias had ever done.

Valeri joined the fray, attacking Gauss from behind to give Ash a break.

Sachi took Elias's hand. "Can I help?"

"I don't know." Elias searched her eyes. "Can you?"

"I have some magic. Not as strong as Fin or Isla, but I want to help."

"Come." Laurence reached out to her with his free hand. "Lend us your strength."

Sachi and Elias drew close.

Laurence beckoned. "Touch my skin. Allow me to draw from you."

Without releasing Elias, she took Laurence's hand. A shiver raced up Elias's spine and morphed into tingles that ignited along his skin. Elias had never touched magic; it felt like air gathering before a storm, wind currents swirling and energy sparking, so much he expected his hair to ruffle, but nothing actually moved.

Laurence shook under the burst of Sachi's contribution. The power of her magic hit Remy, and his barrier wavered then redoubled, the opal sheen thickening.

Finley and Isla were forced back.

Isla screeched her fury. "Sachi! How could you?"

Elias squeezed Sachi's hand. Beside them, Gauss was quickly gaining the advantage over Ash and Valeri. The brawny vampire dealt powerful blows, fast and agile for a man of his size. The tangy scent of blood filled the air. Red on Ash's face. Fear seized Elias's chest. Valeri was a decent fighter, but no match for Gauss's deadly skill.

Aella's chanting grew louder. Magic crackled and snapped. A burst of purple light cast the room and all its occupants in an eerie glow.

"No!" Isla's hands shook with effort. "Bannos, do something!"

At her order, he leapt at the barrier and was repelled from it with such force as to be flung against the far wall.

Faint voices sounded in the distance, a chorus of witches chanting with Aella. *Bran Vigny's witches!* Hope dared to mix with fear. Elias risked a glance over his shoulder. The portal appeared as a vibrating rip of color directly in front of Aella, glowing purple around the edges, the other side too blurry to make out. The fissure expanded in size, just enough for a man to pass through.

Shouldn't they go?

Why weren't they leaving?

Elias's gaze darted from the portal to Valeri, who landed with a sickening thud, sprawled on the stones as Gauss tossed him away. "Valeri!"

Valeri held his ribs, meeting Elias's panicked gaze. "I'll be all right. Stay out of it."

Ash was down, and still. Too still. Elias's hopes were dashed as Gauss's eyes blazed in triumph.

Gauss lunged for Sachi, grabbing a fierce hold of her elbow.

Sachi jerked sideways and let out a yelp.

"Now!" Aella's voice resounded powerfully throughout the hall.

Elias kicked Gauss in the shin, but his body was hard as marble. The strike had no effect. Gauss ignored him.

"Go through!" cried Sachi as she stumbled. "Take Valeri and get out!"

Torn, Elias dropped to Valeri. He took his arm and tugged. "Come on. We must carry Ash."

The three of them were to go through the portal first, with Sachi as well, then Laurence, Remy, and finally, Aella, who'd snap the portal shut behind her. But Sachi was locked in a struggle with Gauss. Their plan was falling apart.

Valeri's movements were sluggish. He grimaced.

Panic threatened Elias's control. With Valeri injured, he'd have to get them out himself. "Up, Valeri, come on." Elias tugged him to his feet. "Go!"

A stubborn edge lined Valeri's hard gaze. "Not without you."

Elias grabbed Ash beneath both armpits and hauled him up. His body was deadweight and blood soaked his collar, but Ash was a vampire. He couldn't be dead...right?

Ash was taller and bulkier than Elias, but he had to get the man through the portal. Valeri staggered on his feet, clutching his side. No help. Definitely injured.

Think, Elias, think.

The battle raged around him. Isla and Finley were not giving up; Remy and Laurence concentrated their efforts on holding them off. Bannos and the other man had both been knocked out cold from Remy's barrier. Sachi used her magic to hold her own against Gauss, but the man fought wildly. Elias couldn't predict who'd win the upper hand.

First things first.

Grunting, Elias clutched Ash's body to his chest with all his strength and dragged him to the portal. He set the bloody vampire down at the edge of the rippling purple fissure. With one last burst of effort, Elias shoved, rolling him through the opening as if he were a sack of potatoes. Elias winced, but he had to trust there was someone on the other side who could help. It wasn't dignified, but it was done.

Next, Valeri.

Elias grabbed the knife from his lover's belt, then took him firmly by the shoulders.

"I'm right behind you. Go!" Elias ordered and pushed him through the rip. Valeri's face froze in a stunned expression of protest as he disappeared into the purple blur.

Sachi had to go next. Remy and Laurence couldn't stop fighting until she and Elias were safe.

Elias wielded the knife as if he knew how to use it. He didn't. "Sachi, we must take him with us. There's no other way."

Her green eyes blazed like jewels, sharp and shimmering. Gauss took advantage of the distraction and grabbed her by the neck. Panic took over her gaze.

Elias put on a burst of speed. He would need every bit of advantage he could muster. He hurled himself at the pair as they grappled, dug the knife into Gauss's flank, and drove them mercilessly toward the portal.

They fell to the ground in a tangled heap on the other side. Cold marble met Elias's cheek as he rolled away from Gauss and struggled to sit up.

The familiar grip of Valeri's hands landed on him, sending a surge of relief through his chest. "Elias! Are you all right?"

"Yes, you?"

Valeri nodded, but Elias knew he'd been hurt. The question was, how badly?

"Where are the others?" A woman's voice. He didn't recognize her right away.

Witches stood in a line, chanting in rhythm.

"Shall I go through?" A man's voice. Elias didn't recognize him either. He glanced up. A vampire, one of The Dozen.

"Yes!" Elias ordered with all the authority he could muster from his spot on the damned floor. "Yes, go through! They need your help!"

Ash was being gently carried away by two vampires Elias didn't know.

Elias turned his attention to Sachi and Gauss. Bleeding from the knife wound to the gut, Gauss was being restrained by two vampires. Sachi was likewise restrained though she put up no fight. Her cheeks were wet with tears.

"Someone start explaining," said the woman. Corinne. That was her name. One of the Dozen.

When Valeri stayed quiet, Elias took it upon himself to handle the explanations. He pointed to Sachi. "She's here of her own free will and wishes to stay." Then he gestured to Gauss. "If there is any way to send him back once Aella is through, do it! He does not belong here."

Corinne nodded, and the rest was out of Elias's hands. Valeri was in no shape to stand, so Elias stayed with him on the ground and waited, terrified for his people still trapped on the other side.

"Are you sure you're all right?" asked Elias.

Valeri's arm tightened around him. "I will be."

"What if they don't make it?"

Valeri's lips pressed to a thin line. "They have to."

The constant thrum of the witch's chanting began to grate on Elias's nerves. What was happening on the other side of that portal?

Laurence burst through the fissure, a wild look in his eyes.

With him came the two Bran Vigny vampires who'd crossed to help. Laurence turned, and as Remy raced through, caught him in his arms. The couple collapsed to the marble.

"Hurry," ordered Corinne, "send him through!"

Gauss leapt into the rip the moment he was released.

They only needed Aella. Elias thought of her, alone on the other side, unprotected without the barrier from Remy and Laurence.

Corinne cast a worried glance to Laurence. "Aella?"

"She's coming," said Laurence as he and Remy climbed to their feet.

Elias's chest clenched with worry. Valeri slumped against his side, breathing shallow.

Everyone stared at the shimmering purple tear in space. Anticipation hung in the air, thick with tension. Behind them, Bran Vigny's witches' chanting rose louder and louder. Their rhythm beat a pulse in the ether Elias could feel against his skin.

What would The Vartija do to her if she was stranded under their roof? After she'd made Sachi's escape possible? Their fury would know no limit.

Elias shuddered at the thought.

The portal crackled. Wind began to pick up, though they were indoors. Aella burst through the spasming whirlpool just before the edges slammed shut with a loud, snapping bang.

Relief rushed over Elias like the welcome tide of a full moon. He took a deep breath and held it, clutching Valeri's hand in his.

Aella had landed on hands and knees with a grunt. Her eyes swept the room, panic in her gaze. "Ash?"

"He's being seen to," said Corrine, her tone ambiguous.

Where the portal had been, there stood only the castle wall.

Elias exhaled.

Was it really over?

21

Mahu, Present, 1432 Common Era

*D*akarai hovered by Mahu's bedside, eyes flooded with concern. He reached for Mahu's hand, but there was no substance with which to touch. Only Daka's astral spirit could make this journey. His body lay somewhere in Egypt. Still, Mahu felt a pleasant flutter of cool air on his fingers at the sweet gesture.

A weak smile tugged at Mahu's lips. "I'm glad you came."

"You aren't an easy man to forget."

"Neither are you."

Daka lifted a dark brow. "I'm not a man."

Mahu waved that away. "Demon then."

Daka coiled his tail around his waist as if to emphasize the point.

Mahu's body hosted a great many pains. His lungs twinged with each labored breath. His chest ached. Fingers and toes tingled with a thousand tiny needles yet failed to turn numb. Perhaps the greatest agony of all was to see Daka without being able to touch him. To run his fingers along the familiar ridges of the incubus's tail. To tease his nipples to hardness and watch him writhe for more.

Daka's expression changed. His head tilted, black hair falling across his forehead.

Mahu longed to brush the silken strands behind his ear.

"Do you hear that? Vampires approach."

Mahu listened but heard nothing. His senses weren't what they used to be, dulled with sickness. Half the time, he didn't know if he was awake or dreaming.

"I must go."

"No, don't." Mahu struggled to sit.

Daka leaned in. "Shh, they're coming to help. Lie back"

"Don't leave," Mahu begged, but Daka's handsome form shimmered, threatening to vanish. "Please."

"Next time we meet, it is you who must come to me."

"Wait!" Mahu put all the force into the command that he could muster, which is to say, very little force at all.

When the door creaked open, Daka was gone. Mahu sank into the bed, eyes closed, ready to surrender to fate.

Voices filtered through the haze in his mind.

"Oh my, he's worse off than I imagined." A woman's voice, light and airy though tinged with concern.

"Can you help him?" A young man. Gentle and timid.

"Yes, Elias. I think I can."

Without opening his eyes, Mahu heard her approach, sensed her presence at his bedside, but all he could think of was his lost love.

"Hello, Mahu. I'm Sachi. I hope we'll become friends."

Did she want him to answer? He could not. *I'm sorry.*

A bright scent caught his attention. Blood. But more than that. Roses. The smell blossomed under his nostrils as the woman pressed her dripping wrist to his mouth.

A spark of strength he hadn't known he possessed coursed through his veins, enough to allow him to part his lips and bite.

Her blood was like no other. Thick and coppery but with a floral bouquet of aromas. She tasted of spring flowers and sunshine, warm like a summer evening, crisp as fall leaves, pure as winter snow. Her offering brought a host of experiences, a hint of the divine, a mother giving life.

Mahu opened his eyes.

Dakarai. I will come for you.

22

Valeri, Present, 1432 Common Era

Seated at his desk, alone in his and Elias's rooms at Bran Vigny, Valeri stared at an unopened letter. All the way from Russia, surely the missive was from Fedor, which was an excellent reason to throw it directly into the fire. Nothing good came from Fedor but money, and the money already belonged to Valeri in the first place.

With a sigh, he ignored the correspondence to stare out the window. The moon hid behind the clouds, its silvery glow outlining the edges. High enough within the castle to see the tops of thousands of trees swaying in the breeze, Valeri wished he felt like he belonged there. But even after the mission had proved a success, he found he was no more accepted by these vampires than he'd ever been. Always the misfit. Forever an outcast.

The part of him that cared was mercifully silenced by the part that didn't. Elias fit in here, and that's what mattered. Elias—as happy as Valeri had ever seen him—had endless engagements with friends and mentors. Letting go of the restraining leash he'd kept Elias on since that fateful night in the barley fields had been easier than he could have imagined. Elias's joyful smiles were all he needed in trade. If only he'd known that sooner. How stupid he'd been. How awful.

Elias and Sachi had become attached at the hip. Together they'd gone to Mahu's bedside, and Elias had watched as she fed him. Elias then reported these details to Valeri.

Slowly, night by night, Sachi's miraculous otherworldly blood nursed the dying vampire back to health.

Mahu had been skin and bones upon their return. His eyes sunken in his skull, his skin paper thin, his constant murmuring unintelligible. But when Sachi opened a vein in her wrist and pressed it to his lips, his garnet eyes fluttered open and he drank.

Her secret was safe with The Dozen for now. Valeri had been threatened on pain of death to tell no other soul, and he'd sworn an oath. He'd had enough of ancient secrets and magic blood to last a lifetime. Besides, he had no one to tell. Elias was his only companion, and soon, he'd lose him too.

His ribs had finally healed from his tussle with Gauss. The thug had crushed him like an insect. Valeri had heard each bone break with an awful chorus of pops. Had it only been one or two, one day's rest would have done the trick, but Gauss had broken the lot of them. It had taken a vat of blood split between several donors and three full days of rest before he felt like himself again. He'd never seen poor Elias more worried.

His gaze drifted to land on Elias's books. Presents from a girl called Clara who Valeri didn't know, but who'd discovered Elias was learning to read. In the early morning hours, Elias would curl up with him in bed, and they'd practice endlessly. Elias was ravenous, drinking in knowledge with the same sort of zeal Valeri had reserved for sex, blood, and killing.

This would never work.

Valeri was going to lose him. He knew it like he knew the sun would give way to darkness each night.

The separation was already happening, one agonizing bit at a time, inevitable. Even now Elias was gone, out gallivanting elsewhere in the castle with his precious new friends. The friends he'd always longed for, finally at his beck and call, so Valeri could be more easily cast aside. Discarded now that his part had been played.

He deserved it. Valeri could admit as much. He'd treated Elias like a possession, allowed his own jealous nature to rule over his better judgment. He'd been cruel. Elias deserved better. But none of that made the slow withdrawal any easier to bear.

Picking up the offensive envelope, Valeri braced himself for the vitriol he assumed it would contain. He tore open the edges, plucked out the letter, and unfolded the paper. Met with Fedor's impeccably neat cursive, he blew out an irritated breath and began to read.

Valeri,

When news of your second failed attempt at guiding a fledgling to maturity came to my awareness, I had to admit my profound disappointment. Though I shouldn't be surprised, considering you lack the much needed common sense that rearing a whelp demands. Not everyone should procreate.

Our mutual acquaintance Lajos has assured me that Elias shows promise in spite of your negligence. I hereby offer to take the lad under my wing. I regret the missed opportunity with Laurence, and seek to rectify the situation without delay. Should you decide to accept, send Elias along to your ancestral lands where I shall begin his proper tutelage upon arrival.

Regards,
  Fedor

Valeri shuddered at the words 'proper tutelage' because he

knew precisely what Fedor meant by them—punishment and deprivation—and he would never let such a curse befall his beloved Elias. Fedor would have to kill him first.

The nerve of his hateful sire to pen such a pompous message. Like he could honestly do any better. Fedor would ruin Elias, and he'd enjoy every minute of it. Fedor was the reason Valeri knew what the cracking of his own ribs sounded like. He'd never lay a finger on Elias, Valeri would make sure of it.

Valeri dipped his stylus in ink.

Fedor,

Though I'm much obliged by your generous offer, I fear I must decline. You see, I prefer my fledgling healthy, whole, and spirited, and you would pluck those virtues from him piece by painful piece. So thank you, but no. Do not anticipate his arrival and know that if you ever touch a hair on his head you earn my wrath (for which I know you care very little) and lose my estate (for which I know you care a great deal).

Humbly and Forever Yours,
    Valeri

He enjoyed a wicked little laugh imagining the face Fedor would make upon reading the words. Then he folded the letter and tucked it safely in its envelope.

Heating the wax for the seal, Valeri wondered how his life might have been different if he'd had a kind sire. Though he wished to be such for Elias, Valeri knew he'd failed. He wasn't a kind man himself. Elias had suffered under his cruel streak, and it was surely the reason Valeri would lose him in the end.

But he refused to hand Elias to Fedor. Such an outcome was unthinkable. No. As much as he loathed to admit it, Laurence was a wise man and a kind sire to his own witchborn fledgling. And

Laurence would not refuse Elias if Valeri came begging. He was too caring, too loyal for his own good. If Valeri must part with his lover, he would do it on his own terms. He would send Elias with Laurence, where he knew he'd be provided for like he deserved. In a sense, the men were brothers. At least, Laurence could be made to see it that way.

Valeri dribbled the wax onto the envelope and pressed his stamp to seal it shut. That done, he leaned back in his chair and let his shoulders slump.

Footsteps pitter-pattered from the hall. The door to their apartment burst open. Valeri didn't bother to turn. Merely looking at Elias's beauty had become painful.

"Valeri," said his lover, voice bright with newfound happiness. "Aella has invited us to her training session with Laurence, Remy, and Sachi. Mahu will be joining us as well. Will you come?"

Elias sounded so hopeful. Did he wish Valeri to say yes or to decline so he could enjoy their company without him? Deciding it had to be the latter, Valeri shook his head.

"Not tonight. I have letters to finish."

"But—"

"Not tonight, I said. You go. Have fun." It wasn't easy to get the words out, but his desire to keep Elias all to himself had crushed his lover's spirit. Valeri wouldn't behave that way anymore. "You can tell me about it when you return."

Elias came closer, his familiar scent a comfort. Valeri longed to bury his face against Elias's throat and inhale, but he sat perfectly still. Hands came down upon his shoulders and squeezed.

"Perhaps I could stay here and watch you at your letters. Or I could practice while you finish. We could join them after. Or not at all," Elias rambled, his voice soft as satin. "We could take a walk instead, or if there's something you'd rather do, we'll do that. Just tell me."

Valeri picked up one of his hands, flipped it over, and kissed his palm. Perhaps Elias had wanted him to come along after all, though he couldn't fathom why. The last thing he wished to do was steal an ounce of Elias's joy.

"Go and watch the training session, Elias. I'm sure you'll have a nice time without me."

Elias gave a huff of annoyance and pulled his hand from Valeri's grasp. "Fine. I shall go by myself. Enjoy your letters."

Valeri watched him go. Then he stared at the door and told himself this was for the best. Better a clean cut than a jagged tear. He would make letting go as easy as he could for Elias. It was the least of the debts Valeri owed him.

Elias, Present 1432 Common Era

Elias met Sachi in the hall outside her rooms, and they headed down the staircase to the courtyard.

"Are you all right?" she asked, her eyes glowing with concern. "You look upset."

Elias gave a sigh. "I suppose I am a little upset."

"It's your lover, isn't it? Valeri." The gentle twinkle of her voice soothed his hurt feelings. "He makes you sad."

They exited the castle and continued downward through the courtyard to the gardens. A warm breeze ruffled the flower beds and brought their sweet scent forward. Crickets chirped merrily, no doubt in search of other crickets to make more crickets with. There was no crunch of snow underfoot. Elias's arms were as bare as Sachi's in the warmth of the late spring night. He loved it here, but Valeri was miserable.

"He doesn't mean to. I don't even know that he realizes it," said Elias in Valeri's defense. Valeri had done nothing to bother Elias since their return. Quite the opposite. He'd been utterly devoted to their reading lessons, indulgent in bed as always, but...something was nagging at Valeri. He almost never left their rooms. When Elias questioned him, he insisted he was fine, only recovering from injury, nothing to worry about. But Elias worried anyway.

Sachi took his arm at the elbow. "Then you should tell him."

"Tell him what?"

"That he's making you unhappy. And what he could do to make you happy instead. He cannot read your mind, Elias."

Fair point, though Elias had difficulty imagining that conversation going well. It didn't help that he wasn't sure what he wanted. He'd been frustrated by Valeri's possessive nature. Angry he'd never been allowed friends. But now? Elias almost felt abandoned. Though he was thrilled with each new freedom, he didn't quite understand the shift in his lover. Valeri had gone from one extreme to the other, and neither brought them contentment.

Sachi let him sort out his thoughts in silence as she led them to the center fountain where they'd meet the others. The pleasant gurgle of flowing water grew louder as they approached, drawing Elias from his thoughts.

Laurence and Remy were already waiting. Aella and Mahu had yet to arrive, so the four of them enjoyed a chat before the lesson began. Elias would miss them, especially Remy, who he'd grown quite fond of. They'd be leaving soon to visit their friends Livia and Clara for a while. Clara, Elias had learned, was the silent benefactor who'd been providing book after book for his new reading habit. One day he hoped to meet her so he could thank her properly.

"How are things progressing with Mahu?" asked Laurence.

Next to Elias, Sachi beamed. "You shall soon see for yourself, but suffice to say, very well. If I had to guess, I don't think he needs me anymore, but we've plans to travel together anyway."

Among The Vartija, those without fae blood like Sachi's had to drink from the halflings at most every few decades to avoid the aging sickness. Elias wasn't sure why he'd assumed a steady supply would be needed, but it wasn't. Occasional small infusions few and far between was enough to keep madness and death at bay. But since Mahu had deteriorated so thoroughly before gaining access to Sachi's blood, he drank nightly at first, until his strength had been restored.

"Travel together?" asked Remy. "That's the first I've heard of such plans. Tell us, where are you going?"

"I want to see Constantinople, and Mahu longs to return to Egypt. Can you imagine your feet in the sand while staring up at an ancient pyramid? I'm going to do that."

Elias had to smile, though it also hurt. He'd known of their planning, and he'd known of Sachi's wanderlust and deep-seated yearning for travel. He'd be sad to say goodbye to her so soon, but she'd promised their paths would cross again, and he believed her.

It seemed everyone would be leaving them, but Elias had been making new friends at Bran Vigny, so he could take comfort in those budding relationships when Laurence, Remy, Sachi, and Mahu were gone.

And of course, he had Aella, who was even now approaching with Mahu. Bran Vigny was her home, and she'd be there if Elias needed her.

Walking next to Aella, Mahu looked healthy and strong. His long black hair, dark as onyx, rippled in the breeze. Behind the polite smile lingered a melancholy in his garnet eyes that never seemed to vanish completely.

He greeted their group with a bow, which Elias found endearing as, aside from Sachi, he was their elder by centuries. But his generosity was well known, and thus he was generous with his courtesies as well.

Elias glanced to Aella. "How is Ash tonight?"

"He's recovered well." She smiled. "Still busily committing

every detail of our journey to paper. Well"—Aella turned to Sachi —"not *every* detail, but he does appear to be penning his own novel."

"I'm so glad he's better." Elias would never forget the dead-weight of Ash's body as he forced it through the portal. He repressed a shudder at the memory.

"Shall we?" Aella indicated they leave the castle grounds for the forest.

Elias hadn't been invited to watch before now, but Remy had told him of their studies. Aella's habit was to conduct most magical lessons among nature when possible. His excitement was only dampened because Valeri wasn't at his side to enjoy the demonstrations with him.

"Tonight Sachi has kindly offered to help with the lesson," Aella began as they reached the copse of enormous evergreens. Old, mature trees with wide trunks that stood a good bit away from each other and left plenty of room for them to maneuver beneath. A dense carpet of pine needles cushioned their feet. The sharp, spicy scent of spruce rose to greet them.

"Between us we've been taught two different methods of gathering water," Aella explained. "I intend to learn Sachi's method, and she will no doubt learn mine. In the process, with any luck, Remy and Laurence will learn both."

Mahu stepped to Elias's side and cast a grin his way. "We laypeople will enjoy the show."

Elias returned the smile, and the two of them sat out of the way, their backs against a massive tree trunk, legs stretched out before them. Neither Elias or Mahu had magic of their own, but that didn't mean they found the subject any less interesting.

While Aella gave her initial instructions, Mahu turned to Elias and whispered, "How fare you, young Elias? You smile, and yet behind your eyes lies sadness."

He'd gotten that right, hadn't he? Elias considered holding

back his next thought, but Mahu was kind. He wouldn't be quick to anger. So he replied, "I could say the same thing to you, Mahu."

Mahu gave a slow nod. "Indeed." A little chuckle. "But I posed the question first, my friend."

In front of them, Remy had his arms spread wide, fingers twitching as he attempted a water gathering spell. Elias watched, waiting for something to happen.

"I suppose you caught me there," said Elias to Mahu. It wasn't that he didn't want to answer the question, it was his own uncertainty as to the reason. "Do you know Valeri very well? Or at all?"

Mahu shook his head. "No, your sire keeps to himself. He's been that way since his first arrival at Bran Vigny nearly a century ago."

"That's not surprising. I've only known him for four years, and until now he has seemed content with only me for company."

Remy began his spell again while Laurence, Aella, and Sachi cheered him on.

"And now?" asked Mahu.

Elias frowned. "And now not even my company makes him happy."

Remy flung his arms up, wiggled his fingers, and brought them slowly and steadily inward. Water began to coalesce over his head from absolutely nowhere. Astonishing.

"I asked of your happiness, Elias, not his," Mahu pointed out gently.

"Oh, well, I am often very happy. I like Bran Vigny. I like the people here. I enjoy spending time with other vampires. Valeri has never allowed that without argument before now, you see, so it's refreshing to make friends without coming home and fighting about it."

"But…" Mahu waited.

"But now it's like he doesn't care at all," said Elias at length. "Before, he cared too much. He never trusted me. And now, it's like…I feel like he is letting go."

"Is that what you want?"

"No!" Elias answered without hesitation and much too loudly. The witches turned to look his way.

Remy lost his concentration and the bubble of water he'd been gathering burst over his head, wetting his hair and soaking his shoulders.

Elias's jaw dropped open. Whoops. "Sorry!"

"Everything all right?" asked Remy, swiping a wet tendril of hair from his eyes. Behind him, Laurence was doubled over with laughter.

"Fine, fine. So sorry," said Elias. "Go back to your water spells. I didn't mean to interrupt." At times like these he was glad he could no longer blush.

Mahu chuckled under his breath. "Elias, let me give you some advice from a very old man to a very young one. You must learn how to communicate. Tell Valeri how you are feeling. Be honest. Hold nothing back. Ask him the questions that linger on the tip of your tongue and be silent until he answers. If you love him..."

Mahu's voice trailed off in such a way Elias was prompted to fill the gap. "I do. Very much."

"Then you must be sure he understands what you need from him," Mahu continued. "Only you can tell him. Will you try?"

Elias nodded. "The conversation won't be easy."

"No, but it will be worth it." Mahu patted his knee. "Take it from a man who learned the lesson too late."

Elias's eyes widened; his mind raced with questions. Had Mahu lost a lover? He opened his mouth to ask, but Mahu shook his head.

"I've forgotten something at the castle." Mahu climbed to his feet. "You stay and enjoy the lesson. Think on my advice."

"I will. Thank you." Elias leaned his head back against the tree as Mahu said his goodbyes to the others. He watched the pine needles dance in the moonlight above him and thought about Valeri, alone, up in their rooms.

What could he say to Valeri to fix the rift between them? The truth was that he needed Valeri somewhere between the extremes of treating Elias as if he owned him and treating Elias as if he didn't care what he did.

Could he tell Valeri the truth? Would Valeri want to hear it?

23

Valeri, Present, 1432 Common Era

ot long after Elias left, a knock sounded on Valeri's door. He wasn't expecting anyone. A brief flash of fear struck like lightning. Fedor had not come himself, had he? Valeri's chest constricted at the thought. His throat tightened. The last person he wanted to see was his hateful sire.

A terrible thought took hold. What if Elias saw him that way? Maybe he didn't yet, but if Valeri wasn't careful, it could happen. The idea that Elias might dread seeing Valeri the way he dreaded seeing Fedor clawed at his heart.

The knock came again.

Too gentle to be Fedor. And the man would not have come all this way on Valeri's account. Though his offer to take Elias was probably some misguided effort to help, it wasn't for Valeri's sake, but rather because Fedor thought he stood to gain something from Elias's company. Even that would not be enough to draw him away from his riches in Russia.

Valeri stood from his desk. "Come in."

The door opened to reveal Mahu, who gave an elegant bow. "Have I come at a bad time?"

Valeri hid his surprise. He didn't know Mahu well and had no idea why the man would pay him a visit. "Not at all. What can I do for you?"

Mahu stepped in and closed the door behind him. "There's nothing I need. I only wish to speak with you."

"Please." Valeri gestured to the furniture. "Have a seat. I thought you were with Elias and the others watching a magic lesson."

Mahu took a chair, leaned back, and crossed his long legs. He ran his hands down the soft maroon upholstery of the arms as he settled. "I was. Elias is still there, no doubt involved in a water fight by now. You can well expect him to return to you drenched."

"Is that so?" Valeri sat across from him. He didn't know what to make of that. Vampires in a water fight? "But why?"

Mahu waved his concern away. "The others are learning water spells. Remy already looks as if he tripped and fell face first in a puddle. What matters is they are having fun."

Valeri did want Elias to enjoy himself, even if it meant he returned home soggy. "Sometimes I forget how young he is."

"Hmm. He and Remy both, but that's not why I've come. I've been meaning to thank you. If it weren't for your valiant effort, I wouldn't be here to enjoy watching vampire-witches learn water spells."

Valeri lowered his gaze. "No thanks necessary. Without Elias, Sachi would never have returned with us."

"And without you, Elias wouldn't have been there to charm her."

Elias could have been killed because of his arrogance. Valeri shivered. "I'm glad it's all worked out in the end."

Mahu leaned forward. "Let me do you a favor in return."

"That won't be necessary," said Valeri, voice crisp. "There's nothing I need."

"I disagree."

Valeri tipped his head. "Oh?"

Mahu gave a grave nod. "You're losing Elias."

Hearing the words out loud and put so bluntly was a jagged blade through his tattered soul. Though he knew Mahu spoke truth, Valeri argued anyway. "I'm not losing him. I'm letting him go."

"Semantics." Mahu waved away the rebuttal. "You're losing each other, and it's making you both miserable."

"He is happy," said Valeri through clenched teeth, then made himself relax. He wasn't mad at Mahu. He had no one to blame for their circumstances but himself.

"Sometimes."

Valeri arched his brows. "What does that mean?"

"Elias is capable of enjoying his new freedoms with his friends, yes, but there's a deep sadness lurking behind his easy smiles. A wound that pains him, and only you can take it away."

The accusation didn't sit lightly, but Valeri knew the truth in it. He supposed he deserved to feel this way for how he'd treated his lover. But why Mahu would rub his nose in his failures, he hadn't the slightest. "The damage is already done. I don't intend him further injury."

"And yet you're causing it right now."

"Now?" Valeri threw his hands into the air, frustration seeping into his tone. "But I've let him go out with his friends. I'm not lurking over his shoulder or demanding he speak only with me. I've given him the freedom he's longed for. What more can I do? Should I leave?"

"You should ask him what he wants," said Mahu gently. "You should listen when he answers. Then you should do what he asks."

A mirthless laugh escaped Valeri's lips. "That simple?"

"It really is. Tell me, have you tried?"

From anyone else, the question would be offensive, but Mahu possessed an earnest face, a sweet voice, and kind eyes. Valeri would like to say that he'd tried, but if he were being honest...had he ever simply asked Elias what he wanted? No. The answer came as a bit of a surprise. Such a simple courtesy, and yet doing so had never occurred to him. "I haven't."

"Admitting as much is a good start," said Mahu. "Don't forget to listen to his answer."

That sounded obvious, but Valeri let it sink in. He was afraid of what Elias might say. Listening to his answer might very well break Valeri's heart. "He'll want to leave. He'll want me to let him go."

"And if that's what he asks of you?"

To his shock, Valeri found himself blinking away tears. Unacceptable. He turned his face rather than let Mahu see.

Mahu rose from his seat. "Make sure to hear what he actually says, and not just what you think he will say. Learn from my mistakes as I did not."

The door clicked softly shut behind him.

Valeri swiped a tear from his cheek.

Elias, Present, 1432 Common Era

Elias hurried through Bran Vigny's corridors and up the stairs to his rooms, all the while dripping a trail of water behind him. He hoped he wouldn't run into anyone, but dashing through the castle soaking wet was worth the potential embarrassment for the fun they'd had.

Though it was hard to picture Valeri in a water fight, Elias couldn't help but wish he'd been there.

He slipped through the door to their apartments, relieved to have made it unseen. He shut the door and leaned against it, giggling out a breath.

His smile faded as he scanned the parlor and found Valeri

sitting rather slumped in his chair, shoulders caved forward, head in his hands. By the look of him, he'd been there a long time. Valeri lifted his head to glance his way.

Elias rushed to kneel in front of him. "Are you hurt? Is it your ribs? I thought they'd healed."

Valeri perked up, but Elias could see the motion for the show of will that it was. "I'm fine." He offered Elias a smile. "I was warned you might turn up wet. You may as well be a fish. What've you gotten up to?"

Elias's eyes grew big. "Warned? By whom?"

"Nothing bad, don't let it bother you." Valeri reached out to palm his cheek. "Tell me about your night. Or would you rather dry off first? Yes, I suppose you should do that. Why don't you have a wash while I fetch you some dry clothes."

"If you're sure you're all right." Elias stood. "You looked as if you were in pain when I walked in."

"I'm not. I was only thinking. Now off with you. You're leaking on the fancy rug."

Elias planted a kiss on Valeri's mouth and took off for the wash basin. Something had definitely been wrong, but if Valeri wouldn't speak of it, there was no use continuing to nag. He'd learned that lesson over and over again. At least Valeri found Elias's soggy condition amusing rather than irritating.

He stripped off his wet clothing layer by layer. Remy and Laurence had fared no better, their clothes were a sopping mess too, but they'd gone easy on Sachi, who squealed when the smallest splash hit her skin. And Aella easily avoided the other's attacks. Mahu had left just in time.

Running the soap over his skin, Elias thought of Mahu's advice and wondered if Valeri was in the proper mood for a serious conversation. He rinsed off, wrapped a towel around himself, and wandered into their bedroom.

Valeri stood with his back to Elias, gazing out the window. A fresh white linen shirt, long gray smallclothes, and thick socks lay waiting for him upon the bed. Elias walked past them, dropped the towel, and hugged Valeri from behind. Words had always been difficult for them, but not touch. Touch came naturally.

Elias squeezed his arms around Valeri's middle and pressed his front to Valeri's back. He burrowed his nose through the chestnut curls to touch the nape of Valeri's neck and inhaled deeply. He pressed a kiss there, then gave the spot a little bite for good measure.

Valeri took a shuddering breath. Almost as if…

Was Valeri crying?

"Turn around," whispered Elias against the soft skin of Valeri's throat.

Valeri shook his head. He grabbed Elias's arms and held them tight against his stomach, keeping them locked together with Elias unable to see his face.

A sniffle. However unlikely the sound might seem, Elias heard the snuffling, then felt Valeri's chest shaking.

"Valeri, are you…crying?"

Valeri didn't answer. Elias hadn't really expected him to. Lately, they didn't communicate well in the best of circumstances, but with Valeri in tears, he couldn't imagine pulling a conversation from him in this condition. He'd never seen Valeri cry. Even hearing the evidence for himself, the reality was difficult to believe.

"Come to bed," said Elias. "Let me hold you."

Valeri nodded. Elias led him to the bed and pushed him to sit on the edge. A tear hovered on his cheek, his eyes watered to the brim. Elias wiped an escaping tear with a gentle swipe of his thumb.

"Darling, tell me what's wrong." Elias stood between Valeri's legs and held his face in his hands.

"I don't remember the last time I shed a tear, and yet tonight I've cried twice." Valeri gave a pathetic little laugh and put on a smile that looked incongruous on his face.

"What can I do?"

Valeri gazed up at him through dark, wet lashes. "Nothing, my sweet. This isn't your fault, nor is it your problem to fix."

"But—"

Valeri put two fingers against Elias's mouth. "No buts. I want to hear of your night. Tell me about the magic lesson and how you ended up leaving a trail of water to our door."

Elias narrowed his gaze. "Is that really what you wish to talk about? It's not important."

"It's very important." Valeri's gaze turned serious. "Your happiness is priceless."

"Not if it comes at the expense of yours, it's not."

"I'm not unhappy," said Valeri.

Elias huffed. "You are lying through your teeth, Valeri. Don't think I don't know."

"I'm not unhappy with you," Valeri amended. "Put some clothes on, please, you're entirely too distracting like this. All that beautiful skin on display."

Elias leaned in. "You can have me if you like. Any way you want me. I'm feeling indulgent."

"Yes," Valeri murmured. His mysterious tears had begun to dry. "Soon. But for now, clothes, please. I want to talk with you."

"All right," Elias consented, backing out from the warm spot between Valeri's thighs to pull on the linen shirt and the soft smallclothes and socks. "Get in the bed though. I meant it when I said I wanted to hold you."

Valeri tugged down the velvet coverlet and shuffled in under the blankets.

Elias joined him. "I can't believe you had me get dressed to get into bed. I hope you'll be taking these off for me later."

"I hope so too." The words were flirty in nature, but Valeri still managed a melancholy note to his tone that made Elias's heart ache.

Curling close, Elias tucked himself against Valeri's side and clung to him like a barnacle. "Tell me what's wrong. Please."

Valeri ran fingers through his short hair, scratching his scalp with his nails. Elias usually loved this treatment, but tonight he recognized it as a stalling tactic. Waiting in silence for Valeri to say whatever was on his mind, Elias closed his eyes and enjoyed the petting.

So quiet only another vampire could hear him, Valeri said, "Mahu came to see me tonight."

"He did?" Had Mahu left their lesson early to speak with Valeri?

"Yes. He said he came to thank me, but truthfully he was here to give me advice."

"What did he say?"

"He told me I should ask you what you want from me, and then be sure to listen to your answer. You wouldn't think I'd need directions on that second point, but apparently I do. I've spent the remaining hours dreading the conversation."

"Dreading it?" There was a lot to pick apart in that statement, and Elias had several questions, but this one stood out as most important. "Why would you dread speaking with me?"

Valeri pressed a kiss to the crown of his head. "I'm afraid I know what you'll say. And I don't want to hear it. I don't want to face the consequences of those words once they're out in the open, but I will. I know I must. I'll do it for you Elias; I will learn to let you go."

Alarm struck. Elias stiffened. "Let me go?"

"Yes," Valeri confirmed.

"What?" Elias sat straight up in bed. "What are you talking about? Let me go where?"

"Fedor has offered for you," Valeri admitted.

"Offered for me?" Elias said it like the words tasted revolting in his mouth. Fedor had been cruel to Valeri. Fedor was certainly part of why Valeri turned out the way he did.

"I'd never let that happen, Elias, I promise." He squeezed his eyes shut. Opened them. "But Laurence…"

He couldn't be saying what Elias thought he was saying. Could he? "But Laurence what?"

Valeri hesitated. Took a breath. Let it out. "Laurence is a good man. He'd take you. Teach you well."

Elias knew how it would pain Valeri to suggest such a thing. Did he know Laurence and Remy had offered to take him with them to Livia's? But he couldn't know that. Who would have told him? Not Elias. Elias had turned them down. He didn't wish to leave Valeri, and he didn't think Valeri would agree to come with them.

Valeri forced the words out one by one. "Laurence would take good care of you."

A flare of anger sparked. "I'm sure he would. Aren't you even going to ask me first? Don't I get a say?"

"Of course." Valeri stroked a soft hand down his flank, perhaps trying to bring Elias's former mood back, but it wouldn't work. "I'm sorry, of course I'll let you say it."

"I'm so confused right now." Elias's nerves jangled. "It's like you've had a conversation with me in your head, played all the parts yourself, and think you get to make all the decisions for both of us, but you don't. I am just as big a part of this relationship as you are, and there are things I need from you."

"Anything," offered Valeri with no hesitation. "You may have anything you ask for. Money, solicitors, land. Everything I have is yours for the taking, Elias. I would deny you nothing. That's not what this is about."

Elias rolled his eyes. "That is the first logical thing you've said so far. That is *not* what this is about! I don't care about your money or your grubby solicitors. What would I do with land when this entire castle is mine to roam? I need you! You, Valeri! You deny me yourself. You do it every night. It weighs on my soul. Why don't you want to spend time with me anymore?

What have I done to offend you so, because I want to take it back!"

Valeri took his turn at confusion, his expression flummoxed. "I thought...I thought you were planning to leave me. I've been waiting to hear you admit it. Any night now, I thought you'd break it off, ask for your freedom. I'd vowed to myself to let you go. To give you my blessing. I—"

"Stop talking." Elias stared down at him, unbelieving. "Since when?"

Valeri's face was the picture of misery. "What do you mean?"

"How long have you felt this way? That I was going to leave you?"

A muscle twitched along Valeri's jawline. "Since I ordered Aella to steal Sachi and run," he confessed. "The way you looked at me after I'd said it...I thought for sure we were over. But even before, at the tavern with Jemma, on the ship when I commanded a halt to your reading lessons. When I nearly drained Frans to death, though I'd promised you I wouldn't...other times. The expressions you make when I disappoint you, like you don't recognize me anymore. I knew I was going too far, and yet I couldn't stop myself."

Elias took that in, flipped it over in his mind, studied the admission from all sides and saw the profound truth it contained. He took Valeri's hand and brought it to his lap to hold.

"I did think about leaving," Elias admitted, to himself as much as to Valeri.

"When?" Such vulnerability in the word.

"All the times you mentioned. I thought of it, but I never really wanted to leave you. I still don't. Especially now."

Valeri blinked. "You don't?"

"No."

"But why? I've been awful to you."

"You have, but you have also been good to me. And I love you —that is no small thing." Elias had an admission of his own to make. "I'm no innocent here. I've been complicit in your crimes. Our crimes."

"No," said Valeri forcefully. He squeezed Elias's hand. "You are innocent. It's I who—"

"Shh, listen. Don't let me off the hook so easily. I knew what you were every step of the way. You never hid your flaws from me. Not once. Not one sin. From the very beginning. Information, yes, you hid that, but not your crimes. And I said yes, Valeri. I had choices, and said yes to you at every junction."

Valeri's brows drew together. "But I have been terrible."

Elias laughed. He couldn't stop himself. Nothing was really funny, and yet. "Yes, you've been your share of terrible. But you have also been loving. You've been generous and protective. You've been attentive and kind as it suited you. None of us are perfect, we are all a jumble of faults and attributes. I happen to think ours could work well together."

Valeri's eyes were shining with tears again. "You do?"

"I do. Ask your question."

"What question?"

"The one Mahu gave you that you are so afraid to ask me."

Valeri wet his lips. "What do you want from me?"

Elias leaned down to kiss him. "Everything, Valeri. I want all of it. All of you. I want your companionship. I want it in our rooms, alone like this, but I also want it at social invitations. I want you to walk by my side around the castle grounds with your chin high and your shoulders back like you are proud to have me as your lover. I want you to support my friendships and my interests, even if you don't share them, as I will do for you. I want it to be the two of us together in the world, not against it. Can you do that?"

Valeri began to look hopeful. "I want to say yes."

The hope in Valeri's eyes was contagious. Elias felt it too. "Just say you'll try, and that will be enough."

Valeri frowned. "It isn't enough if I fail."

"Then don't fail. Commit to trying until you get it right."

"I will try my very best."

Elias let go of Valeri's hand to worm his way into his arms, against his chest. "That is all I want."

Valeri held him close. "I don't deserve you."

"You've put me on a pedestal where I don't belong. Take me off it. Let us start again on equal ground."

"Wise words," Valeri murmured as he stroked Elias's back.

"And what do you want from me?" asked Elias. "This should work both ways."

"I love you just as you are."

"There must be something."

Valeri took a deep breath. Elias rose on his chest with the inhalation and sank as Valeri let it out on a sigh. "I want you to curl my hair again as you fall asleep, as you used to before I stopped you."

Warmth pulsed in Elias's chest. "Is that all?"

"I was a fool to chastise you for it. I regretted my words the moment I said them. I'm sorry."

Elias's heart swelled. "I'd be glad to. I've missed that."

Valeri tightened his embrace. "I've missed you so much."

"This will be a fresh start for us. We've a blank slate to fill." Elias pressed a kiss to Valeri's collarbone. "And now I know all my letters, so we shall have no trouble filling it."

"You learn quickly."

"I've had good teachers."

Valeri reached for a book from Elias's stack beside the bed. "Shall I read to you for a while? Or would you like to read to me? We could do it together."

Elias lifted up enough to take the book, one of Clara's origi-nals. "As much as I want to improve my new reading skills"—he set the book aside and lowered himself back down onto Valeri just so—"right now let's pursue something I've already mastered."

A real smile spread across Valeri's face. He thrust his hips to meet Elias's. "I did promise to try to do as you asked."

"Try *your best,* I believe it was." Elias opened his legs and grinned. "Give me your best. Give me *all* of it."

---

*Thank you for reading Elias and Valeri's happily ever after! Mahu and Dakarai's story begins in the next volume, **Beyond the Ruby River**, which is available for preorder here:* amazon.com/dp/B08ZZXN5TY *and will release in June 17th of 2021. In the meantime, as my gift to you, there is a bonus scene with Elias and Valeri that picks up immediately where **Across the Sapphire Sea** leaves off. To get it, follow this link:* bit. ly/bonus-btss *You'll need to sign up for my newsletter, but you can unsubscribe at any time.*

Forbidden Bond (They Bite Series: Book One)

~A vampire heir at a werewolf university

~An alpha wolf who hates vampires

Can love conquer all—or is war inevitable?

Forbidden Love (They Bite Series: Book Two)

~An esteemed vampire surgeon

~A young, injured werewolf

Can love flourish between enemy species despite a society in turmoil?

Forbidden Need (They Bite Series: Book Three)

~A jaded vampire too damaged for love

~A lovesick shifter who refuses to give up

Will destiny unite them—or will old enemies reign?

A Bridge to Love

~A sweet messenger werewolf

~A lonely troll stuck guarding his bridge

Can love blossom across a massive cultural divide,

or will Arlo and Toby always be alone for the holidays?

ABOUT THE AUTHOR

Lee Colgin has loved vampires since she read *Dracula* on a hot sunny beach at 13 years old. She lives in North Carolina with lots of dogs and her husband. No, he's not a vampire, but she loves him anyway. Lee likes to work out so she can eat the maximum amount of cookies with her pizza. Ask her how much she can bench press.

Connect with Lee
Email: LeeColgin@gmail.com
Facebook: www.facebook.com/groups/leecolgin
Twitter: www.twitter.com/leecolgin
Website: www.leecolgin.com
Newsletter: http://eepurl.com/gJEu35

www.ingramcontent.com/pod-product-compliance
Lightning Source LLC
Chambersburg PA
CBHW061612170626
46811CB00001B/407